"The perfect stoop read! I love to laugh, and this book provided ample opportunity. So now, I'm in love with a book . . . this book. Is that weird? Don't tell my husband."
—Cat Greenleaf, NBC's *Talk Stoop with Cat Greenleaf*

I'm not trying to be rude, but don't we need to discuss *this*?" Coco opened the newspaper, knowing full well that dread was written all over her face. Right there on the front of the "On the Town" section were Sarah Palins One through Four. And a moose.

CJ looked closely at the photo. "How cute we look!"

"Why aren't you freaking out?" Coco asked. "We saw what we thought we saw, he knows we were there, and now he knows our names."

Olivia began to freak out, "Oh shit, oh shit, oh shit!"

"So now you have *Tourette's* too?" CJ said snidely.

Olivia quivered. "That's not funny. Oh, god, we're totally screwed."

"Girl, relax, we were *all* in drag. Nobody's coming after us. We're going to be fine. Have a Xanax," CJ said, pulling a bottle from his pocket.

"Oh, god, I hope we aren't going to be killed. I would hate it if this was the last picture taken of me!" Olivia said.

CJ smirked. "Oh, not me, girl. I looked *fierce*!"

This title is also available as an eBook

Also by Cooper Lawrence

The Cult of Celebrity

The Cult of Perfection

The Fixer-Upper Man

Been There, Done That, Kept the Jewelry

THE YOGA CLUB

COOPER LAWRENCE

G

Gallery Books

New York London Toronto Sydney New Delhi

G
Gallery Books
A Division of Simon & Schuster, Inc.
1230 Avenue of the Americas
New York, NY 10020

This book is a work of fiction. Names, characters, places, and incidents either are products of the author's imagination or are used fictitiously. Any resemblance to actual events or locales or persons, living or dead, is entirely coincidental.

First Gallery Books trade paperback edition December 2011

GALLERY BOOKS and colophon are registered trademarks of Simon & Schuster, Inc.

For information about special discounts for bulk purchases, please contact Simon & Schuster Special Sales at 1-866-506-1949 or business@simonandschuster.com.

The Simon & Schuster Speakers Bureau can bring authors to your live event. For more information or to book an event contact the Simon & Schuster Speakers Bureau at 1-866-248-3049 or visit our website at www.simonspeakers.com.

Designed by Davina Mock-Maniscalco

Manufactured in the United States of America

10 9 8 7 6 5 4 3 2 1

Library of Congress Cataloging-in-Publication Data

Lawrence, Cooper.
The yoga club / Cooper Lawrence.—1st Gallery Books trade paperback ed.
p. cm.
1. Yoga—Fiction. 2. WASPs (Persons)—Fiction. 3. Murder—Investigation—Fiction.
4. Greenwich (Conn.)—Fiction. I. Title.
PS3612.A946Y64 2012
813'.6—dc22

2011017655

ISBN 978-1-4391-8727-2
ISBN 978-1-4391-8728-9 (ebook)

For Joe

ACKNOWLEDGMENTS

My friend Anne once said to me, "Don't just live your dreams, live your wildest dreams." Great advice for sure—but what she didn't tell me was that living your wildest dreams usually requires a collection of special and valuable people in order to make those dreams happen. For me that would be the incredibly talented team at Gallery whose support is the most precious commodity a writer can have.

Thank you to Anthony Ziccardi, my champion and ministering angel from the start. My deepest gratitude to my generous publisher Louise Burke, the wonderful Jen Bergstrom, the quiet genius Jen Robinson, and the magnificent design talents of Janet Perr.

Lucky is the writer who gets to work with one of the most admired and hard-working editors in the industry, Abby Zidle. Thank you, Abby, for getting my jokes, being available whether I had a real question or just wanted to gossip, and always using your powers for good and not evil.

I have to say a special thank-you to Sean and Jon Lee, who are the most generous supportive people I have ever met. Thank you to my radio gurus Scott Shannon and Todd Pettengill, whose humor keeps me motivated every single morning.

Since *The Yoga Club* is about friendship, I wouldn't dream of missing an opportunity to thank my true friends, Emily, Stacy, Jeffre, Liz, Adam, Kim, Eric, and Cheryl, whose friendship and love I take with me every day. Thank you to my parents, Sandi and Robert, who early on called me their "blue-chip investment," and thank you to the person I may be the most indebted to, my partner Joe Clarke, who gets me like nobody ever has.

I am beyond grateful to you all.

CONTENTS

ONE

All Hallows' Eve

He OD'd on the first day of the tour! Can you imagine?"

Coco couldn't imagine. She couldn't really even focus on what was being said, because she was trying to figure out if the guy speaking was an actual fifty-seven-year-old hippie or if he was dressed as one for this godforsaken Halloween party Rory had lured her to. The overly tie-dyed shirt said "costume" but the David Crosby–style goatee and smell of patchouli said "lifestyle."

"The tour manager sets him up with Nestlé Crunch by the truckload—y'know when these guys are in Nar-Anon they need chocolate. Tons of it."

The whine in his voice was a song of discontent and passive aggression, like that of an authentic boomer. "So anyway there's a crowd of about forty thousand people screaming his name and the dirtbag is backstage mainlining with some dickhead roadie instead of eating his chocolate, and he friggin' OD's! Completely wiped out my investment."

Coco gazed on, wondering if this guy could have been likable once, back when he had hair and a social conscience. No question, she thought—at some point in his life, this guy had vowed to never let *the Man* keep him down. No, instead he *became* the Man, in spite of that nasty little soul patch on his chin. Yep, she thought, classic new-money Greenwich.

Nothing grated on Coco's nerves more than hypocrisy—and this town ran on it like it was diesel fuel—so the moment she saw her business partner, Rory, enter the room, she moved to join him. After all, he was the host of this dreadful Halloween party and the sole reason she'd shown up. The sooner she could make nice with him, the sooner she could return home for some quality time with the dogs and Sam. Coco really wasn't cut out for these events. No matter how perfectly coiffed her hair, how expensive her shoes or house, she always felt *less than.* The Greenwich upper class had a remarkable knack for sniffing out those who didn't truly belong, then making sure they were aware that they didn't. Coco probably didn't want to anyway.

Rory was one of the few in this set she could respect. He worked incredibly hard despite having made his money the old-fashioned way: by inheriting it. Even though he was a Thomson, of the Canadian Thomsons who owned Reuters, he still got up early every day and worked for what he got paid. And, unlike typical Greenwich blowhards, he was discreet. "Work is like masturbation," he would say. "Everyone does it, but nobody should be talking about it."

Coco was grateful it was a costume party. She didn't feel as raw and exposed as usual, being in costume. She had decided to go as Sarah Palin, since any crack about looking nouveau riche or white trash would only be a referendum on how well she'd prepared for the role.

Rory was dressed as Superman, which fit Coco's view of him. To her, he fell somewhere between mentor and savior.

Though she'd been no Eliza Doolittle when she first crossed his path, without him she never would have properly capitalized on her success, or learned to live with her sudden wealth. Butt-B-Gone, her derriere-shrinking cream—available not just on late-night infomercials anymore but also on QVC—was responsible for turning her rags into rubies. It was Rory who'd found her at an As Seen On TV trade show at the Javits Center in New York. The two hit it off instantly at a demonstration for vibrating underpants because . . . well . . . who can stand quietly while watching a male model squirm in his underwear? Rory was willing to invest in Coco because he had a gut feeling about her. He insisted that she wasn't a fly-by-night huckster on a lucky streak but someone who could "live the life"—and make him money. There's no free lunch in this town.

Rory's outfit wasn't your schlubby, packaged Superman gear from Ricky's. He was wearing one of the original costumes George Reeves wore in the TV series: boots, cape, red underwear, and all. It even came with that special musty wardrobe smell. Naturally, his wife was dressed as Lois Lane. Though, to be honest, were she not standing next to Rory, she'd have looked like a mousy temp from the secretarial pool.

"Well, well, Coco! You look pretty sharp for a woman who died in Paris last week. What was it I read? 'Scarf caught in wheel of car'? You pulled an Isadora Duncan?" Rory chuckled.

"Washing machine," Coco said, straightening her pencil skirt. "Spin and die cycle."

"Oh, right, washing machine. Pretty ironic for a woman who hasn't done her own laundry in ten years. Okay, let's go find the reporters." Rory wasted no time getting down to business.

It seemed that in Paris a week earlier a woman named Katherine Guthrie had indeed choked to death while leaning over a washing machine; her scarf caught in the works, becoming an unintended noose, and in moments she was dead. News spread that Katherine "Coco" Guthrie, world-renowned inventor of Butt-B-Gone, was the one who died, and for a moment Coco had considered not telling anyone that it *wasn't* her. There were times when she'd wanted to go back to her former quiet, normal life. She dreamed of refound anonymity, where she and Sam could get things right—start anew, take different names, new identities; like a witness protection program for people who had achieved sudden fame and frequently regretted it. No such luck. The news had sent her company's stock plummeting, and though Rory was a decent guy, he wasn't going to lose millions on a rumor so easy to dispel. Besides, only he had the juice to arrange an impromptu press conference at his own Halloween party.

So there they were: Sarah Palin, Superman, and Lois Lane in a makeshift pressroom, setting the record straight about Katherine Guthrie. Back to the limelight.

When the Q & A ended, Coco looked across the room and thought for a second there was a mirror. She'd spotted another sophisticated power updo hovering above those signature Tootsie glasses: a *second* Sarah Palin. *Good god, really?* Now it was definitely time to go. Business was finished and there was no reason to linger.

But then, not two feet from the first updo, she saw the

sharp tailored edges, wide shoulders, and stiffness of yet *another* northern blight. At this point Coco was both mildly embarrassed *and* intrigued. Two was embarrassing; three was amusing.

Nonetheless, home beckoned, so she sought out Rory for a quick good-bye, sending her best to Lois—which, ironically, was actually his wife's name—who had vanished into the amalgam of overpriced, underwhelming rented costumes.

Good-byes accomplished, moments from freedom, steps away from the valet, she felt a dainty hand grab her arm. Lois Lane. *Damn.* Lois wanted one last photo op. Coco figured more photographic proof that she was not, in fact, dead or in Paris was probably good business, so she followed along. Passing by a particularly boisterous and chatty group, Lois reached in and grabbed yet another Sarah Palin.

"Coco, this is my darling nephew CJ," Lois said and beamed.

And, voilà, there she was face-to-face with her fourth Sarah of the evening, though earlier in the day this one had been a man. But, wow! He was stunningly beautiful. *How do they do it?* Lois herded them out to the backyard, grabbing the other Palins as she went.

"Gather ye Sarahs while ye may!" she sang. "Coco, CJ, meet Olivia and Bailey. Or should I say Sarah and Sarah? I think it would be just *dahling* to have a picture of you four by the banyan tree. Isn't that tree just precious? And what a lovely evening. It's not cold at all!"

Coco remembered what it was about Lois Thomson that drove her nuts. Overuse of words like *precious, darling,* and *lovely* brought a bitter bile to her throat. In Coney Island, where she grew up, that sort of talk would have gotten her a well-deserved beating. While Rory was down-to-earth despite his wealth, Lois embraced every affectation, making her not only impossible to have a real, candid discussion with, but completely unbearable.

On their way out to the backyard, Lois also lassoed the photographer from the *Greenwich Ledger,* who remembered seeing someone inside dressed as a moose and promptly headed back into the party to find the beast for his photo. Lois scurried behind, leaving Coco with the other three Sarahs under the banyan tree.

CJ spoke first. "Can you keep a secret?"

"If you tell me, will it still be a secret? And speaking of secrets, isn't your dad . . ." Coco asked. She knew that Lois's sister was married to a bigwig politician.

"Cute. Yes, he's William Skoda, GOP governor candidate." CJ sighed. "But let's not worry about him tonight, 'kay? I'm the only governor who counts right now." There didn't seem to be a big love there, so Coco left it. "Anyway, that Zorro in there, did you see him?"

"What about him?"

"Well! He may be one hundred percent accountant under that swashbuckling costume, but he is a *huge* Mary. Don't let the M-R-S fool you, that boy works it on the down low . . . and from the bottom at that."

"Come again?" asked a shocked-sounding Sarah, the one Coco thought was Olivia.

CJ, happy to accommodate, chirped, "A Mary. A mo. You know—a nancy boy. Gawd, this town, no one here is who they seem at all. Nuh-uh."

Coco leaned in to Olivia and said in a loudish stage whisper, "I think what he's saying is the masked man's secretly a gay. And apparently he likes to be on the receiving end in his interludes."

"Yikes! But Mary? Why do you call him that? Is that what he goes by when he's, you know . . . being gay?" Olivia asked.

"No, no. It's a thing from the eighties, when we used to cruise city parks, gay bars, and rest stops. Everyone was just Mary because you weren't with them long enough to learn their names."

"Oh, my god!" Olivia blurted, then clapped a hand over her mouth as her overrouged cheeks reddened even more. "Gosh, you're really beautiful, by the way," she said after a pause, smiling with embarrassment.

"Well, thanks, honey. But beauty is pain, you know. Between the girdle and the pantyhose, this outfit is like a cheap hotel. There's no ball room!" CJ replied. The girls guffawed.

This caught Sarah Palin the Fourth's attention, causing her to look up from her BlackBerry midsentence.

"Wait, I know you!" she said, looking toward them. "Aren't you in my eight thirty yoga class?"

"Yes," said Coco and CJ simultaneously.

"Wait, I take that class too!" Olivia chirped.

Coco *really* didn't want to know anyone in her yoga class—she always felt her worst there and enjoyed the anonymity. On the other hand, she thought her form was particularly impressive. The instructor, who spent the class pushing the students into various impossible shapes, generally against their wishes, more often than not walked right by Coco and whispered, "Great, you've got it!" just loudly enough for everyone to hear. Coco was particularly proud of her Ardha Chandrasana. Every time she did the half-moon pose—right arm and right leg holding her body rigid and parallel to the ground, left arm thrust straight up in the air, left leg also parallel to the ground and shooting straight back in a beautiful, even line with the rest of her body—she felt like a star athlete and could just imagine, probably falsely, her classmates admiring her perfect poses.

Coco was about to tell her classmates about an amazing yoga retreat she'd gone to in Costa Rica last Christmas when a tall, handsome, well-built man walked out to greet the group. But what was he dressed as? A detective from *Barney Miller* or *NYPD Blue*?

Without introducing himself, he sauntered up suavely and said, "I saw a group of lovely ladies out here alone and wanted to make sure everything was okay."

Coco knew it was common in Greenwich to hire local law enforcement to be a little extra muscle at parties since, lord knows, nobody wanted someone from, say, the upper middle class to get in. *How gauche!* The undercovers were supposed to be inconspicuous, but Coco had this guy made in a minute. Definitely a cop. The Thomsons must have asked him to be at the party since Lois didn't trust anyone—yet another thing about her that Coco couldn't stand. Lois was distrustful of anyone poorer than she, particularly the help. She was still convinced that five years earlier the housekeeper had stolen her four-thousand-dollar Lanvin ruffled coat. And so, of course, with all of those caterers parading around, nothing of hers would be safe tonight.

When he heard the greeting, CJ, who'd had his back to the cop, turned around, looked him up and down, and in as manly a voice as he could muster said, "Oh, honey, now that you're here we are *more* than okay. And by the way, that little outfit of yours is just *precious*!" It seemed that even CJ couldn't resist taking a shot at his aunt Lois, especially since he surely knew she'd been the one to hire this hunk.

Olivia looked right into the cop's big green eyes and immediately perked up. She thrust out her hand and said, "Hi, I'm Olivia!"

"Rob," the handsome newcomer said.

"Hi, Rob," Olivia repeated. "I'm Olivia."

Rob blushed. "Yes, you just said that. Well, seeing that you ladies—and, uh, *gentleman*—are okay, I'm going to head back inside. What are you doing out here anyway?"

"We're waiting for Lois, she wants a photo of . . ." Coco waved her hand dramatically across the four Palins, like a *Price Is Right* girl introducing the full Showcase Showdown package. "Well, you know. Ridiculous, right?"

"No, no. Not at all. Quite clever," Rob replied. "See you around, then. Oh, and it was nice meeting you—both times—Olivia."

"Yes, Olivia," she said and sort of bounced and raised her hand slightly, as if Rob were doing roll call. As he walked away, the four Sarahs watched him carefully, his strong frame disappearing into the crowd.

"I wouldn't mind blowing that man down," CJ said.

"Mmm, I could spend *hours* licking those shoulders," Bailey added.

"He seems nice," said Olivia.

CJ smirked.

"And your name is . . . Olivia? Do I have that right?" Coco grinned. She couldn't resist teasing Olivia. Some people are just automatic targets.

"Oh, and you're purple off-the-shoulder sweatshirt, right?" shot CJ to Coco, as if standing up for Olivia.

"Huh?"

"At yoga. You do retro eighties. You've got a Jennifer Beals thing going."

"Ummmm . . . yeah, I guess that's me. But I don't wear leg warmers or headbands anymore," Coco said, sneering at CJ and putting out her hand to Olivia. "Hi, Olivia, I'm Coco." Apparently Lois's earlier introductions had fallen on deaf—and bewildered—ears.

"Riiight! I've seen you." The fourth Sarah was back and in their faces, crowding between CJ and Coco. "I'm Bailey."

"I'm CJ and she's—drumroll please!—Olivia!" CJ sang, looking at Olivia to confirm. She nodded her head and blushed.

Bailey, done with her important BlackBerrying, wanted to get back to the dishing. "Okay, tell us about Zorro. How do you know him?"

CJ, thrilled to indulge, said, "Okay, well! In high school, he was my first upperclassman and my second lover. We used to meet in the second-floor bathroom every Thursday after AP English."

Olivia and Bailey gasped as Coco rolled her eyes. This sort of thing wasn't new to her. She wasn't a fag-hag by design, but for some reason the gays absolutely *loved* her. They would seek her out in clothing stores, in restaurants, or at the theater. She never knew if it was because they liked her from television or if their gaydar labeled her "one of us."

CJ continued, "He was a bit older, sexy . . . taught me everything. It was my favorite extracurricular activity. Too bad you can't put *that* on a college application."

Bailey shrieked, "Ha! I *knew* he was gay! I tried to blow him after gym class once, and all he kept talking about was how bad my roots were and that he knew a great colorist for me. Totally dried my mouth. But he wasn't bullshitting about the colorist. He introduced me to Juan Carlos, who's simply the best."

CJ started to respond, "Well, if you really want to hear—" but was cut off by the ebullient Bailey.

"I mean, his brother was the most obnoxious kid in our class! He hit a teacher across the head with a hockey stick when she gave him a C, and his parents had the teacher fired. Every member of that family is an entitled snob. When the dad was under investigation—I'm sure you heard about *that*—the mom hid out at our house for two weeks until we got a call from the FBI."

Since Coco hadn't been raised in Greenwich, she wasn't up on the local lore. Mostly, she didn't care or want to know, but the businesswoman side of her realized there are just some things you have to be up on. "What did they want?" she asked.

"They had a search warrant. Said she needed to get back home or they were going to break down the door. All she could say was 'How dare they talk to me like that! Don't they know who I am?' Like who the hell is she?" Bailey made a face in disgust at the memory.

The others were suddenly intrigued.

"Go on," CJ insisted.

"Yes, please," Olivia agreed.

So Bailey continued. "She kept telling us that no matter what happened to her, their ten-million-dollar manse in Key Largo would be fine. 'Florida has those laws, you know,' she kept saying. 'That's why OJ went there.' No regard for her kids or the fact that her husband was about to go to prison. All she cared about was that house and what would happen to her."

"So what happened to the husband?"

"He got twenty years in a minimum-security prison for embezzlement and money laundering," Bailey said proudly, as if she had something to do with the arrest.

"So, who else do you know?" CJ asked.

"Everyone. I grew up here. Name someone," said Bailey.

"Did you know Daisy Neirob?"

"That slut monkey?"

"Yes! She was my neighbor. We called her Daisy Chain because of all the—"

"Okay, yes we got it," Coco interrupted. "She liked lots of men."

CJ and Bailey simultaneously shot Coco impatient looks while Olivia furrowed her brow, confused. CJ *had* to finish. ". . . lots of men at the same time." He grinned. "Who doesn't?"

"Yes. We understood." Coco sighed.

Olivia stood rooted to the spot, astonished.

CJ turned to Bailey. "Oh, what about that weird guy with the pretentious, Waspy name—Tag Wittimore. Oooh! I *hated* him!"

Bailey agreed. "Me too! He was such a tool. He used to drive his father's Maserati to school and park it on the lawn."

Just then there was a loud car alarm, which in a city might go unnoticed but in a posh small town is a conversation starter. The group paused to listen; the very idea that anyone would still have a car alarm was distracting. Then, just as CJ and Bailey were about to go back to their game of haters geography, Olivia, who until now had been silently sipping something pink from a martini glass, blurted out "Wooo wooo wooo wooo," in startling mimicry of the alarm.

They all turned to look at her.

"What. Was. *That?*" CJ finally asked.

"Oh, sorry," said Olivia sheepishly.

"But what *was* that?" CJ asked again.

"It's this thing I have where I have to imitate noises and sounds. I usually don't do it that much. I have medicine for it, but it doesn't really work when I'm drinking and well"—she explained, pointing to her martini glass—"I've had a few. Sorry." She giggled.

"Do *all* noises make you do it?" Bailey asked.

"No, no. Just the ones that stand out, like something out of the ordinary. I can't help it, I just have to mimic them."

CJ was still trying to figure out what the heck Olivia was talking about. "Wait, so you'll just be standing somewhere and there will be a loud noise and you'll have to do the noise?"

"Pretty much," Olivia replied.

"Echolalia?" Coco asked. "It's echolalia, am I right?"

"Pretty much," Olivia repeated. God, she was like a skipping record.

"Are you in our eight thirty yoga too?" Bailey asked Olivia.

CJ interrupted. "No, I haven't seen her there."

Olivia defended herself. "Um, hello? Actually, I just said I was, but nobody was listening to me. I'm usually in the back of the room. That's probably why you haven't seen me."

Just then Lois appeared with her photographer and a moose in tow. "Don't you four just look *precious*!" she exclaimed.

Flash. Flash. Done. And just like paparazzi chasing a gaggle of celebrities into Kitson, Lois, photographer, and moose vanished back into the house.

Coco found her new associates rather charming. Enjoying a fresh glass of Prosecco, she was no longer in such a hurry to leave and decided to stay and get to know them a little better.

"Well, that was . . . unique." CJ looked at the other three and gave a Palinesque twist to his perfectly lipsticked mouth. "So what brings you all to this freak festival?"

"Oh, I'm just a neighbor. I grew up here, further down the lane, and moved back not too long ago. I was little Livy from the block." Olivia smiled. "I saw Lois the other day in town, and she said I just *had* to come. I entered a beauty contest once and still had the dress, sooo . . . this," which explained why she'd come as Sarah in her early years.

Coco laughed. "Well, I guess that's sort of my explanation, too. I have to wear this stuff for business all the time. Rory's a colleague of mine—you may have caught the press briefing—so I was sort of obliged, y'know. Not a big fan of the dress-up thing."

"Well, I can't stand the woman and take any opportunity

I can to ridicule her." Bailey Warfield (Sarah Palin Number Four) explained she was an entertainment reporter and began to tell the group all about the mayor's house next door. Mayor Quilty had hired the visionary architect David Fisher to design a miniature sculpture of Dynamic Tower—the quarter-mile-high rotating tower to be built in Dubai—on his property. The tower was slated to be the world's first prefabricated skyscraper, with individually rotating floors, a veritable architectural wonder of the world. The mayor, one of Planet Earth's wealthiest public officials, was so taken with the project's ingenuity that he wanted one of his very own. Bailey's father had spent a summer in Florence hanging out with Dr. Fisher, so when Fisher was in town working for the mayor, he naturally stayed with the Warfields.

It wasn't unusual for luminaries of all sorts to visit the Warfield home, she said. After all, the family patriarch, Bailey's grandpa, was none other than the legendary journalist Mark Warfield.

Bailey told the by now enraptured gang of Palins a little about her life as the granddaughter of one of the greatest legends of journalism. She explained that way before the Take Our Daughters to Work program, her grandfather thought that, while it was important for all children to understand the working world in general, it was even more important for the Warfield girls to learn early on that they shouldn't be excluded from any business because of their sex. So he brought them to work whenever he could.

"Once, when I was seven years old and my grandfather was on his way to an interview, I cried and cried until my mother allowed me to go with him. See, there was Mark Warfield the journalist and then there was my grandfather. Mark Warfield the journalist had the firmest handshake you'll ever feel, and you didn't want to be on the receiving end when he was about to catch you up. But Grandpa Mark is the sweetest, most nurturing man. He knew that when I was going with him to CBS, I would require a chocolate croissant and one stuffed animal from F. A. O. Schwarz. So, this particular morning he was on his way to do one of the most controversial interviews of his career—you know, the one with General Silvius Venerable, who later sued for libel over it—yet he still stopped at the F. A. O. Schwarz and a deli for me first."

Coco waited out a series of increasingly tangential stories until Bailey finally got back to Dr. David Fisher and the tower.

"Okay, so one of the really cool things about this building is that they just build the core on-site. Everything else is put together in a factory somewhere else and then shipped in," she explained. "Which is exactly how Dr. Fisher did the mayor's version."

"So it's like a big Erector set?" Coco asked, remembering the toy her usually MIA father had given her for her twelfth birthday in the hope it would inspire her to a career in architecture. It was a hodgepodge of beams, screws, pulleys, and other mechanical geegaws, which had completely mystified her. She'd succeeded in making exactly one rectangular "house," also known as a metal box screwed into a platform. Before said house could be seen by anyone, it was put back in its box and stored under her bed. It was probably still there.

"Mmm, Erector sets," cooed CJ.

Olivia stifled a giggle.

"You're such a slut," teased Bailey.

"Takes one to know one," shot back CJ. "From what I hear." He grinned approvingly. Bailey turned away, pretending she hadn't heard.

"Okay, ladies. Enough." Coco didn't want to get involved in the catfight. She was too fascinated by the prospect of seeing the monolith in the next yard. "Why don't we just go check it out for ourselves?"

"Can we get close enough to see it?" asked CJ.

"Absolutely!" Olivia seemed confident. "We should be able to get near the main house down there by that grove of trees. That's pretty much the property line."

Coco didn't know what made her propose such a thing, since she was neither the snooping kind nor all that interested in the lives of others—most of the time anyway. Maybe it was the crisp fall air, maybe it was that last glass of Prosecco, or maybe it was because they were all dressed as Sarah Palin that she felt protected, invulnerable. Anonymous. And for the first time since she'd moved to Greenwich, she actually *liked* some people she'd met. She felt an odd sort of mischievous camaraderie with this inadvertent sorority.

Well, a sorority plus a drag queen.

TWO

Peepers

The mayor's place was less of a house and more of a compound. A fifteen-acre compound, in fact, replete with extensive shrubbery for privacy from the main road, an actual waterfall, and a cobblestone courtyard.

"Holy crap. How much house does one person need?" Coco was incredulous at the enormity of the mayor's mansion. "Look at that—is that a guard booth?" They'd wandered over from the Thomsons' yard, so there weren't so many imposing barriers on the back side. Before they knew it, they were crossing the great lawn.

"Yep." It wasn't such a big thing to Bailey.

"I had an apartment in Manhattan smaller than that. Lot of good it does without a guard, though. I guess he got the night off," Coco said.

From their position at the back and to the side of the mayor's house, they could see what they presumed was the master residential wing and its beautiful ornate balcony overlooking the meticulously landscaped grounds.

"Do you see the tennis courts down there?" Bailey asked no one in particular.

Coco nodded.

"Designed by Ivan Lendl," she said. "He likes this Har-Tru surface so much he comes to play here all the time. I think he gives the mayor free lessons in exchange for playing here whenever he likes."

Off to the side of the manse there was a sizable house that completely absorbed Coco's attention as she realized it was most likely just a guesthouse. She realized in silence that it was probably larger than the home her parents had been so proud to buy once they moved out of her grandparents' two-room apartment in Brooklyn. Originally meant to be servants' quarters, it now looked vacant. There were a curious number of padlocks on the door. Were they there to keep interlopers out—or others in?

The group walked a bit further down the lawn, and there it was. Between the dock reaching out into Long Island Sound and the mayor's classic nineteen-room Georgian colonial was the replica of the Dubai monstrosity. It was like having a small-scale, considerably less attractive Chrysler Building in your backyard. There was simply no rhyme or reason to it. In Dubai, the project was triumphant, a glorious feat of architecture and excess. Here in Greenwich, it was obnoxious and grotesque.

"Ugh, that is *so* new Greenwich." CJ spat. "My mother loved Provence, so she hired some famous landscape architect to re-create a Provençal farmhouse for her, piece by piece, in our backyard. She practically shipped all of southern France over here. But when she got bored with it, two years later, she installed an outdoor kitchen because that was the thing to do. I just hate this shit. This is one of my least favorite neighborhoods. It's so fucking pretentious."

At that, Olivia made a noise that sounded like disappointment.

"Is that your echo thing again?" asked CJ.

"No," Olivia replied. "That was intentional. I live over there." She pointed to the house on the other side of the Thomsons'. "My father left it to me. I've lived there since I was seven." She sighed. "Come to think of it, maybe I hate this block too."

"Well, the house is one I wouldn't mind having. Let's go see if we can peek into any of the rooms," Coco said.

Sharing her curiosity and daring, they deliberately—and as carefully as one must, dressed as they were—strode, ostrichlike, back up the lawn till they were near the back patio.

Just then a light went on in the house, and like a pack of dogs suddenly hearing the can opener, the four went silent and peered through the window. They turned to look at one another, all sharing the same thought. Bailey was the first to speak it.

"At this moment the right thing to do would be to turn around and go back to the party. But we are not going to be doing the right thing here, are we?" she whispered.

CJ chimed in. "Oh, no way. If the interior is anything like the landscaping, I must see it, if only to say that I've seen something tackier than Graceland."

And there they were, four Sarah Palins sneaking past the obsessively groomed shrubbery of the mayor's house to look through his window like common Peeping Toms. It was thrilling.

But it wasn't just the oversize, Rococo-framed painting of

a manic-looking harlequin clown that shocked them. Amid all the nineteenth-century-style gilded furnishings, there was the mayor, frantically moving through the room like a thief, grabbing items and stuffing them in a large duffel-type bag. More astonishing, though, was that he wore what looked like a black studded latex straitjacket, black dress socks pulled to the knee, and ugly white BVD underwear. Around his neck hung what looked like a costume ball mask, but in leather. It was quite the ensemble.

"Um, what is all that?" Olivia asked in a loud, frightened whisper.

"Wow, he's really committed to this Halloween thing! Had I known he was so much fun, maybe I would have voted for him," CJ replied.

"You suppose he's friends with Zorro?" Bailey cracked, jerking her head back toward the party.

"Wait!" Coco exclaimed in as hushed a yelp as she could muster. "Who's that?"

A young woman lay on the Napoleon-style sofa, seemingly passed out cold. She wore remnants of leather and latex gear similar to the mayor's, though her wrists appeared to be bound by some kind of thick black tape. The mayor was freaking out, sweating profusely; he attempted some sort of rudimentary CPR move, looking like someone who'd only seen it done on television. The body remained limp. The mayor put his palms to his temples, then hurried out of the room.

Shortly thereafter, he returned and stood next to the sofa, staring down at the woman, seemingly perplexed. Her body was motionless. Panicked, he disappeared into an antique trunk, frantically rummaging around in it. He finally emerged holding some lengths of rope in his sausagey fingers. The group stood frozen, attempting to peer closer without moving or making a sound. They watched as the mayor dragged the woman's body from the couch onto the Persian rug. He was breathing heavily, sweating, red-faced, and appeared to have tears rolling down his face. Or perhaps it was just sweat. Even his hair was damp. He positioned the woman on the rug, then rolled her up in it, securing it tightly with the rope he'd found in the trunk.

The four were frozen, speechless and horrified. If the busybody gods had been smiling on them at that moment, they could have just tiptoed away and pretended it was all just an awful, terrifying communal dream. But, alas, the godforsaken car alarm went off again.

Totally incapable of self-restraint, Olivia released a high-pitched "Woo, woo, woo, woo!" jerking the mayor out of his nightmarish task in time to see the surreal specter of four faces of Sarah Palin frozen in horror at his window.

THREE

8:30 Yoga

The next morning Coco was jarred awake by the sound of the coffee grinder, which was fine with her for a change. She desperately needed a cup before yoga, especially after the nightmare of the prior evening—the one she'd been awake for—in addition to all those she'd had while asleep. She needed a jolt in order to sort the whole thing out.

As she stared down her mascara-smeared face in the bathroom mirror, the cobwebs began to clear. The four Palins had, recovering from their paralysis of shock moments after Olivia's outburst, turned together as if on one heel and sprinted back for the Thomsons' property. Well, *sprinted* isn't exactly the right word. Considering their skinny skirts and slutty stilettos, they'd more or less shuffle-trotted across the yard, as if rushing en masse to the toilet.

Coco recalled thinking how impressively CJ managed to run in heels. The foursome stopped just out of view of the other party guests, caught their breath, and agreed to melt into the crowd and discreetly leave on their own, as inconspicuously as possible. Numbers were exchanged, and imprecise promises were made to meet soon. That was about all Coco could remember—and then, of course, there was the dread and sadness of realizing that she may have witnessed a horrific crime. Who was the woman on the sofa? Why did she have to die? Her poor mother, father . . . significant other? Coco felt sick.

Having removed the goo from her face, Coco splashed herself with ice-cold water, almost in penance. *Okay, time for coffee. Seriously.*

Sam, her boyfriend—or really, common-law husband by now—was a total coffee snob. He was particular about most things but nothing more than coffee. Coffee in their house had to be made in a French press with freshly ground, fair-trade Counter Culture beans, which had to have been roasted that week. How he could know the difference between beans ground two days or two months ago Coco couldn't fathom, but she had to agree that the stuff was phenomenal.

It had taken her some time to get used to Sam's predilections. The screech of the coffee grinder first thing in the morning had been particularly grating when they first moved in together—every time she heard it she jumped three feet out of bed. Their first fight, in fact, had stemmed from Coco's solution to the problem. She'd had the audacity to buy preground beans in order to preserve her morning peace and quiet, but she quickly got her first lesson in Sam 101: "Don't fuck with my coffee, Princess." He'd meant the comment to be funny.

Sam was sarcastic and jokey about everything, or nearly so. When Coco was angry, Sam laughed; if one of the dogs was sick, Sam made a joke; if she set the kitchen on fire (which she had, three times), Sam poked fun. Somehow, though, he had no sense of humor about his coffee. So, she learned to live with the grinder.

Sam was painfully immature in many other ways too, but that childlike behavior was what endeared him to her. On their first "sleepover," she awoke not only to the coffee grinder but also to chocolate chip pancakes on paper plates and SpongeBob on TV. It was adorable and felt thrilling, as if they were seven and their parents had left them alone for the weekend. Well, except for the sex part.

Their courtship was quick. Really quick. But Sam had come along as if by magic when she'd finally given up on ever finding an ideal life partner. It didn't take long after she met him before she realized she'd found one. So, there didn't seem to be any point to a prolonged period of casual dating. Within two weeks of meeting, they were living together. If it didn't work, she could easily move out, she reasoned. But she didn't, and after all these years he was her one and only rock, a comforting aspect of their relationship that counterbalanced his lack of self-confidence, propensity for the blues, and the no-longer-charming aspects of his boyish immaturity.

In fact, after being together nearly ten years, though they'd never actually made it official, they appeared to be the ideal couple, one of the few content partnerships they knew. It was the strength of the friendship that kept Sam from insisting on making it official despite his having a "five-year plan" that included marriage, as if it were some sort of commodity. Sam's father had died unexpectedly at the age of forty-five, which had left a twenty-something Sam with the conviction that his clock was running out. Consequently, he had a list of things he had to have done in order to feel he'd lived his life to the fullest. Marriage was definitely on the list, but he was enlightened enough to realize that the relationship, not the certificate, was the important part. Their shared view on big weddings was: *what's the point of celebrating something you haven't actually accomplished? Let's do it up big when we've made it twenty years.* Secretly, Coco thought, he just didn't want to spend all that money. About certain things he was a total tightwad. But the same went for Coco, and she had no fondness for being the embarrassing center of attention anyway.

Their relationship was in many ways solid. Sam was always one step ahead, anticipating her every need. If it were pouring down rain, she would come home to find him holding a warm towel to dry her wet hair, a hot cup of tea at the ready. Even after a long day at work, Sam would lay out her pajamas and slippers. (He claimed he only brought the slippers because the dog hadn't yet been properly trained to do it.)

All the attentiveness, the wonderful best-buddiness of their relationship was amazing; it was the sort of thing she'd always dreamed about. But the thrill and the spark that one had with an exciting lover simply wasn't there. In fact, the term *lover* wasn't one Coco would be inclined to use for Sam. She liked the rush of adrenaline, the thrill of newness . . . In fact, what *was* that she'd felt as she hurried home last night and quietly snuck up the stairs? She'd had a high she hadn't experienced in years.

As she brushed her teeth, Coco began thinking again about the night before. *What the hell? Was that real?* Stopping midstroke, she walked herself through the whole thing. No, it wasn't a crazy dream. Nor some exaggeration brought on by too much booze. But *what* really? Had she witnessed a performance? Some bizarre fantasy? She'd heard about couples who staged abductions or *worse* for sexual thrills. The mayor was into some kind of kinky behavior—his outfit (for lack of a better term) made that clear. But this was a bit beyond. So was this some kind of crime? Accident? He did seem genuinely distressed . . .

Coco finished brushing her teeth and went into the bedroom to dress for yoga. The dogs—who'd come racing up the stairs to greet her when they heard the bathroom faucet—followed her anxiously, wondering if they might be going somewhere exciting with her. But she was too distracted to notice. Should she tell Sam? If it were indeed nothing, what would be the harm in telling him the whole wacky story? Then they could laugh at the absurdity of it all. However, if she had indeed seen what she most dreaded, then she would be putting him in a difficult position by telling him. What if she were liable for not reporting a crime? Or, worse, what if the mayor decided he needed to silence anyone who knew anything? Better to keep Sam in the dark until she was sure. Coco prayed it would turn out to be one of those things where you were certain you saw a UFO but then learned it was merely a weather balloon. Maybe what she saw was the mayor stuffing a big weather balloon into a sack. "Yes, that's it," she said to her reflection in the bedroom mirror. "A big, half-naked, dead weather balloon."

But still, it didn't make sense that Coco wouldn't tell Sam, her rock, what had happened. Her rock should know everything, right?

Just then Sam yelled up from the kitchen, "Two eggs or one?"

Usually he knew exactly what Coco wanted at any given

moment, but she was wishy-washy about food, so he didn't take a chance. Why waste an egg?

"Don't you remember? I have yoga!" she yelled back.

Coco smiled at the thought that Sam was expected to know her entire schedule. Yoga meant just one egg. She headed downstairs.

"Did you feed the pups?" she asked.

"Yup," Sam replied.

Coco sat down to her one egg, assorted cheeses, and English muffin. She was not one of those yoga women who looked at a strawberry, sniffed some yogurt, and was full. She was an eater.

"You got home late last night. I don't even remember hearing you come in. What time was it?" Sam wondered.

"After one. I thought I was going to sneak out by eleven, but Lois had to introduce me to everyone on the planet. You know how she can be," Coco explained.

"I'm *so* glad you let me sit that one out. What excuse did you give for me?"

Coco joked, "I told them you were allergic to tedious and frivolous people in costume." She actually hadn't asked him because she preferred to handle business matters on her own. She neither felt a desperate need to have Sam with her at all times nor liked being viewed as half a couple. She was an independent businesswoman. Going solo reasserted her independence and strength, she thought.

"Oh, good. I hope they understood. No, really. What'd you say?"

"I said your back went out again. Rory has a guy he wants you to see. He made you an appointment."

"Aw, man, are you kidding me? So basically I'm screwed whether I go to these things or not. Next time I'll go, since at least I'll get free shrimp. Do I have to see Rory's guy?"

"I think you should. You do have back problems."

"Fine," he said, then continued, "Why did you stay so late?"

"Oh, it was so funny. Lois introduced me to three other people dressed like Sarah Palin. One was a guy, and he looked better than I could have hoped to," she said.

"So much for originality," Sam scoffed and went back to reading the paper.

"Yeah, but they were actually pretty cool and, it turns out, all in my eight thirty yoga class. I'm probably going to see them again this morning."

Coco finished her breakfast, scratched the pups, grabbed her mat, and prepared to head out.

"Back after yoga," she said as she kissed Sam good-bye.

"Oh, wait!" He caught her. "Check this out. You and your Palin pals made the *Greenwich Ledger.*"

Coco gasped. She had forgotten about the photo. Right there on the front of the "On the Town" section were Sarah Palins One through Four. And a moose. Okay, but surely their names weren't . . . *damn!* Stupid slow-news town. Boldly and clearly written under the photo was the caption identifying them all, accurately, by name: "From left to right: Coco Guthrie, Charlton Jeffre Skoda, Bailey Warfield, and Olivia Barnes. Also known as Sarah Palin. Plus Moose." Oh, no, no, no! Coco tried hard to conceal her panic. She began to realize what this information could mean for her if the mayor had seen the photo, especially if he'd done what they thought he did. But what were the chances he'd read the society page the morning after dumping a body? She was probably safe. *Right?* Too many variables. All of these thoughts went through her mind in a split second, but slowly enough to betray her uneasiness.

"You okay?" Sam asked. With him, she couldn't get away with anything.

Coco scrambled to come up with an explanation as her stomach dropped through the floor at Mach speed. "No, no. I'm fine. I'm just shocked by how much weight I put on. You didn't tell me I looked like John Goodman dressed as Sarah Palin. I really need to lay off those mochaccinos after yoga, huh?"

Always use weight as an excuse, Coco thought. It's the one area about which women can appear insecure and nobody questions them, particularly a smart boyfriend who knows to steer clear of such topics.

Across town the mayor sat in the large mustard-colored wingback chair in his living room, the same one he had been sitting in since "the incident." He had watched the sun rise and set from that chair many times before, but this morning was different. This morning he was worried. Really, really worried. He had no idea what the people at the window last night actually saw; he didn't know who they were (though he assumed they were from the Thomsons' party next door), what they knew, or what they would do. He was accustomed to worrying, but this was nauseating. Could these four Sarah Palins end his career? His life? Were these his last days as a free man? And then there was the incident itself. It made him ill.

These thoughts had run over and over in his head all night. Just as he wondered how to make this situation go away, or who to call, he heard the familiar sound of the morning paper hitting the front step. His paperboy was allowed up past the guard booth but not so close to the house that he could place the paper gently. Truth be told, the boy feared the mayor and was happy just to launch the day's dispatch and be on his way. The mayor wasn't ordinarily in a hurry to read the *Greenwich Ledger,* but something told him to today. His publicity whore of a neighbor would surely have had a photographer at his party. He turned to that cloying "On the Town" section—whereupon he immediately made a phone call.

In the car, Coco let her imagination get the best of her. Would she end up like the woman rolled in the rug—if there truly were a woman in the rug? It could have been a Halloween prank. *Couldn't it have?* What did CJ think? Was BlackBerry-gazing Bailey self-aware enough to realize she might be in danger? What must Olivia be thinking? *Is she mimicking absolutely every sound she hears this morning? I sure as hell would be,* thought Coco, and she even considered, for a moment, blurting out the sound of the car horn blaring behind her. It seemed in her pensive haze she had stopped at a green light.

Frustrated that she couldn't phone any of the people with whom she would soon be stuffed in the trunk of the mayor's car, Coco sped to yoga as fast as she could. She needed answers.

When she arrived, CJ was standing outside with Olivia,

grilling her about something. Coco rushed toward them, clutching the *Ledger.*

CJ saw her and kissed her on both cheeks, European style. "Oh, hey, hon, I'm getting the 411 on little miss thing here and why she was flirting with that hot guy last night." He turned to Olivia. "Okay, so go on, dear."

Olivia looked at Coco and smirked. "I was just telling CJ about my *boy.* I have the most beautiful eight-month-old. His name is Simon, and he's the only boy I need." She smiled. "I have, er, *had* a now off-again boyfriend—Simon's daddy—who is presently at one of the poles, South I think, doing some global warming thing. I don't know. He's quite smart but a total jerk. You'd hate him. But it's been so long since I've been single that I don't know how to date. I think I even forgot how to flirt."

"Oh, you never forget how to flirt, hon; it's like wearing a pair of heels. It always comes back," CJ said.

Coco, surprised, looked at Olivia, eyes wide. "Wait. You just had a baby? But, you're so *tiny*!"

"Yoga!" Olivia beamed. "I did it throughout my pregnancy. They have the best prenatal yoga here. My water broke right in the middle of a sun salutation. It's a new position: mountain with waterfall pose. That's probably why we hadn't met. I've been doing baby yoga for the past year or so."

Of course Greenwich had "baby yoga." Coco wondered if there was yoga for her dogs too.

Coco tried to speak, but CJ beat her to it. "Girl, pull the bus over, we need to back up. I want to hear about the boyfriend. So is it over? Or are you gonna two-time your big-pole boyfriend with that hot man muffin from last night?" CJ was so over the top this morning, Coco wondered if he weren't covering something up.

Olivia started to blush. "Oh no, no, he is *at* a pole, South, I said . . . Oh, a joke . . . sorry. Well, was I too obvious last night? I don't know what to do around guys. That's why I got knocked up by a meteorologist and not a rock star."

"Mary, give me a bottle of champagne, a push-up bra, and twenty minutes, and I'll show you what to do," CJ replied.

"Sorry, I'm not trying to be rude, but don't we need to discuss *this*?" Coco finally interjected, shaking the rolled-up newspaper in her hand. And with that she opened the paper, knowing full well that dread was written all over her face. She showed them their revealing photo and waited for a reaction. But it never came.

CJ looked closely at the photo. "How cute we look!"

"Why aren't you freaking out?" Coco asked.

"Should we be?" Olivia started to look worried now.

"No!" CJ answered empathically. "Nobody saw anything. And even if we had," he said a little ominously, "nobody would be able to recognize any of us."

"Our names are right here." Coco pointed to the caption.

"Nobody reads this thing," CJ assured her. "People use it to pick up dog poop and line bird cages, if they actually bother."

"Okay, worst-case scenario. We saw what we thought we saw, he knows we were there, and now he knows our names," Coco said.

Olivia began to freak out. "Oh shit, oh shit, oh shit!"

"So now you have Tourette's too?" CJ said snidely.

Olivia quivered. "That's not funny. Oh, god, we're totally

screwed; we have to go to the police. I think Coco is right. The mayor is going to see this picture and come after us. And last night made it pretty clear he's prone to violence."

"Girl, relax, we were *all* in drag. Nobody's coming after us. We're going to be fine. Have a Xanax. I just got a new scrip," CJ said, pulling a bottle from his pocket.

"Oh, god, I hope we aren't going to be killed. I would hate it if this was the last picture taken of me!" Olivia said.

CJ smirked. "Oh, not me, girl. I looked *fierce*!"

"Okay, if you don't think we should worry, it makes me feel a little better," Coco said.

"Please. We'll be fine. You know what you really need? A yoga class. Oh, and look! A yoga center right here. What luck!" CJ opened the door for the girls with a flourish.

"Yeah, you're right. Maybe I'm panicking for nothing. Hey, do you think Bailey is coming?" Coco asked.

"Knowing her, she very well might be, but not to yoga, darlings," CJ sang.

"Gross," said Olivia as the three ex-Palins walked into class.

Perhaps yoga *was* the best thing Coco could have done that morning. Without it, she might have had a complete breakdown. There's nothing like the centering and calm that overtakes you after a yoga class.

"Good morning," said the instructor, a pixieish, absolutely adorable twenty-something with what appeared to be a yin-yang tattoo on her shoulder. Coco hated her immediately. "For those of you who don't know me, my name is Debbi."

You could tell by the way she said her name that it was spelled without an *e* at the end and possibly a capital "B." "Hi. Today we're going to focus on breathing and working on strengthening our core muscles. Does anyone have any injuries or sensitive areas I should know about?" She smiled beatifically and looked around the room.

Coco rolled her eyes. *Oh, lady, you don't know the half of it.* CJ looked back, grinning knowingly from the front of the class—*he's one of those suck-ups who likes to make sure everyone in the class sees how wonderful he is,* she thought. That and he wanted to make sure he'd be seen by any stray man who happened to wander in.

Olivia raised her hand just above her shoulder and smiled, eyes twinkling. "Uh, hi! I'm Olivia. I just had a baby a few months ago. I know that doesn't count as an injury." At this, several in the class tittered. "But, uh, I've been doing the neonatal classes, so, uh, I'll just adjust accordingly."

Debbi smiled back at Olivia, a bit quizzically and a bit lovingly. "Hey, that's fantastic. Congratulations! Okay, so we'll keep that in mind." Her gaze held on Olivia slightly longer than it should have. "Okay, well, let's get started. Let's close our eyes, legs crossed, and breathing deeply. Great. I want you to focus on someone you want to dedicate your practice to today."

During her "practice"—*if this is practice, when are we going to get to the real thing?*—Coco was agitated, feeling run-down and wondering why the hell she was there. Nothing moved or bent the way it was supposed to. But lying there on her back in what she called the "corpse pose," arms by her sides, eyes closed, room dark, wine-scented sweat rolling off her temples, she was incredibly grateful she'd come. She thought she'd earned the right to dedicate her practice to herself. And that poor girl in the mayor's house.

Bailey woke up at nine and stared at the ceiling. She had to get motivated to attend yet another press junket. As an entertainment reporter for the local ABC affiliate, she had to get an exclusive on every star, young or old, famous or up-and-coming. If they were promoting a film or a TV show, she had to use that legendary Warfield charm to get them to say something they'd not said to anyone else. Her expert grandfather had taught her how to ask questions nobody else was asking and get answers people had no intention of giving. She was *skilled,* and many of her interviews had garnered national press for her and for the station. It was *she* who broke the story that Lindsay Lohan was in a relationship with a woman; it was *she* who introduced thousands of young women to Zac Efron way before *High School Musical;* and when Angelina was pregnant with Shiloh, Bailey was Angelina's choice to make the announcement to the world.

Today she was interviewing John Mayer, Jessica Simpson, and Tom Hanks about an animated Pixar feature with music by John Mayer. She hadn't yet seen the film, which was slack of her considering she usually went to all screenings. As she lay in bed thinking of questions to ask, playing out the interviews in her mind, the warm body next to her began to stir.

"Mmm. Morning," a disembodied, raspy voice said.

"Morning," she replied.

Bailey looked over and saw the bold sleeves of tattoos and

otherwise smooth, tanned skin of John Mayer peeking out of the duvet. He didn't seem to want to move. She fixated on a flower on his shoulder and spoke to it.

"I'm trying to think of questions to ask you guys today. Did you bring the sound track? Can I listen to it while we shower?" she asked.

"Sure, it's in my bag," he said as he slowly rolled toward her. "But why the rush? We don't have to be there until noon."

They kissed. He smelled amazing, even in the morning. Bailey moved closer.

"Well, if we have until noon." She started to kiss the softest lips she'd ever felt when the doorbell rang.

"Shit," she said. "Is your car here for you already?"

"Shouldn't be," said the rocker.

"Let me see who it is and get rid of them."

Bailey had an incredible body, and she knew it. She was anything but shy and loved to show off her perfectly shaped butt; flat, yoga-toned stomach; and muscular legs. She bounced out of bed naked, teasing John by barely throwing on a robe as she went downstairs.

There was no one at the door, but through the stained glass—the security camera was out, yet again; she cursed herself for not getting it fixed—she could see an envelope propped against the door. She didn't want to investigate further; Bailey was always paranoid about strange packages, given her profession and her family's notoriety—what if there were an explosive or anthrax or something in there? Alarmed, she ran to the kitchen and called the police.

While she waited in the kitchen for the cops, she made strong, strong coffee for the sexy, sexy rock star in her bed.

He didn't drink decaf and took his coffee black. She knew it from reading that famous *Playboy* article in which he called her friend Jessica "sexual napalm," although his innumerable tweets about his coffee obsession would have been more than enough information. Nevertheless, she brought a cup upstairs to him.

"Who was at the door?" he asked with eyes barely opened.

"It was an anonymous envelope. I called the police," Bailey said as she handed him the mug.

"You called the police? About an envelope?" he asked.

"Well, yeah. What if it's a pipe bomb? I'm a journalist, you know," she replied.

"You interview celebrities. Who's sending you anthrax? J. Lo?" He was almost laughing. "How exactly do you fit a pipe bomb in an envelope, anyway?"

She waved her hands and said, "I don't know . . . technology?"

"Wow, even I'm not that crazy," he said as he tackled her on the bed and began pulling her robe off.

Just as he started sliding his stubbly cheek down her belly, they heard the police car pull up. Bailey whimpered, frustrated.

"That's fast," he said.

"It's Greenwich. They're not that busy," she said as she headed back downstairs, this time putting on sweats and a T-shirt.

When she got to the door, she recognized the officer's face. It was the guy from last night, the one Olivia had been awkwardly flirting with.

"What are *you* doing here?" she asked.

"You called the police, didn't you?"

"You're a cop?" Bailey asked.

"Detective. Rob Casey." He stuck out his hand, and she shook it carefully, keeping her other hand discreetly across her chest as she realized her T-shirt was more or less transparent. "What can I do for you this morning, Ms. Palin?"

"Oh. Well, I received this," she said, leaning down to pick up the envelope." And I don't want to open it, because I wasn't expecting anything and it's anonymous. And, you see, I'm a journalist, and—" she stammered.

"Say no more," Detective Casey interrupted. "And by the way, if it's a bomb, you probably shouldn't be handling it."

"Oh, yeah. Whoops," she said. "Boom."

"Do you have reason to believe someone would want to harm you?" Casey asked as he took out rubber gloves and placed the envelope in a plastic bag.

"I hear she gave Dakota Fanning a pretty hard time on the red carpet last week," John Mayer said from just beyond the opened door. It was pretty dark inside, but Mayer wasn't shy and liked his conquests known. He wore jeans but no shirt or shoes. His hair was bed-ruffled.

"Shut it, smart guy," Bailey yelled over her shoulder.

"Clearly you're busy, so let me take the envelope down to the police station. Once we're done processing it, we'll let you know," Detective Casey said as he began walking back to his car.

"Thanks, Detective," she said. "Oh, and by the way, Olivia seems like a pretty cool chick, doesn't she? Are you single?"

"Uh . . . yes," he said, caught off guard for the first time in their conversation. "As a matter of fact, I am."

"Good to know. Bye!" Bailey said with a grin as she closed the door.

After yoga, a sweaty Coco and a drenched Olivia stood outside the classroom chugging bottled water as CJ rooted around in his bag for his iPhone.

"How do you not sweat like crazy in there?" Coco asked.

"I don't sweat, I glow," replied CJ. He found his phone and turned it on.

"Of course," said Coco.

Suddenly CJ's mood darkened. "Dammit!" he said.

"What's up?" Coco asked.

"One of my guests just canceled for Monday's show, and I don't know if my bookers can find a replacement. I hate when this happens," CJ said.

"A guest? What are you involved in?" Olivia asked.

"I'm a senior producer for the Rachael Ray show," CJ replied.

"Oooh! I love that show! Is she nice?" Olivia perked right up.

"Totally. She's the best boss there is. I adore her. The only thing I don't adore are the guests who cancel on us at the last minute. 'Scuse me a second, I'll meet you guys outside," CJ said as he walked away, phone already pressed to his ear.

Olivia and Coco collected their things and went into the dressing room to change, emerging a few minutes later, only to find a frantic-looking CJ.

"What is it? More trouble at work?" Coco asked.

"No, worse. I need to get home. Nanny called like ten

times while I was on the phone—some weird guy showed up at our door and left an envelope for me. She's really nervous about it."

"You have a nanny? For what?" Olivia was intrigued.

"No, I don't *have* a nanny, she *was* my nanny growing up and is part of our family. Now she's ill and I'm taking care of her," CJ explained.

"Is she okay?" Coco asked.

"No. I mean, yes, she's okay—she's just freaking out about a guy and a package. But I get some weirdos contacting me because of Rachael Ray. I'm sure that's all this is. I gotta go."

Just then Coco's phone rang. It was Sam.

"You need to come home. Now."

"Why? What's going on?"

"Just get here," he said as he hung up.

Coco looked at CJ, lips pursed, and said in as sarcastic a tone as she could muster, "Well, I'm betting not everyone uses the *Ledger* to line bird cages. Mother fuck!"

Olivia, not quite getting it, looked dismayed. "*What?* Will someone please tell me what's going on?"

"Tell her, CJ," Coco demanded and began hurrying toward her car.

"Wait, what's your number?" CJ yelled.

"203-555-B-U-T-T," Coco yelled over her shoulder as she opened her door.

"Of course it is."

FOUR

The Unwanted Visitor

Screeching into the driveway, Coco leapt from her car and ran frantically into the house. She found Sam sitting at the kitchen table with his head in his hands, peeking through his fingers at the envelope and its contents. Coco moved closer to see dozens of papers spread out on the table.

"What is it?" she asked, trying to sound innocent.

"I don't know. I don't know what all of these documents are or why they're all together," he said. "Who the hell sent this?"

Coco looked closer. She saw piles of business documents. None of them looked friendly. Sam continued, "It's the company's financial data—it's all here. The balance sheets, accounts receivable, accounts payable, budget forecasts. I checked and double-checked every one of these when I signed off on them, yet now it looks like a mess, and none of these numbers make any sense. The dates are all wrong. What the fuck is going on?"

Sam had recently retired from an extremely successful but extremely flawed start-up company that sold health insurance. He began working there with friends straight out of college, but when the company grew too large too quickly, he found himself in over his head. The board and its sinister lawyers had forced him to sign off on a number of specious documents, making him feel more like a pawn than a partner, ultimately prompting him to leave. The entire matter was soul-crushing, and for a long time after Sam seemed frozen, almost afraid of becoming passionate about any sort of career again. For months he scarcely left the house.

Not long after Sam's departure, the president of the company—his college friend—was slapped with enormous fines by the Insurance Department and booted out following a stock option scandal. Several board members were brought up on fraud charges as well. Sam felt he had gotten out unscathed. But these documents suggested something else entirely.

"I don't understand," he said again. "The dates correspond to when I was still there. This is my signature, yet these are the papers that got Mark in trouble for the stock option thing, which happened after I left. Someone has to have doctored this shit. It just doesn't make any sense."

Coco tried to reassure him. "Okay, let's not panic. Call Kornacki, he'll know what to do. He's the best attorney in the world. Let's let him handle this, okay?"

"Yeah," Sam said reluctantly. Even the best attorney in the world couldn't do anything if anyone believed it was his signature on these papers.

"Wait, what's this?" Sam asked, lifting a smaller envelope and handing it to her. "Looks like something addressed to you."

Coco opened the ominous letter and stared at the bold, typewritten lines. It read:

I know who you are.

You have been identified. For now this is merely a warning to keep your mouth shut. If you talk to anyone, especially the police, many lives will be ruined. That includes yours and your loved ones. Say nothing or forever curse the day that the former Governor of Alaska inspired your costume choice.

Oh shit, she thought, *what the hell is going on here?* As the pieces of the puzzle began falling into place, her phone rang. It was Olivia.

Olivia arrived home from yoga eager to relieve the babysitter—if she could just find her stupid keys. Her plan was to spend the beautiful Sunday afternoon in the park with Simon. Getting in and out of the car was always a juggling act for new moms, but Olivia had more baggage than most—on every level imaginable. First, her hypochondria forced her to travel with her version of a go bag, which hung across her body, heavy with nearly the entirety of a medicine cabinet: Advil, Pepto-Bismol, a thermometer, Band-Aids, small umbrella, ankle braces, itch cream, and bug spray, to name but a few items. Today she also balanced her yoga bag full of smelly clothing while she tried not to spill her après-yoga skinny chai latte as she struggled to keep her yoga mat pinched under her armpit.

"Damn. Did I leave my keys in the car again?" she mumbled.

Olivia walked up to the porch of the house that was soon to be hers—once she'd successfully sued her estranged mother for trying to rob her of her inheritance. That her mother was clearly mentally ill did nothing to ease Olivia's pain, or allow her any empathy. Every time she found some peace in her life, the evil witch would swoop in and sabotage her attempts at normalcy.

Olivia and her mother had never been close. When Olivia was seven years old, her mother left the family, moving from Greenwich to L.A. to become an actress. Some people manifest their family stress by being angry and bitter. But not Olivia. Her stress came out in quirks, like her echolalia. Though brilliantly book-smart, she came off to most as a total ditz. She was forgetful, silly, and disorganized. Her great secret was how absurdly intelligent she was.

When her father passed, it was only natural that he had left the house to her with no stipulations. She'd been the apple of his eye, and he'd endured a lifetime of guilt for what he saw as her insufficient upbringing. But, of course, despite not having communicated with her opportunistic, vengeful mother for nearly twenty years, Olivia wasn't surprised that her father's death would stir a sudden interest. The case, as far as her lawyers were concerned, was a no-brainer, but Olivia would put nothing past her mother.

Upon moving to California when Olivia was a child, and changing her name to Sunshine, the teenage model–wannabe was dissatisfied with her baby-boomer status—hippies and love children notwithstanding. Sunshine intended to be the next Twiggy. It seemed to be lost on her that Twiggy had character, personality, and charisma, which drew people to her.

Sunshine believed she would be creating the "ray of sunshine" the modeling industry was waiting for.

Sunshine's real obsession was with Burt Reynolds, and she was sure she was meant to be his costar. She followed him for nearly a decade, landing nothing more than background work in a few of his films and a random shampoo commercial as the before girl. Olivia had heard rumors that her mother tried to get into the porn industry but couldn't even succeed there. *How mortifying.* Galvanized by the fame and celebrity all around her, Sunshine pursued her crazy dream relentlessly, constantly assuring Olivia by postcard that one day she'd be proud to see her mother on the silver screen. But she only succeeded in becoming increasingly pathetic in Olivia's eyes. And Sunshine remained angry and unhappy, despite the oodles of money her "lowly accountant husband" made and by which her deluded fantasies were enabled. Olivia's father, out of a sense of duty, continued to support Sunshine all those years, most likely in the hope that she would come to her senses and return home to her loving family.

Olivia and her brother, Finn, were raised by their faithful father, basically on his own, in this very house; and if she could beat her mother in court, the house would finally be hers. Unfortunately, this wasn't going to be the first time she'd seen Sunshine from a witness box.

At seventeen, just a few months before her eighteenth birthday, when her trust fund would kick in, Olivia received a startling letter from her mother's attorney. It seemed that mommy dearest was suing to be executor of her trust, claiming that Olivia's father was not of sound mind when he drew up his intentions. In court she claimed that Olivia had told her over the phone that she'd smoked pot and was therefore a drug addict who would use that money for her "repulsive habit." The overwhelming irony of this claim was not lost on those who'd gossiped that Sunshine was famous in L.A. for offering movie stars lines of cocaine to be snorted off her breasts and various other areas of her body. Olivia's mother fought ferociously in the courtroom until a sympathetic, and aware, local magistrate dismissed the case outright and ruled that the trust would become Olivia's on her eighteenth birthday just as her father wished. Soon after this, her echolalia kicked in.

She managed her affliction with a prescription medication called clonidine. Echolalia didn't keep her from much in life, but Olivia analyzed scientific data for an environmental organization funded by the government. It was an intense job, and she was asked to speak all over the world on the organization's findings. Given the stress of her work, it was only a matter of time before symptoms emerged.

On the day she knew she'd have to quit, she was in China, a country with one of the few scientific communities that truly appreciated the importance of her work; this, of course, made her visit all the more exciting but also incredibly stressful. When she got up to give her talk to a room jammed full of Chinese geologists and their interpreters, someone in the back, presumably speaking to a colleague, loudly and rather remarkably uttered, "CHAAANG!"—and that was it. The jet lag, her performance anxiety, the moment caused a compulsion that she simply could not suppress. She abruptly excused herself, sprinted to the ladies' room, and repeated "CHAAANG" loudly in the small, dingy stall several times, utterly horrified despite the fact that no one was there to hear her. Compulsion passed, she straightened her suit and returned to the meeting; she was so mortified that she desperately hoped everyone thought she'd had a severe bout of diarrhea. Thank god she'd removed her lapel mic.

Now, on a leave of absence, she had returned to Connecticut just in time for the passing of her father and the hellish new court battle with her maniac of a mother.

Olivia looked up from her front seat after finding her keys still in the ignition, surprised by the presence of a slightly hulking man she had never seen before, holding something she was getting used to seeing: a large manila envelope. Assuming he was an agent from her mother's attorney or yet another process server, she said, "What does that horrible mother of mine want *this* time?"

"I don't know your mother, Miss Barnes, but I suggest you read this very carefully," the creepy looking man said, in a gruff voice with a hint of an accent. Eastern European? Russian? He wasn't quite Boris and Natashaesque but reminded her of some of the bad guys at the port in season two of *The Wire*. He had more hair in his mustache than the slicked-back mess on his head, and he wore a light brown, blazer-style leather jacket, slightly darker than his tan slacks.

"Aren't you supposed to say 'You've been served'? Are you new at this?" Olivia replied.

The creepy man then stepped up very close to Olivia, scaring her just a little, which seemed to be his intention. "If I were you, I would take seriously this papers." He mispronounced the word *seeeeriously* in a way that let Olivia know he was not a process server but something much more sinister.

Olivia felt a chill run down her spine. "Okay," she whispered as if she could barely get the word out and watched the man walk down her driveway to a dark Lincoln Town Car. In any other neighborhood, a waiting limousine would be an unusual sight, but in Greenwich it was beneath notice.

"Oh, my god! Coco was right." Olivia dropped everything she was holding and ripped open the envelope. Inside were an eviction notice and an official letter from the surrogate court stating that while the house was in probate it was the property of the decedent's next of kin, which, according to this document, was her mother, Sunshine. Olivia ran inside to call Coco.

At the same moment, CJ arrived home from yoga with no idea that his three cohorts were now in three separate states of confusion; nor did he know that his world was also about to fall apart. Nanny was in the family room waiting for him to come home.

"Scubu . . . you home, son? I inda television room," she said in her thick Jamaican accent.

"Yes, Nanny, it's me," CJ replied as he walked into the room. "I picked up your medicine. It's on the kitchen counter, and you have a doctor's appointment Thursday at eight in the morning. I'll take you and go into work late that day, don't worry."

"I'm not worried, child, you a good son. Oh, Scubu, there's dat envelope come for you today," she said nervously.

CJ opened the envelope like it was no big deal, but in his heart he suspected it might be. In an instant he noticed it had no return address, just his name. But what really caught his eye was the fact that it was not addressed to CJ but used his full name, Charlton Jeffre Skoda. Nobody called him that. He nervously opened the envelope and went white as a sheet at what he saw inside.

"Dat man come to the door, I seen 'im before, he no good. I tell him so," she said. "I worry you in big trouble."

"Nanny, you spoke to the man? Did he tell you what was in this envelope?" CJ was now incredibly worried.

"No, but 'im notta nice man. I ask whatta goin on and 'im tell me to make sure you see this as soon as you get 'ome. What's the matter, Scubu?"

"I can't tell you, Nanny," he said apologetically. "I'd like to, but I can't."

"You tell me everyting, pleeze, boy," she scoffed.

"I'm sorry, I just can't," he said again.

"Dat mayor tryin' to have some fun wit you?" she asked.

"The mayor? Why did you say the mayor?" Now he was alarmed. What did she know? She always knew everything, but there was no way she could know what they'd seen last night. He hadn't told a soul.

"That man, him work for the mayor, I see them together in town," she said.

"The man who brought this envelope? He works for the mayor? Are you sure?" CJ said, seriously panicking now.

"Aye," Nanny said. CJ kissed her and ran out of the house. Where he was going, he didn't quite know.

Olivia arrived at Coco's house visibly shaken. She was uncomfortable with how unraveled she was allowing herself to be in front of near strangers. She wondered if it was okay to let her freak flag fly with someone who, while in the same predicament, seemed to be handling it so much better.

Coco sat at her kitchen table looking across at Olivia, who twirled and untwirled a piece of string around her finger.

"I can't lose the house, so let's do whatever the letter says and just go on with our lives," Olivia said between nervous blinks.

"This letter is all but an admission of guilt. We can't let him get away with murder! We *have* to do something! Think about that woman. What if it was you . . . or me?" Coco insisted.

"I have a baby to take care of. Why can't you do it without me?" Olivia thought that having a baby would give her an out.

"This isn't a negotiation. We're talking about a criminal—a violent one. He isn't offering an opportunity for separate deals. If one of us caves, he goes down all the same. He's blackmailing all of us, collectively. We're in this together."

Coco now knew that it was not a practical joke, nor was it a Halloween prank. They had witnessed a murder. The mayor's letter pretty much confirmed it.

"Holy shit!" Coco surprised herself with her outburst. "Jesus Christ, we saw a friggin' dead body last night. She'd just been killed!"

"Oh, I've seen lots of dead bodies," Olivia said matter-of-factly and somewhat absently.

"You have? Where?"

"Well, I saw cadavers all the time in grad school. I was going to be a forensic scientist before I switched to geophysics, but I saw my first dead body long before that even. It was at a carnival on the Cape," Olivia told her.

"Really? Well, that was my first, and I'm hoping that I don't become somebody else's first," Coco said, not really joking.

"Yeah, really. When I was a kid we used to spend summers in Hyannis, and they always had these carnivals in Barnstable County. This one summer when the carnival was shut down for the night, my friends and I hopped the fence by the Tilt-A-Whirl. As we headed toward it, we saw a strange lump on the ground. It looked like a big blue blow-up toy, but there was a horrendous smell coming from it. We got closer and saw a woman, clearly dead. We screamed and ran. One of the boys we were with stopped a passing police car and told him what we saw." Olivia stopped and waited for a reaction.

"Oh no. Was she murdered?" Coco wasn't all that interested, but she thought Olivia might be making a point. She responded in a way that she felt would satisfy her new friend.

"No, she probably overdosed; in retrospect, she had all the telltale signs," Olivia said proudly, as if pleased that her forensic schooling had finally proved useful.

As Coco rolled her eyes, her phone rang.

"I'm in my car. Where do you live? I have to come over," CJ whispered frantically on the other end of the phone.

"Let me guess. An envelope showed up at your house."

"Shhhhh, stop talking. The phones might be bugged. I'm coming over, where do you live?" he demanded.

"Well, if the phone is bugged, I'm not giving out my address," Coco joked.

"They already know where you live! My god, woman, where are you?" CJ shouted into the phone.

"Eighty-five Walsh Lane," she said.

"Okay, I'm a few blocks away, don't leave," CJ said.

"Where am I going?" Coco replied flatly, and then, clicking off her phone, she turned to Olivia. "Well, CJ sure has his panties in a bunch. I'm guessing he got an envelope too. He should be here in a few minutes."

"Do you think the other girl . . . Bailey, got one too? She must have," Olivia said.

"I'd bet money on it. Do you know where she lives or her number?" Coco asked.

"CJ probably knows where she lives; they went to high school together," Olivia said. "And I think he got her number last night."

"Right, right," Coco continued. "Well, I think when he gets here we should call her and the four of us should figure this out together, don't you?"

"Okay, good plan."

Just then Coco heard Sam on the staircase and panicked. She hadn't told him about the night before or why they had received this envelope; when Olivia had called, she'd tucked her letter away and walked into the other room. As far as he knew, it was just another document, and he assumed one of his old partners was messing with him or there'd been some gross clerical error. She wanted desperately to keep him in the dark, to protect him from what she now knew. *Okay, think fast,* she told herself. *Who is Olivia, and why is she here?*

In a hushed whisper Coco said, "Olivia, I didn't tell Sam any of this. Please, just don't say why you're here."

"Sure, what are we going to . . ." And before Olivia could finish her sentence, Sam entered the kitchen.

"Hi, I'm Olivia. Coco and I are in yoga together." She tried to remain calm, but calm wasn't in her toolbox. "You must be Sam. Coco has told me so much about you . . . Did I mention we're in yoga together? At the yoga center. In town." She was bombing. "Hi, I'm Olivia," she said, holding out her hand. It was like last night all over again.

"Don't let me interrupt, I'm just getting a soda. Nice to meet you, Olivia." Sam shook Olivia's hand. He looked haggard and worried, and shot Coco a look as if to say, *Don't we have more pressing matters at hand?*

The doorbell rang. Coco could see CJ hopping around at her front door like a kid desperately needing to go to the bathroom.

"I'll get it," Sam said.

Coco jumped up. "No, no, no. Don't worry, it's cool. It's for me. Another one of our yoga buddies is here. We're just, uh, figuring out a weekend for a yoga retreat that, uh, Olivia is helping me put together. You know I've been talking about doing that for a while."

"Oh yeah, right," Sam said half suspiciously. Coco was definitely acting weird, but Sam had learned, as most significant others do, to just let her be. The last time he'd been suspicious of Coco's weird behavior it was because she was planning a surprise party for him; so, with their first-date anniversary coming up, Sam thought it best to just play dumb.

"I'll be up in my office. I'm waiting to hear back from Kornacki," Sam said.

"Okay. Love you," Coco said over her shoulder as she ran to the door.

She opened the door to a very tense CJ, who burst right in.

"Darling, you were right, oh, my god!" he half whispered, half yelled as he paced in her entryway. "This is bigger than I thought it was, and I am *totally* freaking out!"

He was flustered but also had never been to Coco's house, so he wasn't sure which way to go. He settled for pacing in anxious circles around the foyer.

"Oh, my god, what do we do? And where the hell is your living room? I have to sit down." CJ was frantic.

Coco led him to the living room, which was in the back of the house by the kitchen, where she picked up Olivia along the way.

"Come in here, you two. Sam won't be able to hear anything," Coco assured them.

"Oh, my god, you didn't tell him? Did they threaten his life? Yours? We have to call the police!" CJ insisted.

"Hang on, hang on! Nobody is calling anybody until we sort all of this out," Coco said.

She was surprisingly calm on the outside. Inside, she too was a mess, but with two maniacs on her hands she had to become the voice of reason.

"Okay, first off, CJ, what happened? What did you get in your envelope?" Coco needed to know.

"You tell me first," CJ said.

"This isn't a game. What's the difference who goes first?" Coco could tell by the look on CJ's face this was a futile argument.

"Okay, fine. My envelope was filled with information about Sam's company, well, his ex-company, which could get him in a lot of trouble. His partners are from that insurance company who had that stock option scandal last year. I don't know if you read about it, but it was in the *Times, The Wall Street Journal*, all over TV. But all that stuff had happened years after Sam left. Well, there is some speculation that it was going on while he was there, but he never knew anything about it. Even when they subpoenaed him for trial he seriously didn't know a thing and turned out to be a crummy witness. But here's the thing: the documents in the envelope are forged to make him look like he was a part of it. Sam saw the envelope, and he thinks it's his ex-partners screwing with him. Even if the papers *are* forged, it looks really bad for him. Really bad," she said. "And in Olivia's envelope . . . Well, why don't you explain it to him?" Coco turned to Olivia.

"Okay," Olivia began. "Well, I'm in a legal battle with my mother over the house I just inherited. It was my father's house and the place where I grew up. He left it to me fair and square, but in the envelope are papers which, if my crazy, negligent mother got her hands on them, could really help her take the house away from me.

"My mother always claimed that my father was mentally unstable when he drew up his will, and in the envelope are clearly forged papers that say he spent some time in a facility where he was being treated for exhaustion."

"Um, *exhaustion*? Oh, girl, yes, that's the euphemism for either drugs or a nervous breakdown. Which one was it?" CJ pressed.

"Actually, he suffered from bouts of depression, after she had left him and way before he revised his will. He saw a therapist but was never institutionalized. But these papers, real or not, could help her case," Olivia said sadly.

"I'm so sorry," Coco said.

"Yeah, me too," CJ concurred.

"It's okay, thanks," Olivia said.

Coco turned to CJ. "Okay, so, you've seen inside our kimonos. What's in *your* envelope?"

"Oh, honey, I'm so sorry about Olivia's house and your husband's ex-partners and all, but mine's much, much worse. There are photos in here that can bury this entire town. Pictures that I didn't even know existed. In fact, they've *got* to be Photoshopped. I mean, things have happened, but there's just no way . . ." CJ said.

"What are they photos of?" Now Coco was intrigued.

"Yeah, tell us!" Olivia said.

"I don't know where to begin, and frankly I'm afraid to say. I never, ever told anyone about this. I have no idea how anyone could have known." CJ was nervous. "Promise you won't judge me?"

They both stared at him as if to imply that the question was pointless by now.

"Promise me, I said!" CJ insisted.

"Okay, okay! God," Olivia agreed.

"Who am I to judge anyone? I make my money selling butt cream," Coco reassured him.

"That's true, okay. Well, when I was in high school I wasn't out. I'm still not officially out to everyone. I'm reserved with people around here, and I'm definitely not out to my parents. I mean—I imagine people assume, but you just don't go around shouting it around here. Nanny knows, but she was the one who told me I was gay when I was twelve. And I was definitely *not* out in high school, so there was nobody to talk to about my crush on the boy in modern history class, and nobody to nudge when the hot new shop teacher's assistant rode away from school on his motorcycle. He was all *kinds* of delicious." CJ distracted himself for a second.

"Go on," Coco said, intrigued.

CJ continued. "Well, when you're young and gay and living in stuck-up, conservative Greenwich, you have to either keep things to yourself or try to find other friends of Dorothy. Sometimes you suspect another kid, but if they're still pretending to be straight and you make the wrong move, you can get your butt kicked. So, I chose the safe, quiet route. Since the headmaster of the school was sort of out, I told him. This was in the early nineties, and even though everyone was trying to be so politically correct, gay still wasn't okay, which is too bad. I would've made the sexiest homecoming queen that school had ever seen!"

"Yes, you would have," Coco said, reassuringly.

"So, one day I was in the headmaster's office—I'd been working for him when he needed help organizing files or at book signings, or whatever extra help he needed. He had a new book out, and I was in his office a lot, and it was obvious that there was some sexual tension building—"

"Oh, my god, how old was he?" Olivia interrupted.

"I don't know, late thirties, early forties. I'm not sure," CJ said.

"Well, how old were you?" Olivia asked.

"Seventeen probably."

"Oh, my god!"

"C'mon, you promised not to judge," CJ reminded her.

"Right. I'm sorry. Go on," said Olivia.

"Here's how it was in the gay community back then, Mary:

everyone needed a drag mother, and I was extremely lucky to have found one. The headmaster, Ricky, didn't have it as easy as I did. He told me he had escaped rural South Dakota by hopping into an interstate eighteen-wheeler and repeatedly fellating the driver in exchange for a free ride to the East Coast. He had no guidance back then, no one watching his back. He wanted to be the guardian he himself had so desperately craved," CJ explained.

"Did you have to have sex with him? Oh, sorry." Olivia caught herself asking what she realized was a really inappropriate question.

"No, that's fine." CJ continued. "For a brief moment we did, but Ricky was more of a gay mother than a lover—and, until this very moment, I thought nobody else knew. Back then the only person a young gay man could talk to was an older gay man who'd been through it all. And remember, they were there at the worst of it, like at Stonewall."

CJ noticed the blank look on Olivia's face. "Oh, god. You don't know any queers, do you, honey?"

"Well, *you* now. But no, no I don't. Didn't," Olivia said sheepishly.

"Well, it was awful. People were queer-bashed, fired, or publicly humiliated for being openly gay, or even suspected of it; people weren't okay with gays at all. Ricky was one of the only people who understood me; our bond was actually quite common. Ask any of your gay friends how much older their first sexual encounter was and you'll be shocked."

"So what does this have to do with what is in the envelope?" Coco asked.

"In here"—CJ held it up like it was the Holy Grail—"in

here are pictures that appear to be of the headmaster and me in . . . let's just say 'doing stuff.' I had no idea photos existed. I don't even know where these came from, but it certainly looks like me. And it's him. There's no mistaking it," CJ said. "In any other circumstance I would think they're kinda hot."

"Well, surely the statute of limitations is up, if you're afraid of any legal backlash," Coco assured him.

"No, it's not about that. It's about humiliating him, and ruining my family. My father is running for governor. Do you have any idea what it would do to his chances if photos of his fairy son blowing the headmaster of one of the most prestigious private schools in the country were released? There's a Skoda wing there, for chrissakes! My parents practically own the fucking school!"

"Okay. So we all agree that what's in our envelopes can't be released," Olivia said.

"Well, of course. But we also cannot let someone get away with murder," Coco insisted.

"Uhhhhhh . . . yes, we can," said CJ. "I have no problem forgetting all of this ever happened. Besides, I'm not even sure what we saw last night, right?"

In spite of herself, Coco was anxious for the problem to go away, and fast. "I think we're making a mistake, but if you think that's what we should do, we all have to be in agreement."

Before she could even finish her sentence, Olivia jumped in. "That's what I think we should do. Sign whatever he wants us to sign or do whatever he wants us to do and let's just make this go away."

"Agreed! I am not going to sleep a wink until this is under control," CJ said.

"Okay, fine. But there's just one problem. We haven't spoken to Bailey, and we don't know if she got an envelope too, and if so, what's she doing about it? If even one of us is not onboard, we're all screwed. He was clear about that," Coco said.

"Well then, let's go to her house and find out," CJ suggested.

"Do you know where she lives?" Olivia asked.

"Pffft, oh, god, yes. Everyone knows *that* house," CJ said.

FIVE

Michael Bublé

When the threesome arrived at Bailey's family estate, they were so focused on their mission they didn't realize that her driveway looked like a luxury car dealership. There before them was wealth in automobile form: an array of Mercedes SLR McLarens, Porsches, several BMWs, and even one Bugatti Veyron. Coco's little black Mini Cooper didn't fit in, but there was no time to play whose bonus was bigger right now. It did seem odd that there were so many expensive cars there, but one could have assumed the Warfields were an eccentric bunch with a penchant for fancy cars.

Before Coco came to a full stop, CJ shoved Olivia's seat forward so vehemently she nearly struck her head on the windshield, mumbling "sorry" as he squeezed through the small opening from the backseat, then sprang out of the car and dashed to the door without even noticing the server in full uniform with a tray of mimosas at the portico. Barging into the large, well, not living room exactly but more like ballroom on his right, he found himself facing fifty odd people in lavish daywear, mingling and sniffing at trays of hors d'oeuvres as servers nattily dressed in white uniforms wove through the crowd. Quickly recovering from his shock, he made his way through the room, impatiently searching for Bailey—it shouldn't have been hard to pick the flower from the fossils—when suddenly a strong whiff of very expensive musk assaulted his senses. Overwhelmed, he wheeled around to encounter the source of the all-consuming scent: Mrs. Warfield, Bailey's mother.

Mrs. Warfield was old money, first-class-on-the-*Mayflower* old, yet there she stood wearing Rock & Republic skinny jeans tucked into four-inch-high-heeled Gucci platform boots, all topped off with an Alexander McQueen blouse, which showed off her Harry Winston blue diamond drop earrings. She was a hodgepodge of too much money and questionable taste combined with a desperate need to look twenty years younger than her age. Everyone knew that Mrs. Warfield was in constant competition with her youngest daughter, Bailey—except Bailey herself.

Mrs. Warfield knew CJ wasn't there for the party.

"Bailey should be back in a bit. She's in the city at a junket, but you are welcome to stay and wait for her. Have a watermelon gazpacho shooter, they're heavenly," she said as she handed a shot glass to CJ.

"I'm here with friends, we can just come back later," CJ said.

"Nonsense! Invite them in as well. There are tables in the tent in the backyard; get one close to the stage, Michael Bublé should be here any minute," she said excitedly.

"Always the hostess—" But before CJ could finish his thought, she interrupted him.

"I think you know Rudy," Mrs. Warfield said as she

grabbed the arm of former New York Mayor Rudy Giuliani as he passed.

"Of course. Your Honor." CJ smiled slyly. "How've you been?" CJ thrust out his hand warmly, but America's mayor moved in for the bear hug.

"Charlton Jeffre! Come here! We're practically family, cut the formal crap," Rudy replied as CJ returned the hug, trying to mask his anxiety.

They *were* practically family. Not only had CJ's family donated an enormous amount of money to both of the mayor's campaigns but Rudy's cousin was married to one of CJ's relatives. He wasn't sure which one; he just knew that they were always at big family gatherings together and that Rudy always gave him the "Charlton Jeffre" business, like an overenthusiastic uncle.

"Looks like your dad'll be moving into the governor's mansion soon, huh? You must be so proud of him," Rudy said with a grin.

All CJ could think about was how that envelope in the car would ruin everything, but he smiled back easily. CJ excelled in masking uncomfortable truths.

"Yes, of course, it's *very* exciting," CJ stressed his *very,* thinking it would make him seem more convincing, but it only made him seem more gay. "Excuse me for a moment, I have some friends waiting outside."

"Of course, but when you come back, make sure you find me. Judith would love to see you," Rudy insisted.

"Absolutely," CJ replied as he rushed to the car where Olivia and Coco were still waiting. He'd be sure to avoid the mayor when he returned, lest he be regaled with yet another 9/11 story.

"Crap!" exclaimed CJ as he ran toward them. "She's in the city at a junket. Her mom says she'll be back soon and we can wait here. What do you want to do?"

"I guess we can go grab a coffee and come back later," Coco suggested.

"Okay, let's do that," CJ agreed.

Just then a black town car pulled up, and out stepped a familiar face.

"Oh, my god, is that Michael Bublé?" Olivia gasped. "What's he doing here?"

"Bailey's mom said he was going to do a show in the backyard," CJ replied absently. "Okay, let's go get coffee."

"Wait. Wait a minute, let's not be too hasty. We don't know when Bailey will be back, and we really should stay," Olivia suggested as her attention strayed toward the black town car.

"You want to stay and hear Michael Bublé, don't you?" Coco asked.

"Yes, please . . . Can we? Please?" Olivia sounded like a twelve-year-old begging to see Justin Bieber.

"Is that cool? Are we invited?" Coco asked CJ.

"Yeah, sure, Mrs. Warfield said we should stay. She even suggested we grab a table up by the stage if we want to," he replied.

"We want to! We want to!" Olivia half squealed.

"Look, let's not forget why we're here. We've got some serious shit going on, and we're not really invited guests. We should try to stay focused, okay?" Coco scolded.

"We can still stay focused while watching Michael Bublé, right?" Olivia begged.

"Okay, fine. No harm in that," Coco agreed.

The three entered the house, stopping briefly to grab tea sandwiches and salmon tartlettes as they headed for the backyard. That was the thing about Greenwich—while other towns had summer block parties or barbecues on holidays and special occasions, not a day went by in Greenwich when someone wasn't having some sort of soiree, fund raiser, honoree luncheon, or, of course, the obligatory charity event (and the more outlandish the charity the better). Today's gathering was comparatively respectable: it was in honor of the Warfield Library's twenty-fifth anniversary. Despite a performance by a Grammy winner, Coco hated these events. Having never really grown accustomed to the moneyed world to which she now belonged, she was allergic to pretension.

It was the first week in November and unseasonably warm, as it had been all week, yet the tent was heated to guard against an errant chill. CJ waved to Coco and Olivia from a table he'd found for them. As she went to sit down, Coco spotted the celebrity chef Bobby Flay and wondered if he would remember her.

Just then CJ turned around to see the renowned chef and yelled, "Bobby, hey!" at which the chef stopped to say hello. CJ made introductions before Flay continued on through the crowd.

"Who don't you know?" Olivia marveled.

"Oh, darling, everyone knows everyone here, if not by

name, then at least by face. And Bobby is probably the best at that. The man can work a room."

Coco couldn't contain herself. "Oh yeah, well I've met him before, and there wasn't even a glimmer of recognition. I was even at his house in the Hamptons," she said bitterly.

"Really? When were you there?" CJ wanted to know.

Coco took a deep breath. This was the stuff she hated about these social events. It was solely about being seen. As long as you got your name in the society pages or on "Page Six," it wasn't about meeting or getting to know anyone. Certainly not in any *real* way.

Coco's entrée into the world of hobnobbery and her disdain for it all had started one summer in the hollow, pretentious world of East Hampton, where it came to a head at the house of Bobby Flay.

East Hampton was an odd place when you thought about it. It was hard to believe that out on the far end of Long Island, where there was now the Ralph Lauren–wearing, celebrity-obsessed upper class (including Ralph Lauren himself), up until rather recently there had been barely sustainable farms. East Hampton was the third town on Long Island established by colonists, when its primary industries were whaling and livestock. How things had changed. Now East Hampton industries were investing in leviathan capital and spending the day trying not to look porcine.

"Well," Coco began, "I had a good friend, Melinda, who was as lovely as can be while in the cement and chaos of the city, but the minute she went out east to the Hamptons, she became as affected as an air kiss at a polo match."

Olivia laughed.

Coco continued. "Melinda and I used to take one vacation a summer together, and it was usually somewhere warm, quiet, and subdued. But as her career as a fashion photographer expanded, she felt more and more compelled to see and be seen. One summer she convinced me that we would have just as much fun and relaxation time in the Hamptons as anywhere else. I reluctantly agreed and spent an entire week being shuttled from one stuffy party to another, usually getting turned down at the door because we weren't on some list, the party was overcrowded, or we'd arrived too late. Some sort of BS or another made every day of that vacation a nightmare."

"Sounds like it. I prefer beaches in the Caribbean myself," CJ put in.

"Yes, I'm sure you would. Anyway, the problem was that Melinda was not as dialed in as she originally thought. Awkward! The only shining moment in the entire week was an actual—I mean genuine—invitation to *the* party of the summer: Bobby Flay's barbecue at his house in the North Woods. Melinda was friendly with him and got us an invite.

"I suggested to Melinda that we should bring something from the local farmers' market as a gift for our host, but by then we were practically broke—the entire week we'd been living on Pepperidge Farm Goldfish crackers and Diet 7-Up in order to afford our hotel room. So, Melinda goes out and buys the most expensive bottle of wine she could find to impress her famous chef friend. Like what do we know about fine wine?"

"Right! Flowers would have been enough," Olivia agreed.

"Right. So, even though we had no money, Melinda bullied me into going halves on a hundred-and-fifty-dollar bottle of wine. I didn't want to come off as cheap, even though I totally couldn't afford it at the time. All my money was spent on housing. But I figured a meal with Bobby Flay *at his house* was totally worth it; it would cost twice that to eat in one of his restaurants, right?"

"Of course! How was the food? Who was there?" CJ asked.

"Wait, I'm getting to that. So we arrive at his house and get escorted to the backyard, where he's grillin' and chillin', and Melinda gives him a big kiss and introduces me. Bobby Flay turns around, and I immediately see he's not in happy host mode. Something is up. Melinda, of course, misses it entirely and hands him the hundred-and-fifty-dollar bottle of wine."

"Was he impressed?" Olivia asked.

"Actually, he barely looked at it. He puts it down and says, 'Hi, Coco, it's great to meet you, thank you so much for coming . . . but I have some bad news for you ladies. I don't know if you noticed on your way in, but the power is out, so we've had to cancel the party,' and he makes a frowny face with his lower lip stuck out."

"Oh no!" Overly empathetic Olivia was practically reliving the moment herself.

"How did you not notice there was no electricity?" CJ asked.

"It was daytime! A beautiful, sunny summer afternoon in the Hamptons. So why would there be lights on anyway?"

"Couldn't they just flip a circuit breaker or something and turn the power back on?" CJ asked. "How could it have been such a big deal?"

"Melinda asked him the same thing, and he says, 'It's not

that simple,' and tells us that Puffy, Puff Daddy, Sean Combs—whatever he was calling himself back then—lived next door and had been having an all-day party that used up all of the electricity. He had giant speakers, lights, music. It was like a carnival over there, and those woods weren't built for that kind of power usage."

"That sucks . . . Ooh, was Jennifer Lopez there?" Olivia asked.

"Sooooo not the point," Coco scoffed.

"Right, sorry," Olivia said.

"Anyway, Bobby was very sweet and invited us to stay and have whatever he was grilling, and then he motions us to sit with a few people and some children who were waiting for whatever was on that grill. I realize it's probably his family or something. Melinda realizes it too and says, 'No, no, that's okay, we'll go.' She's trying to be polite and looks at me for consensus, but I have this look on my face that just says, *screw that.* I wanted something for my hundred-and-fifty-dollar bottle of wine: cheese, crackers, a drink, an amuse-bouche—anything! By now I was pissed. It was all I could do to hold it in. The whole week was rolling up on me."

"So you left and had nothing?" Olivia asked.

"Me? No way. You *must* be kidding. I wasn't going to let Melinda railroad me again. I immediately fell back on the acting classes I took just after college. 'I'm sorry, Mr. Flay, I don't want to impose,' I lied, 'but I'm afraid I've been having some rather severe bouts of hypoglycemia lately. If I don't sit for a minute and have something to eat, I'll pass out.'"

CJ chuckled approvingly.

"Let me tell you"—Coco laughed—"we had some of the

best grilled summer vegetables I've ever had. That boy can cook! Oh, and the wine was terrific. Though I wouldn't've been able to tell the difference from a twenty-dollar bottle, quite frankly."

"Was Melinda grateful?" Olivia asked.

"Oh, not at all. She was mortified . . . though she didn't say so till later. That was pretty much the beginning of the end of our friendship. To hell with her. I don't care who it is. You don't invite someone to a party and then just turn them away. A good host figures out a way to make do."

"Ah, the Hamptons," CJ said. "I have no idea why anyone would ever go there, let alone stay for the entire summer. Did you know that they allow absolutely *anyone* to use their beaches?"

Just then Mrs. Warfield took the stage to introduce her special musical guest. Olivia noticeably straightened in her chair, as if her slouching would harm Michael Bublé's performance; or, more likely, she wanted him to notice her.

Though she looked forward to hearing Bublé, Coco suddenly remembered why they were there and became unexpectedly anxious. Where the hell was Bailey, and what guarantee did they have that she was coming here straight from her press junket, anyway? But then it hit her—Michael Bublé was famous, handsome, and at her house. Bailey catnip for sure.

At the press junket, Bailey was visibly distracted. She sat in the hospitality suite staring at the shoes of the woman across from her, completely lost in thought. She couldn't focus on the questions she would ask Tom Hanks, nor could she think happy thoughts about her tryst the night before with John Mayer. The envelope had her attention. All of it. *Who'd sent it? What was in it?* The questions ate at her, probably because she had begun to suspect it had something to do with last night. She also wanted to know why the heck Detective Casey was taking so long to get back to her.

Just then a noseful of Fleur de Narcisse hit her like a slap across the face. She turned to find the film's publicist, who was coming to tell her she was "on deck." That meant that she was going to have to move to a folding chair outside the room where all of the cameras were set up and Tom Hanks was being interviewed. She'd be there just adjacent to the makeup person, who was getting almost a grand a day to powder Hanks's nose in between takes.

Bailey also knew that it meant while she was waiting her turn she would have to endure the bravado of the other journalists who came to brag about the last time they'd interviewed Hanks and what they "got him" to say—as if he'd suddenly admitted to some scandalous tidbit about his sex life. Right. These interviews were as predictable as most of the crappy movies they had to sit through.

Finally it was her turn, and the hot little PR drill sergeant reminded her she had exactly four minutes, two of which would be spent greeting Tom Hanks, whom she'd interviewed many, many times before.

"Ah, Bailey, I was wondering when I'd be seeing you," the Oscar winner said as he stood up to greet her.

"Hi, Tom, good to see you," Bailey replied as she hugged him hello.

"I heard your grandfather was retiring for good. Is that true?" he quietly asked as the audio tech mic'd her up.

"God no. Never."

"Wow, that's superb. He's in his late eighties, right?"

"Just turned ninety," Bailey replied.

"Jeez, good for him," Hanks said as the drill sergeant reminded them they had only four minutes and needed to get started. Hanks and Bailey looked at each other like schoolchildren caught by their teacher for whispering in class.

"Yes, ma'am," Hanks joked but then continued, "Oh, Colin asked about you, by the way."

Bailey ignored that last comment and began asking questions as the drill sergeant counted her down: "Three minutes . . . two . . . one . . . Wrap it up! Wrap it up!" Good timing, since Bailey didn't want to talk to Tom about his son. She had dated Colin Hanks briefly. Well, *dated* was a strong word. She'd met him when he was doing press for *Orange County,* and they did the long-distance thing for about two months, but she'd had to break it off with the young Hanks when he suggested moving her in. Bailey wasn't looking for commitment back then. Come to think of it, she still wasn't. Well, probably not, anyway.

Her final interview of the day was with Jessica Simpson. This would be the last one for both of them, since the girls had texted each other earlier to make plans for coffee when the junket was over. Jessica was one of those celebrities who had rules about what you could and could not ask on record. Bailey looked forward to hearing which of her competitors had been asked to leave when they crossed the line and asked Jessica a question on the forbidden list: usually about Nick

Lachey, or something equally gauche, like her breasts, the time the media called her fat, or whether she was responsible for the Dallas Cowboys' losing games while she was dating Tony Romo.

As Bailey waited on deck once again, her phone rang. It was a private number, which Bailey normally wouldn't have answered, but she hoped the call was from Detective Casey. It was.

"Miss Warfield, this is Detective Casey. I need to speak with you about this envelope. Is this a good time?" he asked.

"Yes, of course," Bailey said as she stepped out into the hallway. She hoped he was calling to resolve her anxiety—finally.

"You should know that the envelope wasn't laced with anything—no bomb, no anthrax, nothing like that," Detective Casey assured her.

"Oh, good. Thank god." She felt lighter now. "So what was it, then?" Bailey asked.

"Well, that's the tough part, Miss Warfield. There was a DVD inside, so I felt obligated to take a look at it."

"Okay . . ."

"Well, it contained video footage . . . of . . . *you*. And another individual in, shall we say, rather compromising positions. It was—*ahem*—quite graphic," he continued. "But I can assure you that nobody saw it."

"Well, you obviously did."

"Uh, yes. Yes, I did. I'm afraid that, as part of my investigation, I had to," he said. He almost sounded as if he were blushing.

"Yes, of course, I didn't mean anything by that," Bailey assured him.

"But I wanted to assure you that no one else saw this footage," Detective Casey said carefully.

"Thank you, I appreciate that," Bailey said. "Can you tell me more? Did you recognize the other party? Do you have any idea who could have sent it to me? I honestly don't know how I was . . . recorded. Maybe it's doctored up."

"Miss Warfield . . . not only is the video content of a delicate nature but I think I may have some information that we really should discuss in person."

"Great. Please get to the bottom of this, Detective, and spare no expense. Find out who sent it and let's go after the bastards," Bailey said as adrenaline rushed through her veins.

"Absolutely, Miss Warfield. When will you be at home?"

"I'll be there in about an hour. Can you meet me then?"

"Yes, that's fine. I'll see you in an hour," Detective Casey said as he hung up the phone.

Bailey's stomach dropped.

As Olivia swayed dreamily to "Me and Mrs. Jones," Coco fidgeted with her wineglass and stared off into nowhere. She glanced over at CJ, who didn't seem all that enthralled with Michael Bublé either but instead was fixated on a couple off to the side who were dancing.

"Do you know them?" Coco asked.

"No. I'm just thinking about what they would think about

me if I were dancing with a man the way they're dancing with each other. So close and touchy-feely," CJ said.

"My guess is they'd be wondering who'd lead," Coco quipped.

"You ever do that? Do you ever look at people watching you and imagine that they're thinking about you, and wonder what it is they're thinking?" CJ asked.

"Can't say that I do, no," she said. A half-truth, really.

"I do it all the time. I have some sort of ESP, where I know what they're thinking about me. It came with the gaydar. It's like this sketchy paranoia that I have about how they're judging me and what they're saying about me—even Michael Bublé. I think he's looking over here and wondering what it would be like to be with a man, but he is disgusted by the very thought of it, or the fact that he even considered it. It's okay, Michael, I'm not after you. I'm saving myself for Cheyenne Jackson."

"Of course you are," Coco said.

"Seriously. Would Michael Bublé sing at my twentieth anniversary with Cheyenne?" CJ asked rhetorically as he gazed longingly at the Grammy winner.

Coco looked up and saw Bailey arriving to kisses and hugs from various guests. She tapped CJ on the shoulder, pointed him in Bailey's direction, awakening him to their original mission, and rose from her chair.

Olivia was still enjoying Michael Bublé, and as much as they hated to interrupt her, CJ nudged her back to earth. There were more pressing issues.

The trio charged Bailey. CJ grabbed her by the arm and with a stern look that said, "We need to talk," gracefully led her away from her adoring fans.

"What the heck are you guys doing here?" Bailey asked.

"Waiting for you!" CJ exclaimed. "Did you get an unexpected envelope with no return address delivered to your door this morning?"

She'd been distracted by the party, but Bailey's anxiety returned immediately, though she maintained a seemingly quiet cool. How did they know about the sex tape if Detective Casey hadn't told anyone? Was the tape sent to all three of them, and if so, why? She barely knew them.

"Maybe . . . Why?" Bailey had learned long ago never to tip her hand. For all her indiscretions, discretion was her forte.

"Because all three of us received envelopes this morning, and we assumed you did too," Coco said flatly.

Now Bailey was starting to panic, discretion be damned. *Why on earth would someone send video of me having sex to these people I just met?* she wondered, eyes wide.

"So are you here to blackmail me? Because the police are on their way over, and I will have all three of you arrested," Bailey threatened.

Olivia knitted her brow, completely confused.

Coco caught it before the others did. "Wait. What? Did you ask if *we* were blackmailing *you*? What are you *fucking* talking about?" In consideration of the party guests, she said *fucking* quietly and through clenched teeth.

"Well, why else would you be here?" Bailey asked.

"Oh, for god's sake. It's always about you, isn't it?" CJ said, rolling his eyes.

"Oh, Jesus. No, we didn't receive information about *you*. We *each* received an envelope with information about each one of us . . . personally . . . you know, as *individuals*? Why the hell would someone send us information about *you*?" Coco was incredulous. Bailey's level of self-involvement was disgusting.

"I got an envelope about the house I am fighting to keep. Coco got one with papers about her boyfriend's company, and CJ got some tawdry pictures," Olivia explained.

"*Tawdry?* Really, Olivia?" CJ asked.

"I'm not judging, I'm just saying."

"Oh, wait. So . . . you only know that I got an envelope. Not what's in it?" Bailey asked.

"Nope," Coco said.

"Oh, okay, great. Well, I've got my situation under control. I appreciate your concern, but I'm going to handle it on my own," said Bailey.

Coco sucked in her breath. "Yeah, well, that's just the thing. You can't, you see. We have to be a united front here, because if just one of us tries to fight it, we're all screwed."

"This is obviously about last night, darling," CJ jumped in. "The envelopes all came with a letter presumably written by someone working with the mayor. It says that we have to keep our mouths shut about what we saw last night or they will make our lives miserable—ruin us, so to speak. So, we're all going to have to go along with his demands."

"We decided it was going to be easier for us to go along with them and keep quiet. We need to get on with our lives—none of us can afford to have any of this get out. But you're going to have to agree also," Olivia said.

"No."

"What?" Coco asked.

"You heard me: No. I'm not giving in to blackmail. Besides, it's too late. Detective Casey already saw what was in my envelope and has started an investigation. You three are on your own, I guess," Bailey said.

"You are *such* a selfish bitch!" CJ yelled. "You can't do that."

"I'm sorry. It's my life they're going after, and I can do whatever I see fit to defend my reputation and honor," Bailey responded.

"*Your* reputation? As what? Some trollop who fucks any celebrity who would have her?" CJ yelled. "I'm the one with a real reputation. If anyone at Rachael Ray found out what was in that envelope, I would lose my job and my father would lose his bid for the governorship. It's not about you!"

"I'm not listening to this anymore. The three of you get out before I have you thrown out," Bailey fired back.

"Bailey, wait. Please. We have to talk about this. We all have something at stake here. We have to be on the same side," Coco pleaded. "Just give us five minutes. Please."

Bailey stared at the three pairs of confused, distraught eyes. "Fine. Five minutes," she finally said and reluctantly led the interlopers upstairs.

SIX

Corrupt Cops

Bailey led her unwelcome guests up the grand staircase, which was lined with eighteenth-century Flemish tapestries. The second landing revealed a second-floor parlor that defied all conventional interior design rules. It was lavish and exaggerated, replete with rare marble, bronze, and stone sculptures and one impressive buon fresco painted wall. Across from that was an entire wall covered with built-in chests and shelving adorned with carved woodwork. The delicate chandeliers and fixtures hung gently; gold and antique brass abounded; yet the room, much like the house, felt up-to-date.

Several photographs of Bailey's grandfather adorned the walls. In them, he posed, all smiles, with heads of state, religious leaders, celebrities, and the celebrated. It was hard to tell who was happier to be photographed: was Bill Clinton grinning because he was with Mark Warfield, or the other way around? Coco focused on a particularly startling photograph of Warfield with Malcolm X. It felt familiar, and it was—it was the famed photojournalist Bill Ray's iconic *Life* magazine shot from 1964—one of the last professional shots taken of him.

Bailey didn't take her three new adversaries to this room by accident. She wanted them to know who she was, who her family was, and who they were dealing with—a trick she'd learned from her mother. Mother was the master of the subtle jibe, the underhanded hint, and the passive-aggressive *screw you*.

"I'm not changing my mind. I *won't* be blackmailed, and I certainly won't be bullied by anyone," Bailey announced to start the discussion. She settled into an odd but strangely elegant curved chair with a striking ladder back. Coco's minor in art history suddenly kicked in, as she realized it was most likely an authentic Frank Lloyd Wright Barrel Chair. Bailey was laying it on.

Coco couldn't quite focus on the matter at hand. The mix of styles and genres in the room was dizzying. It was so typical of the Greenwich filthy rich: a synthesis of modern and ancient that disregarded tradition yet, defying logic, somehow worked.

"I don't think you are fully grasping the gravity of this situation," CJ said. "We are being blackmailed by the mayor, who, if you'll recall last night's little theater, is not averse to lethal violence."

"Please. I'm begging you." Olivia was nearly in tears. "I can't lose my house. If we just go along with this, he won't release your tape either. And who'd believe our word over his anyway? I haven't seen any reports about a missing girl . . ."

"What makes you think that if we agree to keep our mouths shut he wouldn't humiliate us anyway? And for god's sake, he's capable of *murder*! How on earth does that make him a man of his word? He's the last goddamned guy we should trust! It doesn't make sense," Bailey said. "We go to the police. It's the right thing to do, and really our only choice."

"That's what I said all along. We have to do the right thing for that poor girl," said Coco, snapping out of her reverie. Growing up in a tough neighborhood may have hardened her as a youth, but it also gave her a deeply ingrained sense of community, and respect for others.

"Yeah, I guess you're right." Olivia sighed. "Point taken. It's not like he's given us a reason to trust him. On top of everything else, he's a politician."

"That's what I'm telling you," said Bailey almost convincingly. "We have all the evidence. There's got to be a fingerprint, something on one of our envelopes, or some kind of forensic material. Maybe some article of her clothing is still in his house. I say we don't give in and we nail that bastard. And, of course, you know, stand up for that poor woman who no longer can."

"Okay, so it seems like we agree." Coco had changed direction. It really hadn't taken much to convince her—her conscience had been nagging her all along. "Bailey, you said you'd already spoken with a Detective Casey. Who is he, can we trust him, and what does he know already?"

"Well," said Bailey, lightening up momentarily, "you won't believe it, but the officer who came this morning when I called about the envelope was Olivia's crush from last night! And guess what, sweetie. He's single!" She winked at Olivia.

Olivia gasped. And blushed. "That guy was a *detective*? A real one?"

"Yep. He was working. Hence the just-making-sure-you're-okay business," said Bailey, attempting to imitate Rob's deep, manly voice.

Coco and CJ were cracking up by now.

"Anyway, on the way over here, I had Detective Rob Casey checked out. I've got a guy who knows how to get info fast. I totally had to after I found out what was in my envelope and he said he'd seen it. So, here's what I know: ex-Marine, was in training at Quantico to become an agent in foreign counterintelligence for the FBI, but had to quit when his mom got sick. He moved back to Stamford to care for her, got a job here with the Greenwich police, and has a completely clean record as far as I know."

Olivia opened her mouth to ask more questions, but before she could, they were interrupted by a dainty knock at the door. Bailey looked up to see Amihan, her mother's Filipino house manager, who, from what Coco could gather, was the equivalent of a female butler or a modern-day lady-in-waiting.

"You have a guest," Amihan said, narrowing her eyes at Bailey. "But I work for your mother and not for you; so if he wants a cocktail, you will go and get it for him. If he wants any food, you go make it for him. I don't work for you."

Oh yeah, Amihan was a bitch.

Not only that, but she had particular disdain for Bailey. There had always been tension when Bailey was growing up, but the final nail in the coffin of their relationship had come three years earlier. Amihan's twenty-four-year-old nephew came to visit for a summer. Bailey had never before seen such a sexy, gorgeous specimen of a man and promptly seduced him and smoked all his pot. Both were the best the Philippines had to offer. When her nephew complained bitterly to his aunt over the loss of his weed, she blamed Bailey for everything. Amihan didn't know that her nephew had been smoking for years and insisted that Bailey had corrupted this innocent young man. But by the way this guy was in bed, Bailey knew he hadn't been innocent in a long, long time.

"Fine." Bailey glared. Before she could ask who it was, Amihan stepped aside to reveal Detective Casey himself.

"I'm sorry I'm late, Miss Warfield. Can we talk? I only have a minute."

"*Thank you,* Amihan," Bailey said as the house manager rolled her eyes and walked away.

"Detective Casey, you may remember Coco and CJ from last night. But, uh, I'm not sure—did you meet Olivia?" She grinned devilishly.

Olivia awkwardly held out her hand as if to be kissed, and while Detective Casey couldn't completely conceal his interest—a flicker of a wide-eyed smile breezed across his face—his training immediately took over, so he firmly, if awkwardly, turned her hand counterclockwise as he politely shook it and said hello. He was here on business, and it was his priority to be taken seriously. A true professional.

"Yes, of course. We did meet. Very nice to see you again, Olivia," the detective said as their eyes met. "Nice to see you all, in fact, now that you're no longer the same person."

Bailey was all business. "Thank you for coming, Detective. Okay, so who sent me that tape? What did you find out?"

"I, uh, maybe we should speak in private."

"It's fine. Just tell me, who was it?"

"Well, it's still unclear who sent it or how it was obtained, unless . . . well, unless it was the other person on the tape."

"Well, who was it?" She looked at him as if he should

understand that it could have been any number of people.

"Miss Warfield, do you have any reason to believe that Ryan Reynolds would want to blackmail you?" he asked.

"The actor? Ryan? No, why would he?" Bailey replied.

"I'm asking because . . ." The detective trailed off, looking around the room uncomfortably. "Maybe we should discuss this privately."

"Fine. Let's step out into the hallway," Bailey suggested, then turned to the others. "Excuse us. Sorry." She was getting frustrated.

With the heavy wooden door closing behind them, Detective Casey looked at Bailey. She felt like he was trying to read something, and he was.

"Okay, so if it wasn't him, then it had to be Alanis," he said.

"Why her?"

"Because I cross-checked the time stamp on the tape with his personal life. He was cheating on her with you."

Bailey was instantly incensed. "No fucking way! Not possible. I can prove it."

"Miss Warfield . . ." He looked at her closely, wanting to see if she would lie to him. She knew the trick; good journalists always know when they're being bullshitted, and they know when someone is trying to find out if they're bullshitting. "Did Miss Morissette know about the affair? Suspect? Could she have secretly taped you? The tape, is uh, really high quality, but it looks like a stationary camera, probably hidden. But you can see . . . the whole thing, both of you. Quite clearly."

"No way. That's wrong. I was with Ryan way, way after he and Alanis broke up. As a matter of fact, he ended things with me when he met Scarlett Johansson. That date stamp isn't right," Bailey insisted. "And there's no way that tape can be real."

"I don't think you can readjust a time or date stamp, Miss Warfield. Are you sure?" the detective had to know.

"I am one hundred percent sure." Bailey was firm. "And, trust me, I know techie guys at the station who could change the date stamp no problem. Someone switched it deliberately."

Casey knew she was right. And telling the truth. "Well then, with your permission, I'd like to investigate further. It seems like this goes much deeper."

"No way am I letting this go. Nobody blackmails a Warfield and gets away with it," Bailey said as she led him back into the room.

"Well, I'm sorry to interrupt you folks. Have a wonderful rest of your day," the detective said. As he swung the door open to leave, he stopped, thoughtfully, and turned back. "One more thing, Miss Warfield."

"Yes, what is it?"

"Could you be having any issues with a member of the local government?" he asked.

Olivia let out a slight gasp but held it back when CJ shot her a look and gave her leg a quick tap with his foot under the table.

"Why would you say that?" Bailey asked, calmer than she should have been.

"The envelope that your tape came in is government issue, and there is a particular watermark on the stationery that was familiar. We have them in our office," the detective said.

"You mean like this one?" Olivia took her envelope out of her bag. She was bringing Rob into their party whether the others liked it or not.

"Why yes, actually. Do you work for the government?" Detective Casey asked.

"No, I received an envelope as well," Olivia replied.

"Excuse me?" He let the door shut as he stepped back into the room. "You also received one of these envelopes?" His eyes widened as he realized the case was becoming much more complex . . . and much more interesting. Small-town detective work was normally on the dull side, quite frankly. He also realized he would now have a reason to work with Olivia.

"We all did," Coco chimed in, looking askance at Olivia.

"Hang on a second. You all received *what* exactly?"

At that they invited him to sit down and explained the whole thing. Detective Casey convinced them to come down to the precinct and talk to the chief. Besides, this was *huge*. There hadn't been a big murder in Greenwich since Martha Moxley in 1975, and he was eager to sink his teeth into a real investigation. If only he'd stayed long enough last night to walk next door with them!

On their way out, CJ pulled Bailey aside and asked her in a hushed tone, "What was on that tape? Can you tell me?"

"It was a sex tape, but don't tell the others," Bailey said. "Anyway, it had to be a fake."

"Oh, precious, there have got to be *dozens* of tapes of you doing the nasty out there. Why on earth would this one be a problem?"

Bailey smirked, looked in CJ's eyes, and extended her middle finger in front of his face.

"Bitch." CJ loved to sass.

On the way to the police station, Coco began to regret being involved in the whole affair, though she dared not express her misgivings, as the rest of the group—taking their emotional cues from a suddenly animated Detective Casey—seemed a little too excited by being part of a big "investigation." She felt like she was riding in the Mystery Machine van instead of a limo. All they were missing was Scooby-Doo. She'd heard Olivia mutter the term *sleuthing,* for pete's sake; and CJ said he couldn't wait to get to the "bottom of this caper," then made some off-color joke about always liking to get to the "bottom." Even Bailey began asking about Coco's boyfriend—a big step for Bailey, since it suggested that she might actually have an interest in something besides herself.

It had been ages since Coco had felt part of something—like a group or a social circle—that had nothing to do with work or Sam or the dogs. It seemed like most of her adult life had revolved around being the creator of Butt-B-Gone, or Sam's girlfriend, or a doggie "mommy"—but where was *she* in all of that? Despite all she had going on, she'd recently spent an entire night staring at the ceiling worried that Farnsworth, her new Italian Spinone puppy, wouldn't like his gigantic, overpriced, new doggie bed, which took up a sizable portion of the room. If he didn't like it, she'd have to hire a crew to help lug the offensive eyesore back down three flights of stairs. She had finally fallen asleep when, around 4:00 A.M., she heard clumsy feet walking on the hardwood floor toward Superbed. And just as abruptly, Farnsworth plopped his goofy, oversize body right down in the cozy abundance of his goofy, oversize bed. She didn't want to wake the sleepy pup and stifle her exuberance, so she woke Sam instead.

"Sam, Sam! The puppy's sleeping in his bed!" she whispered.

"And I'm sleeping in mine," Sam grumbled and turned over.

There had to be more to life than this, she thought.

When they moved to Greenwich, she'd let many of her friendships lag. This wasn't entirely her fault. Many of the women she grew up with had had children or moved away like people do, but she'd never bothered to make new friends, or at least none who weren't connected to her work. She found now that it was nice being with a group of people who didn't want anything from her but conversation.

Coco gazed absently out the limo window at nothing in particular, momentarily indulging herself in the thought that this foursome could become the inner circle she had so desperately needed. She was reminded of an old boyfriend whose family owned the Rainbow Room at Rockefeller Center, one of the grandest established restaurant-ballrooms in the country. When she first met him, she thought he was pretentious and spoiled, but soon she learned that he was only one of those things. He was spoiled, but in a way she never would have imagined. He had this wonderful, supportive group of friends who had known each other since high school and looked after one another like family. They visited each other in college, went on vacations together, were in each other's wedding parties, and took summer shares together. She had never seen such a close group and was instantly jealous that she didn't have these kinds of friends, ones you could always count on, trust, and share secrets with. Not that she couldn't do that with Sam, but she would have liked a sisterhood of sorts. There was something to be had in a female bond that she didn't think was possible with a man. Any man.

One thing stood in the way, Coco thought. What did this yoga group even have in common, other than they'd happened to be dressed the same way at a costume party? Sure, they'd witnessed a murder, but was that enough? Look who she was talking about, after all. To hear CJ tell it, Bailey Warfield didn't need friends so much as lovers—and many of them. Olivia seemed to be one of those new moms who would end up like all the women Coco grew up with, ditching her friends to become Super Mom. And CJ. While they seemed to have hit it off, he probably wasn't looking to add any more females to his busy life, and could she really handle his apparent constant drama?

So, was there a basis for any kind of relationship, let alone a close-knit friendship? Probably not. *Pop.* Burst that bubble. Back to the matter at hand.

The car stopped in a part of downtown Coco hadn't yet been in and was not at all familiar with. Detective Casey led them into a very small, antiseptic building that looked more like a museum than a place where law was enforced. It actually took a moment for Coco to recognize the Greenwich Police Station, clearly not the nerve center she had imagined it would be. *Jeez,* she thought, even the precinct was a bastion of immoderation.

On their behalf, Detective Casey informed the chief of police that his presence was requested immediately for a sensitive matter being brought by four of Greenwich's most prominent residents. That's how he put it: "most prominent." Coco laughed to herself as she watched the chief look over the detective's shoulder at them and purposefully not smile. He didn't seem happy about this at all; as a matter of fact, he looked downright upset they were there. He asked the detective to come inside and shut the door. It stayed shut.

It soon became apparent that the police chief wouldn't be seeing them right away, if for no other reason than to communicate his power over these Greenwich elite. Undeterred, Bailey tried to play the reporter card, CJ flirted with an officer he was sure was gay, and Olivia and Coco shared a soda out of a vending machine that took their money four times before finally giving up its booty. It was an exercise in futility for all. Now they had *that* in common, Coco thought.

An hour and twenty minutes later, the police chief opened the door with a big, gleaming smile pasted on his face. Obviously, Coco thought, he didn't care for Detective Casey; that was what his original grimace must've been about. The group was asked into the chief's office.

"Come in, sit down, welcome! Can I get you a coffee or a drink of some kind?" the chief said exuberantly.

"No, we're fine, thank you." Coco made herself the spokesperson for the group.

The chief continued. "Detective Casey told me quite a tale about you four, but he is always a bit overexcited when it comes to his cases. That's what we love about him, we call him the molehill mountaineer, heh, heh, heh." He laughed a strange little laugh under his breath.

"Well, it's not a tale so much as it was . . . oh, what's the word for it . . . a *murder*?" CJ said sarcastically.

"And blackmail," Olivia added. "Is that the other word you were looking for?"

"Yes, it was, thank you, Olivia," CJ replied as he folded his arms and glared at the chief.

"Heh, heh, heh." There was that creepy little laugh again. "I'm sure that isn't what you saw," the chief assured them. "Why don't you tell me the story?"

"Last night we were all at a Halloween party at the house next door to the mayor's," Coco began.

"Which side?" the chief asked.

"What?" Coco asked.

"Which side of the mayor's house were you on? Were you at the Thomsons' or at the Williamses'?"

"What's the difference?" Coco said, knowing full well he was trying to assess whether they were friends of the pain-in-the-ass Thomsons or the goody-two-shoes Williams family, who had roots in town dating back to colonial times.

"The Thomsons'," Coco offered.

"Uh-huh. Go on," the chief said.

Coco shot CJ a look. She didn't have a good feeling about any of this, since everyone in this town knew what a whack job Lois Thomson was.

"Well, we were at a Halloween party at the Thomsons' and went outside for a photo in the yard. We started walking toward the mayor's house when someone suggested that we had to see a rather unusual statue the mayor had on his property—" Coco got out before being interrupted again.

"Who suggested going to the mayor's house?" the chief asked.

"I don't remember," Coco replied.

"Well, if you weren't invited and were trespassing, then we have a different story here, now, don't we?" the chief asked.

"Nobody had an invitation, nobody was trespassing. We just looked through the grove from the Thomsons' property," CJ countered. "Besides, you know it's impossible to tell where one property ends and the other begins out there, certainly not well enough to make that sort of accusation."

"What were you there to see again?" the chief inquired.

"A sculpture of some kind. We weren't on a mission. We were just wandering over to have a look. This really isn't the point, sir," CJ said.

"I'm just trying to get a clear picture and all the facts," the chief said.

"We witnessed a murder," Olivia jumped in. "Is that clear enough for you?"

"No need to get upset, heh, heh, heh," the chief said.

"No? Well, I'm upset. *Very.* For those of us who aren't on the police force, murder is rather upsetting. I'm sorry! Did *you* ever witness a murder?" Olivia asked.

"Yes, yes I have, actually. So what do you think you saw?" the chief asked.

"What do I *think* I saw? I know what I saw," Olivia replied. "I saw the mayor rolling a body into a rug. A *dead* body."

"Heh, heh, heh. C'mon. The mayor? I don't think so. I've known Jim for over twenty years. Impossible," the chief replied.

"We know what we saw," said CJ.

"No, you know what you *think* you saw, and if you weren't trespassing, then how on earth could you have seen such a thing? Was the mayor outside his house with his dead body?" the chief replied.

"Well, no, he wasn't," Olivia said.

"So I will ask again. Were you trespassing?" the chief asked.

"If we were, why would it matter? Doesn't murder trump trespassing?" CJ asked.

"If it were an actual murder, then of course; but this sounds to me like you were somewhere you shouldn't have been. Am I right?" the chief said smugly.

Finally Bailey, who had been silent until this point, could no longer contain herself.

"Listen, mister. We are here to report a crime. A murder, in fact, which we *know* we saw. And our proof is that now we are being blackmailed. So you explain it to me: if there was no crime, then why would someone be blackmailing us? Huh? Huh?" Bailey asked, using her reporter's gotcha voice.

"Simple enough. It was a Halloween prank," the chief replied.

"Excuse me?" Coco said.

"Absolutely. C'mon, don't be so naïve. It's obvious someone is playing a Halloween prank on you guys, heh, heh, heh." There it was again.

"So what do we do?" Olivia asked.

"Remember when you were little and other kids would pick on you?" He seemed to be insinuating that all four of them were bullied as children. "What advice would your daddies give you when the meanies were bothering you? He'd say, 'Ignore those kids, and they'll leave you alone.' Look, someone's obviously trying to get a rise out of you, and it appears to be working. Right? So just ignore them and they'll get bored and leave you alone."

"But the envelopes . . . the threats . . ." Olivia began to plead.

"Well, these guys are good, I've got to admit. It's just a really good prank. We used to play the best pranks at Colgate. One time we duct-taped the quarterback of an opposing team to his bed in the wee hours of the morning before a playoff game. Nobody could find him, and they had to send in the second string. Heh, heh, heh, we slaughtered them." The chief chuckled as he put his feet up on the desk. Bruno Magli wingtips, not the Tony Lama cowboy boots one would almost have expected. "Ahh, I miss those days."

Detective Casey stood still behind them, betraying no emotion. When they had shared their stories with him at Bailey's, he'd clearly believed them and didn't even mention the possibility of the whole thing being a prank. He struck them as being intuitive and intelligent—Quantico, after all—so what came out of his mouth next felt to the four like they'd been walloped with a polo mallet.

"You know, that makes perfect sense to me," Casey said. "Look, I know none of you are familiar with police work, and you're certainly not accustomed to being involved in matters such as these. But, having discussed these details, the chief and I have both concluded that nothing is going on here. Trust us, no murder took place."

Coco and CJ spun around so fast they almost gave themselves whiplash.

"*Really?*" CJ practically hissed.

"You think it was a prank too?" Olivia asked him.

"Sure. Doesn't that make more sense than thinking you saw the mayor of Greenwich commit a *murder*?" Detective Casey asked her. "C'mon now. Would he be involved in such a thing? This is a nice town, full of nice people."

Olivia looked him in the eye, wanting to believe. "Well, I . . . Sure. I guess so," she replied, unconvinced.

"But what about the faked documents in my envelope? Those were as real as I am standing here right now," Coco asked Detective Casey directly.

"I say ignore them. The chief is right. This whole thing is just an elaborate prank. Someone is screwing with you," Detective Casey replied evenly. He was having trouble making eye contact with her, glancing past her at the wall instead.

"I would *very much* like to believe that," Coco said.

"Me too," CJ agreed.

"Look, go home. And if anything else happens, you come back here and we can look into who is fooling around with you and get them to knock it off, okay?" the chief said.

It seemed nobody believed them anymore. How had the chief turned this all around to make them look foolish?

"Okaay, then. Thank you for your time, I suppose," Coco said as she stood. Detective Casey put out his hand, but this time it was she refusing to look at him; she pretended not to notice the handshake.

"My pleasure. Let me walk you out," Detective Casey said to the group.

Casey and Olivia momentarily made eye contact as they

walked out the door, but the dick quickly looked away. The hurt in Olivia's eyes would have stung any man.

If Casey didn't actually agree with the chief, Coco thought, he certainly couldn't show it. Protocol was a matter of honor, and keeping one's job depended on making your boss believe you had no interest in contradicting him. But it was no excuse, she decided. She was steamed.

As they opened the door to the limousine, Detective Casey reached into his pocket. "Here is my card," he said as he handed one to each of them. "Please call me if anything else happens, okay?"

"After all we told you, do you *really* think all this was a *prank*?" CJ asked again, out of earshot of the chief.

"Sounds like a reasonable explanation to me," Casey muttered as he gazed at his shoe tops.

Bailey pulled Casey aside. "If you're not onboard with us, then you need to give me my fucking tape back—*now,*" she hissed.

"It's in my safe for private case evidence. *Not here,*" he emphasized the last part quietly, through almost closed lips. "Would it be okay with you if I dropped it by tomorrow morning?"

"Okay, fine. After eight thirty yoga," Bailey said. Something in the way he said "not here" made it seem he might still be on their side. "Just promise me: nobody else's eyes but yours."

"Promise." Detective Casey pressed his hand to his heart when he said it, as if he were saying the pledge of allegiance. He seemed solemn, but there was a flash of the strong, friendly detective she'd admired before this whole fiasco in the station house. The way he did it stirred Bailey, and made her squirm ever so slightly. She was simultaneously touched by his gentleness and inflamed by his manliness. Was he flirting with her? Or did she just wish he was? Of course she did. She'd slept with Jesse L. Martin when he played a detective on *Law & Order,* but how much fun would it be to play with a real one? The fact that Olivia had a thing for him gave Bailey pangs of guilt. But only Olivia had shown interest in him. There wasn't necessarily any mutual interest. All's fair in love and war, right? For the moment, he was fair game.

Detective Casey watched as the four of them climbed into the car and drove away. He walked back into the station and saw the chief on his private phone, the one with the number given only to the mayor, a senator, and a few Greenwich celebrities who had donated generously to his election. The chief looked directly—one would say almost menacingly—at Detective Casey as he slowly shut the door. Casey knew what he had to do.

SEVEN

The Nervous Nelly

CJ woke up nauseous. He knew he wasn't sick, but he had an uneasy feeling that reached down into the pit of his stomach and told him something wasn't right. *Well, I know I'm not pregnant,* he said to himself as he made his way to the kitchen. *I haven't had sex in months!* He laughed at his own corny joke. Nanny wasn't up yet; if she were there'd already be fresh hazelnut coffee and warm, buttered scones out on his favorite blue Jasperware Wedgwood plate.

He still had two hours before yoga, yet he debated whether he should go because he felt a Nelly coming on. CJ didn't get anxiety attacks like the rest of us, he got a case of the Nellies, as in the nervous Nellies. They were purpose-driven hissy fits that started in the stomach and festered all day until they hit the brain and burst. CJ recognized this feeling immediately. Normally he would react to it—well, *overreact* to it, to tell the truth—but since the police chief and the man he trusted, Detective Casey, said there was nothing to worry about, CJ decided to ignore his impending Nelly and headed into the family room for some important TV time.

Part of CJ's job as a *Rachael Ray* producer was to watch recently aired episodes looking for ways to make the show feel fresh and ever more exciting, lest the audience lose interest. CJ loved Rachael Ray. She was one of the few genuinely nice and caring hosts he had ever worked with who was also totally involved in the production. Simply not true of most hosts. He'd been with the *Ricki Lake* show for years and had vivid memories—toward the end of the show's run—of Ricki showing up moments before airtime, hopping out of her town car in sweatpants, dashing through hair and makeup, then doing the taping as quickly—and poorly—as possible. Seconds after the show ended she'd be back in her still idling limo and off into the night. Ricki clearly had no interest in being there anymore. But not Rachael Ray. She was at every meeting, every brainstorming session, every photo shoot, and had a say about everything that went on air. CJ loved that. He loved his job and his boss so much that here he was on a weekend watching old episodes in order to improve the already Emmy-winning show for his queen. Well, his princess, actually. He preferred to be the only queen in the room.

CJ usually *loved* watching old *Rachael Ray* episodes, but today he simply couldn't concentrate on anything. That Nelly was nagging at him, growing worse and worse until he just couldn't take it anymore. He had to make a decision: should he get his Nancy Drew on and pursue what they saw together that night? Or should he just let it drop as he had been instructed? He had to talk to Coco—CJ could tell she was the voice of reason, even though they'd just met. Coco was one of those people who could talk him off the ledge. He decided that if she were willing to drop it, shrug her shoulders and move on, he would too. As he began looking up her number on his BlackBerry, he heard Nanny coming down the stairs.

Now that he was back staying in the house he grew up in, familiar sounds were a comfort. But something this morning didn't sound as he had remembered. Instead of the familiar sound of his saintly Nanny's feet moving along on the carpet, it was as though a herd of injured elephants were stampeding toward him. The sound went *boom, boom, boom . . . shuffle . . . boom, boom, boom . . . shuffle.* What the hell could that be?

CJ knew he heard the comforting voice of the woman who'd raised him, but who was she admonishing now? She couldn't see him, and he hadn't done anything wrong, but she was most certainly addressing *someone.* CJ peered around the corner of the TV room. From there he could see both the landing at the bottom of the staircase and the kitchen.

"You be careful, you a go outta de back door by de keetchen," he heard Nanny say.

He couldn't imagine who she could be talking to. She was alone—precisely why he had moved back to the house. He knew that Nanny's husband had died years ago and her children lived in England, so who was there? Had she gone mad?

As he watched, CJ saw Nanny lean over, and then there were smooching noises. From around the bend of the staircase, a man appeared. There was CJ's tall, robust Jamaican Nanny in her dressing gown, bending over a bit to kiss her short, balding, two-hundred-year-old Jewish cardiologist! *Whaaat?*

"Wow, even Nanny's getting some," CJ muttered. He wanted to yell out *Good for you, girl!* but realized it might not be a good idea, considering her heart condition. Then again, at least she was with her cardiologist.

The man was so old CJ wondered about the mechanics

of the act itself, but imagining his Nanny and the codger in any sort of sexual union made his stomach even worse. With the Nelly coming on and Nanny in congress with this fossil, he felt overwhelmed and let out an uncomfortable, gagging cough, just loud enough for Nanny to hear and rush her paramour out the kitchen door. Well, *rush* was a strong word in this case. More like schlep.

Nanny returned to find CJ standing at the entrance to the kitchen. "Oh, Scubu . . . Lawd 'ave mercy! You not supposed t' see dat," Nanny said.

She kissed his forehead, which grossed him out a bit, thinking where those lips had probably just been.

"Well, good morning, lady! Don't you worry." He smiled slyly. "I think it's great. You *go,* girl!" There! He got to say it. "But how did it happen? Has it been going on awhile? Give me the dirt, lady!"

"Me and dat man? Yes, Scubu, 'im and me. It had been a long time since I been wit a man and a long time for 'im as well. And thanks to Viagra—" she started to say.

"Okay, TMI, TMI, I get it, but . . . good for you," he blurted out.

"What you doin' up so early, Scubu?" Nanny asked as she cinched her robe tighter.

"I couldn't sleep. That man who came by with that envelope . . . I went to the police with it. They said it was just a practical joke and I should forget it," he said.

"And you nah wanna, is dat it?" Nanny asked.

"You know me, Nanny. I can't just drop something because someone tells me to. I have to know for myself," he replied.

"Ah, you don wanna be involved wit dose men, trust me. You let it go, son, take my word for dat," Nanny said.

"Okay, for you I will," he assured her.

"Now put on our show. Me wanna see me li'l strawng mahn," she said.

On Saturday mornings their thing was cartoons, which they'd watched together since he was little. At first, she'd hated the shows he watched: *G-Force, Transformers, Power Rangers.* But one day he had on the oldies—*Heckle and Jeckle, Merrie Melodies,* and the *Popeye Hour*—and she happened to sit down with him. She remembered many from her childhood and took anew to Popeye. They both enjoyed the aspect of the little man vanquishing the bully, but she saw Popeye as a gentleman and told CJ he would do well to learn from the sailor's good manners and love of spinach. But CJ was strangely compelled by Bluto, the bully, a giant of a man with a hard beard, a deep, rich voice, a dominant personality, and a hot, tight sailor uniform. Spinach be damned, the only thing CJ wanted was to be Olive Oyl, chased down by this big bad wolf.

But this morning CJ couldn't focus on the shows and his mind wandered to bigger problems.

Coco's plane was delayed. It sat on the tarmac nowhere near the gate it had left a mere thirty minutes earlier. The flight crew was all abuzz, serving drinks and snacks early in an effort to distract the passengers. She was on her way to Arkansas. Bentonville, Arkansas, to be exact, home of Walmart, which had been considering putting her Butt-B-Gone product in their stores on the heels of her great success on QVC and her "bomb-diggity" Dun & Bradstreet rating, as her accountant—who clearly watched too much of that tool Jim Cramer on *Mad Money*—put it. He was one of those insufferable white guys who fancied himself a bit "gangsta." For years he'd been the accountant to major hip-hop stars from Salt-N-Pepa to LL Cool J to Jay-Z, but he also worked with celebrity products, so her lawyer had introduced them, and he'd managed her money ever since.

Coco wasn't in a hurry, but she was anxious to get off the plane, if only to readjust her seat belt. She had several odd quirks, or obsessions maybe, which made no sense to anyone but her. Her latest one began when she started traveling for work. She needed to readjust the seat belt to make it smaller when she left the plane in order to make it seem as if a very skinny woman had been sitting there. She would do it in the hope that the next passenger in that seat, despite never having seen her, and not knowing her, would think *My goodness, the person who sat here before me must've been* so *tiny!*

Ever since her products took off and she became a recognizable spokesperson and talking head, her privacy was scarce. So she sublimated her discomfort with fame and recognition into these private quirks. She knew she'd be judged if others became aware of her idiosyncratic concerns, so she never shared them. Instead, she embraced them, and other such foibles, as her very own special little humors. Granted, she was no Kate Winslet, but her media-wide omnipresence did screw with her anonymity.

As Coco sat there obsessing over her quirks, her relationship, her trip to Walmart, whether she'd take coffee or Coke Zero, her phone rang—it was CJ.

"Hey, what's up?" Coco asked.

"Where are you? I'm in a state," CJ said.

"What state?" Coco couldn't resist. "Okay, sorry. I'm on the runway in an airplane that's going nowhere, apparently. I think I see someone stealing the hubcaps off the plane. What's going—" Coco was interrupted.

"Ladies and Gentlemen, this is your captain speaking. We apologize for the inconvenience and delay. We have just been given clearance for takeoff. We will begin taxiing shortly. We should be in the air in about five minutes. Once again, we apologize for the delay."

"Hello?" Coco said. "You still there?"

"Yeah, yeah. Listen, this isn't sitting right with me, I think we need to . . ." Coco strained to hear him over the drone of the P.A. system.

"The captain has turned on the fasten seat belt sign. So that we may secure our place in the departure queue, please return your seats to their upright positions, stow all tray tables, and turn off all electronic devices." The flight attendant's voice calmly but firmly filtered through the P.A. system.

"Sorry, CJ, I couldn't hear you. Listen, we're taking off. Can I call you when I land? It'll be three or four hours, okay?"

But before she could get a response, the flight attendant was all over her. "Miss, you'll have to turn that off *now*, please," she said.

Not even waiting a beat, a woman sitting behind Coco—whose garish pink tracksuit and purple fur boots had horrified Coco during boarding—huffed in an accent that was pure hick, "Great. We finally get a chance to leave, then missy here can't get off the gol'damn phone. Didn't we sit here long enough already?"

Brooklyn would stand for no such thing, and Coco immediately wheeled around and snapped, "Lady, I'll turn off my phone just as soon as you turn off that excruciating outfit; it's the loudest thing in here. Were you planning on working out on the plane?" The woman was silent for the remainder of the flight.

On the floor of the baby's nursery, Olivia was asleep. Her normally perfect eight-month-old baby, Simon, had had another terrible night. Feeding him didn't calm him down, changing his diaper didn't change his mood, and the purple elephant that usually made him smile just wasn't doing it for him today. Olivia didn't think it was possible, but maybe her baby was depressed; or perhaps she was projecting. She hadn't slept much either and had been quite sad lately. Since her father's death and her return to Greenwich, the choices she was making hadn't felt like her own. Benjamin had become intolerable and moved to the South Pole, and the only good man in her life was constantly colicky and not allowing her to sleep nights. When Simon had finally fallen asleep, at 3:30 A.M., she'd leaned against the wall and sunk into a ball on the floor, and slept. She awoke, confused, as the sun seeped through cracks in the blinds, and wiped the drool from the corner of her mouth. These had been her first moments of real sleep since she'd received that envelope and realized that her crazy mother was back in her life, trying again to take it all away from her.

Maybe the contents of the envelope were indeed a practical joke, but her mother's lawsuit was not. Being a mom herself, she could not imagine in what universe a woman would go after her own child the way her mother did. True, Olivia preferred, by leaps and bounds, her father. But what choice was she given? During Olivia's childhood, when Sunshine returned for "visits"—also known as ATM withdrawals—she was terrifyingly irrational and ill-tempered; quite frankly, Olivia had come to loathe her.

She didn't have the strength for much these days, but she knew that her father wanted her to have this house. So, in honor of his memory, coupled with the fact she had nowhere else to go, she decided the best defense was probably going to be a good offense. She was going to stay and fight. There was a lot to lose at this point, and she didn't want to part with the only things she could give her son: a house and a loving mother. But how could she counter this hater mater?

Olivia was always a person who asked permission before forgiveness, always followed rules and laws, never made an unconsidered move. Heck, she'd never even tried drugs—not because of what they could do to her brain cells, or the fact that she might not like being out of control (though all of that was true); mainly, she'd never tried drugs because the law said she couldn't. That was enough for her. That was Olivia, through and through: a law-abiding, echolalia-afflicted, gifted-but-absentminded scientist who never wanted anyone to be angry with her. And yet, here was this *mother.*

Though Olivia always did everything correctly, somehow she had little to show for her do-good nature. Her opening profile quote on Chemistry.com might as well have read:

"Educated, single mom with nothing to show for it." She had put her prolific career on hold for a man who didn't love her as he'd sworn to, didn't honor the commitments they'd made, and then disappeared to the farthest reaches of the planet, leaving her with her precious yet impossible-to-raise-alone son, Simon. And now here was her mother, out of nowhere, messing up her life even more. *The wrong parent died,* she thought, hating herself for the wrongness of the thought. But as she continued mulling over her seemingly endless troubles, something clicked inside. Maybe it was the lack of sleep, maybe it was the light coming through the window of the baby's room, making her feel the warmth of a brand-new day, or maybe it was spotting those papers on the table again, reviving her rage, but Olivia's palpable frustration grew into a seething, churning monster. Her soul responded with an almost audible pop. She was going to fight that bitch, and she was going to do it head-on. No lawyers, no courtrooms, just mother and daughter mano a mano. Olivia, propelled by her newfound rage, darted straight to the phone to call the woman out; and if she had to punch her out, she was prepared to do that too, decorum be damned. Olivia held the receiver to her ear with no idea what she would say and no care for consequences—

"Crap, do I even have her phone number?"

Olivia went to her phone book, the old Filofax with people's numbers written in ink; they were probably out of service by now, since they were the ones that didn't get moved into her cell phone.

"Damn!" The number wasn't there.

Racing to the kitchen, she reached into the back of a

drawer and retrieved an envelope full of slips of paper with numbers scrawled all over them.

"Shit!"

Olivia was beginning to lose steam. This was not her plan. She meant to call and blast through the receiver with *Listen here!* or *Over my dead body.* But now she was already beginning to second-guess herself.

"This is my problem—I have no backbone and I'm too cautious. Okay, I'm calling Jake," she exhaled.

Jake Sachs was her attorney. Surely he'd have that wretch's number. But he'd also try to talk her out of calling.

"He works for me, he is *giving* me that number!" she insisted, planning the fight she would have with Jake since she needed practice asserting herself.

Jake's number she knew, no problem; it was in her iPhone. He was current.

He answered on the first ring. "Hello," he said kindly.

"Jake, it's Olivia. I need Sunshine's number, can I have it please?"

"I'm not giving you Sunshine's number," he said flatly.

"I'm not asking, I'm telling you. As your client, I demand it," she snapped back.

"Well, Miss Client, as your lawyer I am advising you that phoning her is not in your best interest, and I won't let you screw this up. Trust me, don't call her." He was getting angry now. "And incidentally, *good morning*. What the heck has gotten into you?"

"I'm sick of being taken advantage of. This is *my* house, and I will burn it down before I let her take it from me!" Olivia surprised even herself with her forceful language.

"Liv, I know this is hard on you. I thought you were handling it all much too well, so I'm glad to see you fired up, but you are not an impulsive person. You don't do things like this, so you're just no good at it. Sunshine will eat you alive, and you may accidentally say something to her that she can use in court against you. I can't let that happen," Jake cautioned.

"It will be my word against hers," Olivia said smugly.

"No, darling. Sunshine tapes every conversation." Jake was the smug one now.

"Damn. Shit!" Olivia responded.

"Olivia, please, just chill out. Know that I'm handling this and that I know what I'm doing. Now why don't you go do what every other stressed-out mother in Greenwich does and take a little yellow pill, or a big glass of wine?" he suggested.

Olivia sighed loudly into the phone as a tear rolled down her cheek. She didn't know what to do with her overflowing anger. She knew Jake was right, and all of a sudden she was at a loss for words. Not good when you are about to tell someone off.

"Damn" was all she could muster.

"I'm seeing you on Tuesday, right? We can talk then. I promise everything will be fine. But listen to me, Liv, *do not* call her. Don't look her number up, don't ask your brother for it, don't—"

"Finn has her number? Why?" Olivia was shocked and pissed.

"Oh, god, Olivia, let's talk about this on Tuesday, please? Just don't call her, okay? I gotta run, cupcake. Bye."

Olivia clicked off the phone and sank back down the wall. She figured the day might as well end where it began. She sat on the floor, grabbed a bottle of trendy Basque wine, and pouted. She wasn't taking just some of Jake's advice, she was taking all of it.

Bailey wasn't going to let a little rain stop her from a much-needed shopping spree. She had the month from hell with junkets in L.A. and London, and then a premiere in Paris, since everyone was desperately trying to get their films out there before the December deadline for the Oscars. She was exhausted, but never too tired for a bit of retail therapy. Finally back at her pied-à-terre in New York City, she had lined up her personal shoppers at both Bergdorf Goodman and Manolo Blahnik on Fifty-fourth. With a few minutes before her first appointment, she decided to make a mad dash into Christian Dior since she'd spotted a peplum jacket at Dior in Paris that she was convinced had been designed for her alone.

Outside Dior the paparazzi were buzzing. Bailey was used to this ordeal since she was in the business and regularly worked events alongside some of them. She wondered who was inside, and if she knew them. As she approached Dior, she recognized a familiar face amid the photographic barnacles, someone with an impeccable reputation. His good humor about his profession endeared him to even A-list celebs, and as a result he got the money shots every time. If he was there, there was obviously a big name nearby.

"Victor, what's the good word, buddy?" Bailey said, as friendly as she could.

"Oh, Miss Warfield. Nice to see you again. Did you enjoy our friend's performance at the Paris premiere?" he joked.

He was referring to Brendan Fraser and his film *Inkheart.* He'd shown up on the red carpet on a Vespa; dipped Dame Helen Mirren, indulging her in a deep, long, passionate movie kiss; and behaved like a rascal the entire way down the red carpet. Victor had been in love with Brendan Fraser ever since *Gods and Monsters,* and he talked about the actor constantly. For some reason, he had the idea that he and Bailey were partners in their Brendan Fraser obsession. Bailey liked Brendan just fine and had had some terrific interviews with him over the years, but she was more of a Johnny Depp girl.

"So who's in there?" Bailey asked even though she was about to walk in; she wanted to be prepared. Her grandfather had taught her that.

"Sienna Miller."

The hair on the back of Bailey's neck stood straight up at the mention of that name. Bailey had nothing against the actress; it was more what she might have against Bailey. It seemed that during one of Jude and Sienna's many breakups, Bailey may have had a small dalliance with the male star. It was just one night—okay, and again the next morning—but that was all. The fact that he got back together with Sienna two days later should have suggested how minor a thing it truly was; but there was the chance that Miss Miller had found out since Bailey was photographed leaving Jude's hotel room the next morning. The camera phone that took the picture was so antiquated you could barely make out her face in the photo. As far as Bailey knew, the investigation had gone no further; and why would it? She was being paranoid. After all, Sienna Miller was a world-famous actress with a busy schedule—today, a busy shopping schedule—and Bailey was just a single gal trying to make it in an overwhelming business. Sienna probably had no idea who she was, what had happened, or even cared at this point.

Bailey waved good-bye to Victor and entered the store. Sienna Miller was in the fitting room. Bailey began to look around. The coast seemed clear. So she chatted with the salesgirl with the Dita Von Teese haircut, whom she'd seen there many times before. She asked after the coveted beaded-sleeve peplum jacket she had seen in Paris. Dita knew the jacket and went to retrieve it in Bailey's tiny size, asking her to have a seat. As Bailey turned toward the chairs, she found herself face-to-face with the glamorous, pocket-size actress. Sienna Miller.

"Someone get this skanky bitch out of my sight," the British star said.

For some reason, Bailey's heart sank. Normally she was unfazed by divas' catty behavior, but today it got to her. She was tired of women hating her, tired of worrying about the next scandal. The blackmail video may have been the last straw—she didn't want to think about what other women, or the public at large, would say about her. She wished she could have camaraderie like she'd had with the Palins. Just to be with a group of girls who seemed to care . . . at least a little.

For the moment, however, at least Bailey no longer wondered if Sienna Miller had ever found out about her and Jude.

CJ couldn't deal with his Nelly anymore, and nobody seemed to be around to tend to his neediness. He liked being paid attention to, so if he couldn't get attention at home, there was only one place that made him feel special: the gay bathhouse on Twentieth Street in Manhattan. And what admirers they were. With a name, West Side Club, that didn't give a hint of its primary function, it was CJ's place to get his ego—among other things—stroked. Great-looking men walked in carrying gym bags, allowing passersby to assume it was another Chelsea gym. Women who tried to enter never made it past the elderly, slightly dotty Indian man at the security desk in the lobby. "Trust me, miss, this is not the club for you," he would say as kindly and as firmly as possible. Even he had no inclination to visit the place, but he had a pretty good idea what went on inside.

CJ had a great body, which, ironically, he didn't like to show off, given how loud he was about everything else in his life. He liked to say that it was "an unexpected snack once you've taken off the wrapper." Only in the comfort of the bathhouse did he show off his stuff and freely "get his gay on."

In the beautifully appointed, multilevel wood sauna, CJ sat wrapped in an absurdly thin white towel, sipping ice-chilled vodka, sweating, and feeling ambitious when he noticed three men to his left who were quite loud for a group of gay men in a sauna. He looked closer and realized that he recognized one from Greenwich. A shortish, compact, yet muscular guy who was beautifully endowed. CJ had trouble taking his eyes away from the ridge in the guy's towel. It protruded along his leg, looking like an extra muscle lying on his quadriceps. CJ was not shocked to see someone from Greenwich at this club. Aside from the fact that it was upscale and advertised like crazy in the Connecticut gay publication, CJ remembered a study they'd done on an episode of *Rachael Ray.* The study said that you are the audience for everything you do, so everyone around you who does what you do is probably just like you. So, if you are a misplaced Californian living in Long Island with your banker husband and three children, you are more likely to run into other married misplaced California mothers in your everyday life than if you went back to California and sought out those people. CJ remembered how true this had been when he went to Rome too. He was in an out-of-the-way restaurant on a small side street in a hip new area called Trastevere. The eatery had all of ten tables, yet at four of them sat gay American men from the New York metropolitan area.

CJ thought he'd seen this man before at one of the bars in Greenwich, though he'd never spoken to him. As he held court with his cronies, the man looked directly at CJ, but with no sign of recognition. So the group continued to talk, presumably not caring if CJ listened in. From what CJ could glean, the compact man worked for a government official or had something to do with local politics, since he was discussing an incident that had happened at the local beach over the summer. When the conversation got juicy, CJ discerned that this man was, of all things, the mayor's aide! This sparked not just CJ's curiosity but his Nelly. Nanny had said she recognized the man with the envelope as someone she often saw with the mayor. Could this be the man? CJ moved closer as his mind raced. How could he get in on the conversation? How could he find out what the aide knew about the four of them? Did this man know about the envelopes and the police chief? None of this was helping address CJ's Nelly, making it the first time the bathhouse had denied him the comfort he sought; but still, he couldn't walk out. He had to hear the whole story from the other side, and he realized he might be able get it out of the sexy, hard-bodied little mayor's aide. But how to approach him?

CJ weighed several options. *"Hey, I'm from Greenwich, haven't I seen you there?"* Ugh, too cliché. *"I'm gay, you're gay."* Duh, too obvious. They were in a gay bathhouse, for crying out loud. Even the towel boys here were gay. He could start being loud and dramatic, but again, gay bathhouse. No shortage of drama queens, and who really wants to hook up with *that*? Maybe, he thought, he could just move closer to the men and try to get in on the conversation as naturally as possible, no differently than if he were sitting alongside them at a bar. That seemed the least aggressive option, and if one of the minions tried to pick him up, he could start right in with the drama queen stuff. He drew closer.

The stocky gay man looked up. Again, he didn't appear to recognize CJ per se, but he knew what a perfect body looked like and he couldn't stop staring at it. In a bathhouse, if you stare just long enough at someone and they stare back at you just long enough, there's a tacit understanding that you're both up for some action. And though CJ's Nelly had subdued his carnal urges, he didn't want to violate bathhouse etiquette or be rude, so he knew he had to follow through with the ritual. His principal interest now was in getting information about the mayor and those damned envelopes. He was willing to sacrifice his body in order to find out what this compact, yummy, naked gay man knew about him. Coco and the others had better appreciate his efforts.

EIGHT

Rao's and Rivals

I just got this in France. It's the best there is. Would you care for some?" the little man asked as he held up a bottle of absinthe, set out two reservoir glasses, and reached for a box of sugar cubes and a lighter.

CJ could tell immediately that this Barney Rubble of a man was one of those characters who had to have "the best" of everything. He found it a bit tiresome, frankly. Didn't anyone just want to fuck anymore? Just looking around the apartment, CJ knew that this guy worried about the impression he made on others. Otherwise, why on earth would he adorn his room with MacKenzie-Childs furniture, a style that was way beyond even the gay man's aesthetic? It felt too fine and precious, more like dollhouse furniture. The whimsically painted cabinet next to the bed was giving him a headache.

It was 4:00 A.M., and Barney was still drinking. Apparently, he wanted to seem nonchalant about the new workday quickly closing in upon them. The guy was partying as though he didn't want the night to end, while CJ, who'd stopped drinking a few hours before and had even napped briefly, already felt a hangover coming on. So much about the little man seemed designed to create the impression that he was a certain person with a certain lifestyle, and not the boring political aide he was. Even the location of the apartment betrayed the man's neediness. The Tudor City neighborhood was such a cliché, but why would he live in the city and commute to Greenwich? Maybe being gay was one of the few instances when having a Greenwich address wouldn't be the best possible way to get you laid. Mr. Rubble was under the illusion that the Ralph Lauren silk drapes and the John Varvatos suits hanging *outside* the closet were the sorts of things that could turn on some wretched hick queen who knew nothing about *real* style or luxury. Though CJ might have laughed at the thought, there he was, naked in this stranger's bed, bleary-eyed and freshly ravaged.

"What's your name, by the way?" CJ asked.

"Malcolm," the man answered. "So, do you want some absinthe?"

"No, I'm fine," CJ replied as he rolled over in Malcolm's king-size Marge Carson Hampton bed, trying not to agitate his looming hangover. CJ watched Malcolm's muscles contract as he poured himself a drink. He may have been short, but his shoulders rippled with every move he made. It was downright distracting, and CJ thought Malcolm's sexiness might make him inherently annoying as well. Stretching his arms up and behind his head, CJ felt the excruciating leather upholstery of the headboard. *Gross,* he thought. He'd found a way to be alone with the guy but hadn't managed to glean any helpful information.

"I have a work event tonight and then dinner at Rao's afterward. Why don't you meet me there? Do you know where it is?" Malcolm said, not meaning to be condescending but kind of sounding that way.

"Yes, I know where Rao's is," CJ said, a bit thrown off by the question since usually such circumstances were of the one-night variety. "Okay, what time?"

"Eight thirty on the dot. You can't be late," said Malcolm seriously. CJ held back a gasp. This guy didn't even know him, so why on earth would he have the audacity to assume that CJ would make him wait? It wasn't an argument worth having—CJ was interested in information from this affected, pretentious elf, so he'd put up with what he had to.

"I won't be late, don't worry about it," CJ assured him.

"Great," Malcolm said as he and his annoying muscles got back into his pretentious bed with his pretentious glass of absinthe and its flaming sugar cube.

Sobering up, CJ realized he was no longer interested in round two (okay, let's be honest, round six), but the bed he lay in was just three blocks from work. Why go all the way home to Connecticut when he'd have to come back to Rachael Ray in just a few hours? He decided to tolerate Malcolm's further ministrations only with the intent of getting his information at the dinner at Rao's, and then never seeing this little man again.

Coco rushed home from the airport as quickly as traffic would allow. She felt terribly guilty about having to leave Sam home alone once again with the dogs, especially the new puppy. Things had been so tense between them after he was pushed out of his business and then when his partners were indicted. He was clearly depressed. He spent his days padding around in SpongeBob pajama bottoms and an ugly orange T-shirt, never wanting to do anything. Coco was such a doer that living with someone despondent drove her more than a little nuts. Sam had been growing increasingly hard to be with, and consequently so was she. For a while they spoke little, each doing a sort of dance around the other, communicating through the dogs: "Look what the puppy did!" and "Farnsworth doesn't seem very happy today. I think he needs some cheering up. Maybe we should get him a new toy." Finally, just as Sam seemed to be letting go of his feelings about the business, and Coco's company seemed to be taking off—pulling them both out of the tailspin—the goddamned envelope had shown up, sending Sam back into a state of confusion, sadness, and ultimately, stupor.

On the flight home, Coco resolved to spend time working on their relationship and on making Sam feel happy and whole while getting the business of the envelope behind them. She would make him think it was all a big prank, whether it was or not. In a hurry to get started on a weekend of healing, she leaned forward from the backseat of the limo, like Katharine Hepburn in one of those old TCM movies. "Step on it," she barked. The driver looked in the rearview mirror, eyebrows imperceptibly arched. "Yes, ma'am. Right away," he said and continued driving at the exact same speed as the forty vehicles crawling along in front of him.

Almost at her exit on the Merritt Parkway, her cell phone rang. It was Rory.

"Hey, kid, how was your flight?"

"Fine, smooth. What's up?" Coco knew Rory didn't care about air travel experiences; he was obviously calling for a reason, and she didn't care much for small talk anyway.

"Walmart called. You're in!" Rory was downright ebullient.

"But I just got off the plane! They made the decision that fast?" Coco asked.

"Oh, they knew the minute you left the room. You're one of the best pitchmen in the business, and this product is right up their alley. Not to mention the low marketing and delivery costs now that we're producing domestically."

"Wow, this is huge. Butt-B-Gone will be in Walmart? I can't get my head around that," Coco said and then thought for a second. "How many stores?" she asked cautiously. Surely they were only going to try her product out in a dozen or so stores to see how it went.

"Well, that's the even better part. Twenty-five hundred," he said.

"Oh, my lord," Coco replied, almost under her breath.

"Okay, kiddo, good news for us then. Go home and we'll hash out contracts tomorrow. Hi to Sam," Rory said and hung up.

Coco sat in the back of the car, incredulous. The little product she'd worked so hard to invent and promote was now a grown-up on its way to Harvard. She couldn't wait to rub it in Billy Blanks's face at the trade show next week. Blanks was her arch frenemy. They were certainly cordial on a casual level, but those who were on the inside knew of the intense mutual hatred.

Coco called Sam from the car to tell him the good news but also to get the pups ready for her arrival. The older Spinone was mildly amused and contented when she came home.

But little Farnsworth went berserk when she came back from anywhere and peed with excitement—"glee pee," they called it—so they tried to arrange reunions outside the house.

As the car pulled into the semicircular stone drive, there stood Sam with Farnsworth tugging at his lead, stubby tail and hindquarters wagging wildly, and Milo, the elder, standing just apart, sans leash, with a look on his face that seemed to indicate he was embarrassed to be seen with the other two but happy to be outside.

Coco was also familiar with the look on Sam's face and knew that she had her work cut out for her trying to avoid a fight.

"Say hello to the newest member of the Walmart family!" she said, kissing Sam on what turned out to be the side of his face. Farnsworth had better aim, delivering a big, wet kiss, complete with sloppy beard, right to her lips and on up into her left nostril. "Oh, for god's sake, Farnsworth! Breed standard! *Spinoni don't kiss.* How many times do I have to tell you? Blech!" Farnsworth wagged happily anyway and placed his forepaws on her upper thighs. "Okay, cute bunny pose. Good boy."

"Good job, hon," said Sam, pulling the dog back. "So proud of you." She'd never have known it by the tone of his voice.

"Okay, what is it?" Coco wasn't going to let this simmer.

"Kornacki says I'm fucked if those documents get out. He doesn't know where they're from, and says it's obvious to him they're forged, but there's no way he can prove it. Someone could just as easily say our original, legitimate documents are the fakes." Sam appeared ready to cry. He was, no doubt, imagining years in federal lockup, fighting over extra pudding cups with Bernie Madoff.

Coco sighed and realized she was going to have to take charge, as usual. "Look, honey, it's going to be all right. You let me handle this, okay? I'll get to the bottom of it. Trust me."

Sam looked at her quizzically, unconvinced but grateful. He handed her Farnsworth's leash and took her bags inside.

At 8:29 P.M. CJ stood outside Rao's checking his watch. He had been there since 8:00 so as not to upset his envoy, yet the snotty little imp hadn't shown up. CJ didn't mind waiting in plain sight on a Monday night at the legendary eatery, since he knew that nobody who mattered would see him there. Rao's is a hundred-year-old Italian restaurant on 114th Street in Manhattan with ten tables, one seating, and the greatest eggplant parmigiana you've ever tasted. The catch, though, is that no one can eat there. That is to say, it's invitation only. No ordinary schmo gets a table at Rao's. There's no phone number, they don't take reservations, and you can't walk in off the street and expect to get a seat. It is simply the most exclusive restaurant in New York, possibly in the whole country. Even so, Monday night is for amateurs. The real power brokers eat there on Wednesdays and Thursdays, the nights CJ ordinarily went. After all, his father was a well-known politician and major power broker, so CJ could get a table whenever he liked. Monday nights were for people like a mayor's aide or lower castes from all walks of life.

Finally, at 8:45, the mayor's car showed up, and out hopped little Malcolm with an entourage of pretty young men who were treating him like he was a Kennedy—or, in this case, Jackie O.

"There you are. C'mon, let's get in there, we're late," Malcolm said to CJ as if it were his fault. He was so convincing CJ actually thought: *Was I supposed to meet him somewhere else first?*

They were rushed to their table, whereupon, in an effort to speed things along, as he often did, the maître d' squatted down next to Malcolm, who gave him the entire order for the table rather than wait for the infamous Frankie No to take his drink order. Malcolm chose what they would be drinking, ordered appetizers for the table, and decided what they all would be having for dinner. CJ was there on a fact-finding mission and had deliberately eaten a late lunch, so he wasn't feeling choosy about his meal; not being hungry also kept him from being as put off by this alpha behavior as he should have been. But, as a potential dating partner, Malcolm wasn't doing a thing to impress him.

"Thank you, Mr. Marconi," the waiter said when Malcolm palmed him some cash.

"My pleasure," Malcolm replied and then turned his attention to CJ. Leaning in and placing his hand on the upper portion of CJ's thigh, he said discreetly, "I would introduce you to everyone at the table, but they're not important to me tonight. My only interest is you. I don't know a thing about you. Except how fucking great you look naked."

"Well, I guess we didn't do much talking last night." CJ smiled.

"No, I guess we didn't," Malcolm said as he rubbed CJ's leg under the table, which gave CJ chills, though he still wasn't enjoying Malcolm's aggressive behavior. Was this guy a 'roid head? That would explain all those ripply muscles.

Then, before Malcolm could ask again, CJ interrupted. He realized that he couldn't let the man learn too much about him if he wanted to get any information out of him. "So, Mr. Politician, tell me all about working for the big man. You must know some really juicy dish!"

Tell a man who thinks he's important that you think so too, and you can get him to talk for hours.

The others at the table were busy gabbing away, presuming Malcolm and CJ were discussing important business matters.

"Well, I do, but of course I can't divulge. That's why they pay me the big bucks." Malcolm winked. "I know *everything* but say nothing. It's what makes me so valuable."

Damn. Not what CJ was hoping to hear. He tried again.

"Well, you can't know *everything*. Wouldn't that be too risky? I mean, you're just an *aide* after all. What if you had a falling-out—he'd have to bump you off," CJ teased.

Malcolm's face turned beet red, and not from the Chianti. He moved closer and squeezed CJ's thigh tightly, stared fiercely in his eyes, and spoke in a low, thin-lipped voice that somehow reminded CJ of Giuliani. "Just an aide? Listen, you whore, I run that guy's life. I know everything. *Everything!* From the way he takes his coffee to his sexual proclivities. He trusts me with all of it!" CJ watched as a vein in Malcolm's forehead protruded.

Checkmate, CJ thought. He had the man where he wanted him. He gave Malcolm a sly smile and a look that said he'd had no idea how powerful he was, and excuse him for the lack of respect. "Oooooh, what's he into?" CJ asked.

"I can't say, but trust me, I know some wild stuff!" Malcolm assured him, his manhood satisfied as he relaxed back in his chair. He was a hot-tempered one.

"C'mon, what could he be into? Keeping his black socks on while he does it? Whores? Men? Jeez, come back to me when you have a story," CJ said. He scanned the room as if bored, checking out which other nobodies were there that night.

"Oh, you'd be shocked!" Malcolm said, leaning in a little desperately.

"Yes, yes, I'm sure I would," CJ said sarcastically and even feigned a yawn. He was back in control and knew this was the way to get this pretentious little goat's goat.

"Oh, he's gotten himself into a lot of jams. I'm getting him out of his biggest one right now, and it's a doozy. I'm not even sure he's going to make it out this time. I live a very exciting life; you have no idea."

"You know what? Bullshit. You pretend to know everything, but you and your overdone Ralph Lauren apartment, it's all bullshit," CJ growled.

"Oh, it's bullshit, is it? Well, I think the mayor killed someone!" Malcolm hissed. They were practically having a lovers' quarrel.

CJ just stared at him and let those words hang there for a second while Malcolm stared at the floor, praying that no one else had heard him. CJ's Nelly was back. He had been hoping against all hope that the police chief was right and what they saw had been a Halloween prank, but deep down he'd known different. His Nelly had told him so, and now here was proof.

CJ collected himself. "Oh, gosh, I'm so sorry," he said sincerely. He could see the panic in Malcolm's eyes and gazed at him, attempting to soothe. "Can I help?" CJ said, even though he knew he couldn't. He did mean it, though.

"No, no. There's nothing you can do, of course. Oh, god, I shouldn't have told you, but I've been holding this in. It's eating me up. That's why I couldn't stop drinking last night. There's something familiar and comforting about you, though, you know? I feel connected to you." Malcolm seemed relieved as the words tumbled out of his mouth.

"Yes, we do have a connection," CJ half lied.

"I'm freaking out, but I think I handled it. I just wasn't prepared for this. Can we talk about it later? I don't want anyone to hear," Malcolm whispered.

"Yes, of course," CJ said, almost feeling sympathetic, though he was still more concerned about his own predicament. How he kept from vomiting he didn't know. He reached under the table and pinched his own thigh *hard* in order to retain his focus. Tears started to form in his eyes, and he turned to look at Malcolm, who appeared to take the moistness as sympathy.

"Come over afterward, will you?" Malcolm was almost begging.

"Yes, of course," CJ said again and then sighed loudly. Malcolm smiled, again mistaking CJ's sigh as support, though that couldn't have been further from the truth. CJ's mind raced. He couldn't go to the phone now, it would be too obvious. He would wait until they were back at Malcolm's place and lie, saying he was calling home to let Nanny know he would be spending the night out again.

"Hey, did I tell you about the time I was here and Kate Hudson tried to get in?" CJ said as he attempted to lighten the mood. And what a stupid thing to say. Of course he hadn't told Malcolm since they'd only just met, but Malcolm played along.

"No, what happened?" he politely asked.

"Well, it was when she was dating Lance Armstrong, and they came in expecting to be seated, but Frankie No showed them the door. It was brilliant!" CJ beamed.

Malcolm cocked his head inquisitively. He'd thought he was bringing CJ here for the first time to impress him, but now it was clear CJ was something of a regular, though the overly discreet staff hadn't dared give him away.

The appetizers arrived, and the hanger-on next to CJ began talking to him about some political crap that CJ couldn't care less about. But he appreciated the distraction.

After dinner Malcolm let his entourage take the mayor's car back to Connecticut while he and CJ took the car service Rao's provided, but not before asking for a better night. He didn't want to do the obvious pleading, so first he handed the guy a fifty and said, "Such a meal, Frankie! The best in Manhattan. Next time I have to have that *Fish Alla Puttanesca*, eh? So when's my next date?"

Frankie wasn't terribly fond of the little fanook, but considering Malcolm's position, he respectfully scrawled a date on a small piece of paper. Malcolm took one look and frowned, then desperately angled for a different night. But the man is called Frankie No for a reason, and that was it—Malcolm's fate was sealed. He would forever be a Rao's Monday night guy. Malcolm graciously said good night to the waiter, the cocktail waitress, and anyone who would listen, but the second he got in the car he exploded. "Motherfucking son-of-a-bitch!" he screamed. "That's it, I'm done with that stupid place!" and vowed never to eat at Rao's again. Or at least not until the Monday night in March that Frankie had given him as his next reservation.

Eventually Malcolm calmed down and opened the window to let the cool November air wash over him as the car hissed down a damp, quiet, and practically empty Fifth Avenue. The remaining bright oranges and yellows of Central Park, in its final throes of fall, glowed in the incandescent bishops' crook streetlamps.

Malcolm broke the silence, somewhat sullenly. "I hate this fucking job, you know."

CJ started. He opened his mouth to respond, but there was nothing he could think to say. Better to let the rest flow out, he thought.

"The mayor, he's . . . well, I guess he's not an entirely awful guy, but he's a snake. Not a sly, stalking cobra, but did you ever see the video of the stupid king snake that eats its own tail? He's kinda like that. Typical politician. There's nothing about him you can trust. Everything he says is a platitude, and it's impossible to know whether he means a single thing he says. Does 'good job' mean *Good Job!* or does it mean he's trying to con me into something? Know what I mean?"

"Oh yeah. More than you can imagine. I like politicians about as much as I like dirty socks. They stink, they're uncomfortable, and they ruin your shoes."

Malcolm looked at CJ in the dark of the car and smiled. He seemed a bit relieved, CJ thought.

"God, so true. Makes me wonder if I should still be doing

this. It always seemed like the right career for me. I thought it would be a way to do some good in the world. And I know you have to pay your dues, but the shit I've had to go through . . . I'm starting to think it's just not worth it."

CJ suddenly found himself with a bit of a soft spot for the stocky little boy-man. Well, in any case, he was finding himself fond enough to spend the night again, but not enough to tell Malcolm who he really was and what he was really after. When they arrived at the apartment, CJ excused himself to make a phone call before going in.

"I'm sorry to call so late," he said into his cell phone.

"No, it's fine, I'm awake. And I missed talking to you today, so I'm glad you called. But why are you calling at eleven P.M. on a school night? Is everything okay?" Coco replied.

"No, girl, not at all. We need to get that ragtag Scooby-Doo group together. We've got a mystery to solve," CJ said half jokingly.

"Why? What's going on?"

"That police chief lied to us. The mayor killed her, and I have proof!"

"What? You have real proof?" Coco was getting nervous now.

"Well, not real proof, but I'm with his aide right now, and he's told me enough."

"Can you tell me more?" Coco asked.

"C'mon, lover!" Malcolm yelled out playfully.

CJ covered the phone with his hand. "One sec, sugar!" he said to Malcolm and then continued. "Coco girl, I gotta go, but I'll call you in the morning. Can we get together tomorrow night?" CJ asked.

"Well, it sounds like we have to. I'll call Bailey and Olivia. Let's meet at my house at eight, okay . . . sugar?" Coco said, laughing.

"Shut up. Yes, okay, see you then," CJ said as he hung up, hearing Coco give a quick "Okay, bye."

His night was just starting. He was going to get the full story from Malcolm, even if he had to pound it out of him.

CJ walked inside the apartment, took off his jacket, and sat down momentarily. Malcolm wasn't in the kitchen or the bathroom, so CJ got up and looked in the bedroom, where he found Malcolm lying facedown in the middle of the bed, completely naked. He was clearly waiting for CJ, but he appeared to have drifted off. CJ sighed, quietly covered Malcolm with a blanket, and turned off the lights. Taking a spare quilt to the sofa, he removed his shoes and settled down for a few hours of fitful sleep.

NINE

Scooby-Doo and Malcolm Too

Detective Casey couldn't sleep. He was usually a very sound sleeper, but tonight he just stared at the ceiling thinking about something his chief had said, something that didn't make any sense. It was one of those rare moments that made him proud to have been with the FBI. His training had given him a way of thinking that was different from that of an average cop; his thoughts raced between how lucky he was to have had those experiences and the strange little world in which he now found himself.

What kept playing over and over in his head was his chief on the phone, bragging to someone about his job security: "Oh, no, no. Don't worry about a thing. This guy's goin' *no-where*. Heh, heh."

Casey had heard Bruno walk toward the door and close it, so the detective quickly and quietly moved to the wall next to the door to listen, his back against the wall.

". . . nah, I've got City Hall in my pocket. Trust me, this is a big one. They're not going to replace me—probably ever. The search is off. I just earned myself some *very* long-term job security . . . heh, heh, yeah . . . Just like Kennebunkport. Ha. You got it!" Casey moved back to his desk and sat with headphones on, engaged, or so he made it seem, in a review of a witness interview he'd conducted earlier that day.

Damn. How'd he get that kind of job security? There had been talk of the First Selectmen appointing another chief when Bruno's contract was up in July. This was the first Casey had heard otherwise. He'd even thought of applying for the job.

The chief had been insistent that Coco and her friends were mistaken about the mayor, yet Casey's investigative instincts told him otherwise. And now the chief's phone call seemed to tie it all together. Casey's love for his work and his need for an excuse to contact Olivia were propelling him to take a next step—one that could jeopardize his career in Greenwich.

Coco sat in front of her dressing mirror scrutinizing her skin and trying to decide what "type" it was. She'd always been a tomboy, never a girlie girl; attempting to be liberal and understanding, her parents had respected her seeming lack of feminine graces, but at that moment she wished they hadn't. She wished that her mom, or an aunt, or the sister she never had, had taught her something about looking girlie and pretty, how to do her makeup for any occasion. She knew how to make it work for business and how to look like an Ann Tayloresque professional, but what was sexy or exciting about that? CJ's stinging rebuke about looking like she'd stepped out of the eighties made her realize that she needed to update her look—perhaps doing so could even revive something in Sam—but she didn't know the first thing about any of the pricey products laid out in front of her on the bathroom counter. They were all promotional items that came without instructions. She evaluated five shades of foundation as if one of them would jump out and say, "Here I am, *alabaster honeysuckle*: use me!" She knew that her biggest critic would be CJ. *Let's face it,* she thought, *women don't dress for men; they don't even dress for other women; they dress for gay men.* Then there was the matter of figuring out what to wear. She called out for Sam.

"Honey?" she bellowed.

"Yes," he screamed back.

"Can you look at what I'm wearing and tell me if it's okay?"

"Where are you going?"

"Nowhere. The living room."

"Then *garble garble garble garble*?" He was yelling, completely inaudibly, as if he were walking away.

"*Whaaaaa?*" she screamed back.

"*Garble, garble*, wearing?"

She'd had enough and started walking through the house looking for where poor Sam was being forced to yell from. She found him in the kitchen eating an apple.

"I couldn't understand that last thing you said," she said calmly.

"I was eating. I said: If you're staying in, how could it possibly matter what you're wearing?"

"CJ, Olivia, and Bailey are coming over. I want to look good for them. I got platters made at Le Gourmet, and I have to look as good as they do," she replied.

"As good as the platters or the people?" he asked.

"Well, both I guess, but I meant the platters. Did you see

them? They look incredible. I can't be upstaged by foie gras terrine on toast," she joked. "I want to look like canapés, not a can of peas."

Sam groaned. "So, what outfits will we be choosing from?"

"Well, the one I have on, I was thinking."

"The simple black dress is always a good choice. What is it you call it again?"

"The LBD," she said. She knew that much, at least.

"Right, the little black dress, perfect. What's on your face? Have you been eating Cheez Doodles? Ooh, do we have Cheez Doodles?" he said excitedly.

"No. It's makeup."

"Oh, gotcha. So we don't have Cheez Doodles?"

"Oh, for god's sake, I don't know. Check the cupboard!" She was mad at his comment but figured he just knew nothing about the new winter colors. She headed back upstairs to finish getting dressed. Just then the doorbell rang.

"I'll get it," Sam yelled again from the kitchen.

He went to the door and saw Olivia.

"Hi, Olivia," he said.

"Hi, I'm Olivia, we met once before," she said nervously.

"Yes, that's why I said 'Hi, Olivia.' Coco will be right down." He led her into the living room. "Can I get you something to drink?" he asked politely.

"An Orangina?" she asked.

"Ummm, I don't think we have that. Do you just want some orange juice?"

"No thanks. I think I'm good?" Sam hated people who made statements that sounded like questions, but Olivia was cute, so it was okay.

"So, it's Orangina or nothing?"

"Yep." Olivia smiled.

"Oh-kay. Well, Coco will be right down . . ." He trailed off as he started to leave the room.

"So, what are *you* doing tonight?" Olivia caught him.

"Library."

"Oooooh, nice!"

In another city going to the library might seem a punishment, but the library in Greenwich, like everything else in Greenwich, was *spectacular.* Big, yummy, comfy chairs that caress and cuddle your backside, making it hard to leave their embrace. Every book imaginable is available, there's free Internet and a coffee bar modeled on the fabulous Hotel Sacher Café in Vienna. Sam looked forward to being kicked out of the house just for the opportunity to spend his evening at the library.

"Can you get it?" Coco yelled from upstairs.

"Get what?" Sam yelled back. Just then the doorbell rang. Coco must've seen Bailey's car pull up in the driveway from the upstairs bathroom.

"Hi, I'm Sam, Coco's, er, boyfriend, nice to . . ." But before Sam could get out the rest of the sentence, Olivia came prancing in from the other room like an excited puppy.

"Hi, Bailey, it's so nice to see you again!" She beamed.

"Uh, you as well," Bailey said cautiously. Within seconds Coco and the two Spinoni came barreling down the staircase.

"Hi, hi, you guys, sorry I'm running late. Come here, come here!" Coco said as she waved hurriedly for them to follow her into the living room. "CJ just texted, he's late too. I have food, can I get you a drink?"

"Orangina?" Olivia tried again.

"Sounds good, I'll have one too," Bailey said.

"Okay, two Oranginas," Coco replied as she walked into the kitchen and fielded Sam's sneer along the way. "What?" she asked, trying to interpret his quizzical stare.

"We have Orangina?" he asked, stunned.

"Of course we do, duh," Coco replied.

"Oh. Okay. Well, all right. Heading to the library. See you later," he said as he kissed her forehead and walked out the kitchen door.

Coco came back in with her beautiful food platters and three Oranginas. The dogs trotted along behind, then sat patiently staring at the food platters, as if willing the food to come to them, though they dared not grab it on their own.

"Who's got your baby tonight?" Coco asked Olivia.

"I have this wonderful sitter. She lives on the block. I'm so lucky," Olivia replied.

"How old is . . . Gosh, I don't know your son's name," Coco said.

"Simon. He's eight months," Olivia said proudly.

"So what *did* happen between you and the baby daddy?" Bailey asked bluntly.

"C'mon," Coco scolded. "Maybe she doesn't want to talk about it."

"Oh, please, you know you want to know too," Bailey chided Coco.

"No, no, it's fine. I've made peace with it, and actually our relationship had been on the skids for at least the last two years. I'm glad it's over. Really. I don't have any problem talking about it," Olivia said.

"So things started going bad while you were pregnant?" Coco asked.

"Well, things were going bad for a long time before that. But, yeah, it was a rough pregnancy all around. But I wanted a baby. I didn't care if he was staying or not," Olivia said.

"God, why did you wait so long to get rid of him?" Bailey asked.

"That's a good question. I guess I wasn't ready to be without him, but in a way maybe I was. Every time something went wrong, or he treated me like shit, instead of being a woman about it and talking it out, or even letting him know, I just logged it in my brain. Like 'Okay, he spent my birthday in Vegas with his friends, gotcha.' So I let him pile straws on my back, waiting for that final one. It was cowardly, I know, but I had to get to the point where I didn't care anymore. In the back of my mind I knew he would get me there eventually," Olivia recounted. "And, of course, he did."

"So what was the big issue?" Coco asked.

"There were a few. First, he was a huge narcissist. That was the biggie. I don't know if you've ever dated someone who has a personality disorder like that, but it's impossible to deal with. I knew about it early on, but it got harder to accept that *he* was always going to be his own priority; and I had no option but to go along with that if I wanted to be with him. The other thing was his bizarre new religious stuff," Olivia said.

"What does that mean?" asked Bailey.

"His father was Protestant and his mother was Jewish, so he wasn't raised one way or the other. As he got older, he decided to embrace his Jewish heritage, which at first I thought would be lovely for him . . . and I thought that it might tame his narcissism. I also kinda thought it might be valuable for our child, since I was a nonpracticing Presbyterian. But he took me to this weird cultlike temple all the way out on Long Island that was as orthodox and fundamentalist as Jews get. I guessed it would be fine, but this felt totally creepy and culty. The women and men sat separately, and the rabbi preached about the need for women to keep the family together by not working, staying at home to raise the children, and, most important, catering to their husbands' every need. Hah! Really taking too literally all that Old Testament stuff; and he seriously wanted me to buy into this crap. *As if!*" said Olivia, disgusted.

"Oh, like Hasidic Jews?" Bailey asked.

"No, that would have been one thing, but this was creepier, and the temple demanded a certain amount of money from him regularly, like the Mormons and their heavy tithing; this felt more like Jewish Mafia. Plus, Benjamin was a total hypocrite. He had a baby out of wedlock with a woman who had a full-time career and with whom he didn't live. So much for the subservient woman, right? And then, to top it off, he had a sleeve of tattoos up his arm of . . . I kid you not . . . two Warner Brothers cartoon characters and a Mercedes logo!"

"I'm actually more shocked that you'd date a guy with those tacky tattoos," Coco said. "But, hey, people do stupid stuff when they're young, right? God makes exceptions for things you do before you found him I guess?"

"No! He got the tattoos after he became a Super Jew!" Olivia explained. "And, get this: he asked the rabbi how he could be buried in a Jewish cemetery even with his tattoos. So the rabbi gave him a number."

"What do you mean 'gave him a number'?" Coco asked.

"He gave him a number, as in an amount of money he could give to the temple so that he could keep getting tattoos and still be buried in a Jewish cemetery!" Olivia laughed.

"So I don't understand. You broke up with him just because he got religion? That's kinda cold," Bailey scolded.

"Bailey, that's rude!" Coco admonished.

"No, I just meant . . ." Bailey began to explain.

"No, stop. I hear what you're saying. But that isn't what broke us up. I'm just setting it up so you understand what kind of guy he really was," Olivia said.

"Oh, okay, sorry, didn't mean to judge you," Bailey said.

"Well, yes you did, but we can let it go. Here's what happened," Olivia continued. "I accepted that this was his choice and just another aspect of what, at the time, I was willing to put up with despite the hypocrisy of his life and his religious choices. The final straw was New Year's Eve a year ago. We were living in Chicago, and there was this beautiful church where every year they did the blessing of the animals and lots of other secular events. They were known for their really wonderful New Year's party. There would be live music, food, dancing. It was a nondenominational good time, and everybody went: Jews, Catholics, Baptists, Buddhists—everyone. As a matter of fact, the bands they had that year were a bit of a shock because some of their music was rather risqué—but they didn't play any of those songs that night out of respect for the church they were in."

"That sounds like a lot of fun, actually. New Year's Eve is usually such a bummer," Coco interjected.

"Right? Yes, it *was* fun. And there were dozens of families there. It was really lovely. So we show up and they hand us a program, with descriptions of the bands and some of the events and games of the night. But the front of the program has an angel on it, you know, it's sponsored by a church after all, and Benjamin completely flips out! He starts yelling at me in front of everyone, saying: 'You said this was nondenominational, what is this bullshit angel on here? You lied to me! You're a liar!' He starts calling me a liar over and over, in front of all of these people," Olivia said. "I just started crying right there, and I'm like, almost seven months pregnant. I was completely mortified, inconsolable."

"Holy crap, what did you do? I would've stabbed him on the spot," Bailey said. "Tell me that's what you did."

"I wish," Olivia said, cracking a slight smile, though still clearly traumatized by the memory. "No, I was so humiliated at that point I tried to stop crying in front of everyone and just said let's go home. So we went, him screaming at me the entire way, the baby kicking, me nauseous. It was the worst New Year's Eve I've ever had, and I'd thought it was going to be so nice."

"Oh, my god." Coco was horrified, but she privately started to think some of the troubles she had with Sam weren't so bad after all. "What happened when you got home?"

"Oh, well, that was the best part. He started telling me that if I ever took him to a church again, he would walk out the door and never speak to me. He'd just sue for custody and that would be it. And I'm like '*What? Over this?*' and he said, 'Yes. You need to convert to Judaism so you can understand why we can never go to a church again.' So I said, 'Ben, you go to friends' weddings in churches all the time!'" Olivia said.

"Yeah, I was gonna ask about that. What did he say?" Bailey asked.

"He said, 'I sit in the back, come late, and leave early so they know that I disapprove.' Can you imagine?" Olivia chuckled.

"So really, he's not a religious fanatic, just a douche bag," Bailey said.

"Yeah. What a *dick*," Coco added. "Sorry, honey, but *jesus*."

"Pretty much. But the final, *final* straw took place a few weeks after the New Year's Eve fiasco. He kept harping on that night, and he bought me this video called *The Rise of Anti-Semitism* that I refused to watch. He said to me, 'Watch it, Olivia, it will help you with your soul.' He wouldn't let up. It was like he was fighting a Jewish jihad. If he hadn't been sleeping with a nineteen-year-old student in his religious studies class at the same time, I might have taken him seriously," said Olivia.

"*What?* Oh, my god, this guy is too much," Coco said.

"Good thing you dumped that asshole," Bailey said.

"Not soon enough. But thank goodness I've moved on and away. He left Chicago when he got the opportunity to go work at that station at the South Pole, and I came back here," Olivia explained.

"Oh, I thought his moving there was what broke you guys up," Coco said.

"No, clearly we were doomed way before that." Olivia laughed. "Now he's some teenager's problem."

"That nineteen-year-old went with him?" Bailey asked.

"Not that one, another one. But at least they're at the same maturity level. The only sad part is that Simon doesn't get to see his daddy. He was a crappy boyfriend, but a boy needs a daddy. Makes me sad he doesn't have one," Olivia lamented.

Just then the doorbell rang. Finally, the man of the hour had arrived. The women were anxious to hear everything he had to say.

Olivia and Coco ran to the door. Bailey was too cool to budge from her relaxed pose on the couch. They expected to see CJ walking in bursting with information, but what they got instead was him walking in with welts, hives, and red blotches all over his face, which he scratched furiously.

CJ pushed the door open and practically shoved Olivia out of his way. "Oh my god, I have to use your shower immediately, I'm freaking out! The Benadryl isn't working!" He was indeed frantic.

"Okay, okay, follow me. Oh, my god, what happened?" Coco said as she led CJ to the guest bedroom.

"Malcolm has this five-thousand-dollar Bengal cat named Shakira," CJ said as he began to strip down, "that I am *deathly* allergic to. I never saw the cat until this afternoon. It was hiding in the closet or something, so when I broke out, I just thought I was having a food allergy. Please, I have to wash off these cat oils and hair and whatever else is on me. I'm dying! I'm going to die!" he said, panicky.

"No, you're not dying, you'll be fine. Here's a towel, I'll get you some of Sam's clothing so you don't have to wear your cat-hair clothes," Coco said calmly as she exited the room.

CJ stopped her before she walked out. He brought his hissy fit to a screeching halt and looked directly at her. "Honey, *why* is your face orange? Have you been eating Cheez Doodles?" CJ asked.

"Oh, god. It's foundation," Coco said in an exasperated tone. "It's supposed to be the good stuff."

"If that's foundation, honey, then let that house collapse! You look like an Oompa Loompa!" CJ quipped.

"Don't you have cat hair to wash off?" Coco snapped as she slammed the door and headed back to the others.

Detective Casey spent his day doing his usual police work. This generally consisted of vital tasks such as filing complaints about noisy neighbors, or dealing with the woman who called to say her gardeners had trimmed her hedge an inch shorter than she wanted, yet they were still demanding payment. But today he was so distracted that he kept filling out the forms incorrectly and having to start over. His suspicions of the chief were nagging at him, and he was feeling like he was going to get to use his brain and his FBI training for a change. He was afraid of overly scrutinizing the man and raising his suspicions, so he did his best to avoid him. If he were going to investigate his boss, the Greenwich chief of police for crying out loud, he would have to do so surreptitiously. Crossing the blue line is frowned on not only by the officer you're investigating but almost as much by your fellow officers. So he waited for the chief to leave before making any phone calls.

He didn't have to wait long. Chief Bruno frequently cut out early, since the bulk of his job seemed to involve his many social engagements. It was clear to Detective Casey that the chief was a social-climbing, starstruck leech; he was allowed to hang around with the überwealthy not because he was one of them but because they were willing to buy his influence. When you are very, very rich, it's not a terrible idea to have the local police chief in your pocket. This fact, however, was totally lost on Chief Bruno, who was under the delusion that they considered him an equal when they actually thought of him as nothing more than hired help. What Detective Casey needed to determine was just how "hired" he was. And if the chief were being greased, then how closely involved was the mayor?

Casey knew that at the first mention of his suspicions he would be labeled a paranoid conspiracist. *But,* he thought, *paranoia is not such a terrible quality for a detective to have, despite the fact that there's really not a lot of crime in Greenwich.*

Which there wasn't.

The most cops did in that town was break up rowdy parties thrown by dilettante trust-fund kids. The big joke in Greenwich was that, when you saw a police car screaming by, someone would always say, "Ah, there must be a kegger."

Detective Casey was used to real police work, serious cases that had life-and-death consequences; so a side of him thought that maybe he was looking for trouble where there wasn't any in this quiet burg. He'd had to leave Quantico when his mother was diagnosed with cancer and had no one to care for her while she underwent chemotherapy. He took the job in Greenwich (the department was happy to boast that it had one of the FBI's finest on loan, because even city employees had a taste for the elite) so that he could be close enough to commute to her place in Stamford. So the thought of pursuing a real case and uncovering something truly scandalous here got him excited.

There was most definitely something about his boss and

the story of Bailey and her rather, er, stimulating, doctored sex tape and the whole mayor/murder story that got his dander up. He didn't want to stir up something that on its face sounded almost farcical and make a fool of himself, but he just couldn't leave this alone. He thought if he just started with those envelopes—and he'd spent several years at the Bureau becoming an expert in fingerprint analysis—he would be able to dispel his suspicions . . . or give them strength.

Go with what you know, he thought.

Police work is one of those fields where your particular training determines how you assess a situation. A deceptions expert would want to do interviews to see who is lying; a forensics specialist would want to gather as much material evidence as possible to run through microscopes and machines. Detective Casey would certainly have to rely on those investigative techniques later, but right now he had his strongest skills to put to use, and he did fingerprints. And, like all guys with toys, he wanted to try out some of the new fingerprinting techniques he recently learned.

The first thing he knew he had to do was get ahold of the envelopes without arousing suspicion. He had built a bond with Bailey, and she seemed to trust him, so he started with her.

"Uh, good evening, Ms. Warfield, Rob Casey of the GPD here." He'd gotten her voice mail. Funny how she always carried that BlackBerry around yet she couldn't answer the damned thing.

"I was just, uh, hoping to get a chance to meet with you. There is some . . . follow-up I'd like to do regarding your case. I basically need to put some paperwork to bed and ask you to sign off on a thing or two so we can close everything up properly. It'll only take a minute since there's no longer any investigative work to be done."

He paused, realizing he was overcompensating, and thought for a bit, then added, "I'd certainly be happy to come out to your place so as to not be an inconvenience. If you can give me a call and let me know what time would work best, we can wrap this right up. My number is . . ." Well, it seemed plausible enough in case anyone was listening to him. *I'll just take it from there when I see her,* he thought.

One more call and he could get the heck out of there. The office was giving him the creeps, and he was starting to feel like he was being watched. This time, though, he discreetly pulled his FBI-issued cell phone—the one with the secure SIM chip in it—from his pocket, punched in an access code, and called.

"Gary, it's Rob."

"Casey, you bastard! How the hell are ya? How are things at the country club? Golf game improving? How's your mother?"

"She's getting through it, thanks. Yeah, it's kind of a bore here, but I got a little something going that I need your help on."

"You're shitting me. You need real FBI work for a town full of blue bloods?"

"Yeah, I might be onto something big. There are a couple of young ladies here who are being extorted, and there could be some big players involved. I need you to do a background check for me on the police chief and a few of his colleagues. This guy smells dirty. And I have to crack the network here."

"A couple of women, eh? You sure you're not trying to get a sugar momma?" Gary was a kidder, but the silence on the other end of the line assured him Casey was serious. “Okay, okay. You got it, pal. Give me names and a secure line where I can e-mail the code. You still have your kit, right?” He meant the ultrasecure FBI-issued laptops that used the highest level security and could be accessed only with an iris scan and a 128-bit key card.

“Yep. You know the address. I’ll get back to you with additional names as they come up. And I’ll need you to run some fingerprints through the database, okay, bud?”

“You got it. Take care of yourself and get your ass back here. You’re missed.”

CJ walked into the living room with wet hair wearing Sam’s long-sleeve J. Crew T-shirt, an orange cotton roll-neck sweater, and a pair of Gap jeans.

“Are these the guy version of ‘mom jeans’?” CJ grimaced.

“Oh, my god! They are!” Olivia squealed.

“Don’t get me started. I’ve been trying for years to get him to throw those away. He likes high-waisted jeans, what can I say? That I got him to stop buying clothes from the five-dollar bin at the Salvation Army was a major victory,” Coco replied.

“Okay, sorry, not really interested in Sam’s fashion tragedies. Can we please get to why we’re here?” Bailey said impatiently. “I don’t mean to be rude, but I’m meeting with my lawyer tomorrow, and if you have information that can help me, I need to know now.”

“Okay, fine,” CJ began. “Then I’ll just be as blunt as I can. The mayor *did* kill that girl. We saw what we saw and it wasn’t a prank. The police lied to us. Period. What are we gonna do about it?"

"Hang on, what?" Olivia said. "How on earth do you know that?"

"Well, Romeo here," Coco said, "has been 'romancing' the mayor's right-man hand. I mean right-hand man." She grinned.

CJ interrupted. "I met Malcolm, the mayor's aide, out the other night and seduced him—as a favor to you three, of course . . . I enjoyed none of it." He winked. "That's why we called the meeting. I didn't think we should be talking on our phones. I'm worried they're tapped."

Coco chimed in. "But the good news is that apparently CJ will do anything to get information, so we may just have the upper hand."

"This is unbelievable," Olivia said. "How did you manage that? You met him 'out' where?"

"At a bathhouse. I figured out who he was, and then I let him take me home." CJ smiled.

"Huh? You did what in the where now?" Olivia was confused, so she turned to Bailey. "What's a bathhouse?"

"Why would you assume I know?" Bailey replied.

Coco interjected. "It's a nice clean place where very dirty things happen."

"That's a lovely way to put it. Thank you," said CJ.

"What do you mean 'dirty things'? Are you saying guys hook up there? Tell me more! Who goes? Is that even legal?" Olivia asked, clearly titillated.

"Oh, so now you want to hear about the gay bathhouse? Look at you, missy!" CJ teased.

"I'm kinda curious as well," Bailey said.

"Look, we really have more pressing matters at hand. I'll give you all the lowdown on the down-low tomorrow morning in yoga."

"Umm, okay," said Bailey, confused. "Then tell us how you met . . . Malcolm? Maybe I should be afraid to ask, but I'm curious. How did you know who he was? How was it you both were there?"

"Oh, I really didn't know who he was at first. But I've seen him here in Greenwich and suspected he might play for my team. He didn't appear to recognize me at the baths. I was curious to know what his story was, so I sat close by, and then I overheard him talking about last summer when the lifeguard called the cops on those women who were doing yoga on the beach. Remember?" CJ said.

"Oh yeah. Crazy!" Bailey replied.

"What? What happened?" Olivia asked. "I wasn't here last summer."

"Four African American women from Greenwich were doing yoga with their instructor on the beach, and the clueless, racist lifeguard called the police on them, saying they were loitering and trespassing," Coco explained.

"God, nothing changes here. They're all a bunch of rich, white bigots," Olivia said.

"Yeah, so you can imagine how important it is for me to stay in the closet here. Not to mention, of course, that my father is running for governor," CJ said.

"Oh, wow, that suuuuuucks," Bailey replied.

"So, wait. I don't get it. This gay guy from Greenwich just opened up to you and told you all of this in a sex club? He just tossed off that his boss committed murder while he was in the steam room?" Olivia was incredulous.

"Oh no, honey, he didn't tell me at the *bathhouse.* It was the next night, while we were cuddling in bed," CJ said.

"Why would you even see him a second time? I thought the bathhouse was all about one-night stands. How did you swing a second date?" Bailey asked.

"He invited me to Rao's, so I went," CJ replied.

"Rao's?" Coco was almost drooling. "He invited you to *Rao's*? You don't just take a one-night stand to *Rao's.* Oh, my god, he *liked* you if you went to *Rao's.*"

Coco drew the *Rao's* out breathy and long like it was the name of an exclusive Parisian salon, instead of the basic little Italian bistro that it was.

"Is that a special place?" Olivia asked.

"Oh, c'mon, it's not that big a deal." Bailey sighed. "The exclusivity is the thing that gets people excited. But, trust me, if you could go whenever you liked, you wouldn't get too excited about the place. The food's okay, there are a few celebrities there, but it's kinda divey, really. I'll take Per Se over Rao's any day."

"Oh, you can't get a table at *Rao's,* Olivia, it's invitation only. Unless you're a Warfield, of course. And you don't just take a one-night stand to *Rao's,*" Coco repeated. "You take someone you want to impress."

"Oh! So is this something? Do you like the guy?" Olivia was suddenly curious.

"I'm not sure. That's sort of beside the point right now," CJ said, slightly bashful for a change.

Olivia was hurt. She loved hearing about new romance.

"Well, if you don't want to discuss your love life with us, I won't push it."

"Thank you," CJ replied.

"I mean, you can trust us, you know. We *did* witness a murder together. That's kinda special. But if you really think it's none of our business . . ." Olivia pursued before CJ interrupted her.

"Okay, fine. I am really not sure what to make of this guy. He's a bit of an asshole, actually. But then when we're alone he's kind of vulnerable and sweet. You have to understand, it's really hard to live up in Greenwich being gay. It's like being in a secret club that almost nobody around here belongs to, so when you meet someone who's in it, it's exciting. But I'm not sure who he really is: the sweet, vulnerable guy or the idiotic, political, suck-up guy. It's one of those situations where either the occupation makes him an asshole or he was an asshole to begin with so he chose politics. Hard to tell," CJ explained.

"How did you get him to talk about the mayor so quickly?" Coco asked.

"Oh, honey, one roll in the hay with the right guy and I'll find out where Jimmy Hoffa is buried. Malcolm was easy to work. He *needed* to tell someone. I knew that if I challenged his fragile ego, he'd offer me *something*. I just didn't realize how vulnerable he was and how much I was going to get out of him. He really has nobody to talk to," CJ said tenderly.

"How much did he admit to you? What does he know?" Coco asked.

"Yeah, did he know all of our names?" Olivia said.

"I'm not sure. I didn't want to push it, so I just let him talk. I thought if I asked too many questions, it would make him suspicious. He started out by telling me all about his job and how high-pressure it was, but later, while we were playing, he got to talking about how the mayor confided in him that he was into BDSM and that he thought he might have hurt someone 'by accident' in the midst of a recent escapade and that there might have been witnesses. Malcolm intuitively knew it was more than a minor injury, and when he suggested a solution, the mayor told him it had already been taken care of and that he should drop it and never mention it again," CJ explained.

"So did he drop it?" Bailey asked.

"He did until the mayor withdrew a large sum of money from his campaign fund. This usually meant there was going to be a new advertising push or that the mayor had stuck his foot in something ugly and had fences to mend. But instead, he had Malcolm give the money to Police Chief Bruno," CJ said.

"Oh, my god, how did you keep from screaming?" Olivia said.

"It was tough, but at the time Malcolm was a complete mess and I was comforting him. Remember, I was just some new guy he met at a bathhouse, so he was feeling pretty vulnerable. I had to let him keep thinking that, because we need to know what else the mayor is planning and if we're still on his radar."

"We also should get justice for that poor girl. We can't let the mayor get away with bribery and murder!" Coco insisted. "Okay, who do *we* know?"

"I'll talk to Detective Casey," Olivia volunteered.

"No, I will," Bailey insisted.

"Why you?" Olivia stuck her lower lip out, almost pouting.

"Because he called me saying he had some follow-up paperwork to do on the case," Bailey said.

"He called you? Why did he call *you*?"

"Because I'm the one who got him involved in the first place. He wants to close the case, and he needs my sign-off since I'm the one who had him open it," Bailey replied.

"Oh, okay." Olivia slumped back in her chair.

"Who else?" Coco asked.

"Well, obviously I'll keep working Malcolm. But we need an outside source, someone who can help investigate the mayor and the police chief," CJ said.

"I actually happen to know someone with amazingly good resources," Bailey said. "Saul King."

"Saul King, the 'Problem *Saul*ving' guy from Channel Seven? Really? He seems like a bit of a doofus," Coco said.

"I know, I know, but he has amazing connections. I have no idea how, but he's *the* go-to guy for us at the station. He wanted to be a crime reporter, but nobody would take him seriously," Bailey said.

"Maybe it's because he looks like he's wearing a Groucho Marx costume and talks like a cartoon character?" CJ said.

"Right. So now instead of going after embezzling bankers he goes after unscrupulous wedding photographers," Bailey replied.

"Tomorrow you and I will talk to Saul to see what he can help us find out about the mayor and Bruno," Coco said. "And, CJ, you need to get Malcolm to tell you more, like about us and those envelopes, and how they got that information on all of us."

"What about me?" Olivia asked.

"It's too dangerous for you at this point. You have a baby to take care of. Besides, don't you have to meet with your lawyers tomorrow about the house? Concentrate on that for now. I don't trust that crazy mother of yours," Coco said.

"True," Olivia agreed.

"Gas up the Mystery Machine, Scooby-Doo, we're going on an adventure," CJ exclaimed.

"Which one of us gets to be Velma?" Coco wondered.

TEN

The Yoga Club

The next morning the four gathered in the yoga studio and laid their mats out together for the first time. CJ and Bailey were in front and Olivia and Coco behind them, all off to the side and back of the room so they could talk more freely.

"Okay, we're all here," Olivia whispered. "Tell us about the bathhouse now. You can't begin to imagine what I've conjured up without all the facts."

"Oh, honey"—CJ frowned—"please. I really *do not* want to know. Okay, so, this bathhouse in particular is known for having men who work out . . . a lot. No bears, no fatties, just the guys you see at the gym who are obsessed with themselves."

Even though the class hadn't actually started and everyone was quietly preparing their mats, stretching ropes, blocks, and towels, Kristi, the instructor for the day, walked by in her bare feet and bent from the waist toward them with a finger to her lips, shushing them quietly with a wink.

CJ gave her the sweetest smile, which melted away as he stuck out his tongue the moment she turned and walked to the front of the class. "The problem is when you get a guy who is obsessed with how he looks," he continued, "he's usually a total douche, so it's a double-edged sword . . . or a double-edged swordfight."

Olivia stared at him blankly.

Kristi sat cross-legged in front of the class. "Good morning, everyone. Thank you so much for starting your beautiful day with me. Let's begin our session with three *Oms* to clear away the cobwebs and awaken our inner spirits with that beautiful vibration."

"Ommmmmmmmm, Ommmmmm, Ommmmmm" went the class. Coco shot a look at Olivia, who did not echo.

"Om, my god," whispered Olivia, finally understanding what CJ meant.

"Anyway," CJ stage-whispered, cracking a smile at Olivia, "you show ID and your membership card at the door and they ask you if you want a room or a locker, and then you get a towel and a key."

The class began to do a set of sun salutations.

"A room? I thought it was all saunas and hot tubs," Coco said, tilting her head up at CJ from a downward dog.

"Well, you have that there too, and it's where I met Malcolm, in a sauna. You can go to these places just to pamper yourself and take a swim if you like; or, if you'd like to play with someone, that's always an option too.

"Am I making you uncomfortable, sweetie?" he asked Olivia.

"No, no, I'm good. I had a baby. I am very comfortable with body things. Go on," she insisted.

"Oh-kay!" said Kristi a little more loudly than usual. "Why don't we work on opening our hips up today. Let's start with

the pigeon pose. I know you all like that." Several people in the class groaned at the thought of the painful stretch.

"O-kay. So, anyway, other times you just get a room and you sit there in your towel, and it's like 'rib eyes on sale, honey.' You just leave your door open, see what choice cut walks by, and then he nods, and you nod, and in he comes. From there you just point your toes, girl!" CJ looked for a reaction, but only Coco got the reference.

"Ladies—and CJ," said Kristi, half smiling, half glaring in the most beatific, passive-aggressive way possible, "this is a yoga class, not a yoga *club*. If you could try to center and focus yourself a little more, then we'll all get a lot more out of today's practice."

Bailey rolled her eyes, muttering, "If this were a yoga club, I'd beat you over the head with it."

Only Coco was within earshot, and she snorted out a laugh so hard that she had to mask it with a coughing fit.

Bailey was at the studio waiting for Coco to get in from Greenwich. Coco had a business lunch in midtown, so they'd decided to meet there to discuss their strategy with Saul King. But something other than their case was on Bailey's mind. Of course she was worried about this whole thing with the mayor, but she was also thinking about how poisonous her work environment had become.

Bailey sat in the edit bay angrily banging on the keys as she put together a package on the latest Samuel L. Jackson movie. It wasn't the movie that enraged her but her job—the job she'd once loved. There was a time when this part of the process was exciting to her, but here she was loathing every second of it. She blamed her new boss for taking away the joy. It seemed that her new executive producer, a relatively attractive failed actress who claimed she looked too much like Winona Ryder to get work, had made Bailey's job nearly impossible. At first Bailey thought the Winona wannabe was just a hard-news snob who didn't understand the value of entertainment news in the midst of so many stories on death and destruction, but she quickly learned this wasn't the case. It was her boss's own need to be famous that drove most of her ill-advised decisions. Not until Winona began sending herself, instead of Bailey, the show's entertainment reporter, on junkets to Los Angeles did it dawn on Bailey that she was not an employee but the competition. Everyone around Bailey warned her that Winona was jealous: of the job, of Bailey's access, and of Bailey's built-in fame. Winona's jealousy caused her to make spiteful choices, from sabotaging Bailey's work to cutting her segments in half, keeping Bailey's airtime to an absolute minimum. It was contentious.

Bailey didn't want to go over the woman's head, despite the fact that she could do so quite easily. The person who ran the network was indebted to Bailey's grandfather for launching his network news career. One phone call and Bailey could have a new executive producer, but she wouldn't make the call. Since Bailey was starting to feel the Warfield curse—the need to report on more meaningful, hard-news stories—anyway, she was beginning to see her lousy boss as a way out. She was mulling over the possibilities when the front desk called to tell her Coco Guthrie was on her way up.

Bailey rang Saul King's office knowing he would pick

up—he always did for her. Saul loved Bailey like family, like an older brother . . . a very bizarre, cartoonish, overprotective older brother. Bailey wondered if she should warn Coco about Saul's little eccentricities, but she didn't really have a chance because Coco was already on her way up.

Bailey went to meet her at the elevator. "Saul is waiting for us. Let's get right over there, I have so much to do today." She was tense.

They entered Saul's office, where they found him playing garbage can basketball. Coco took a quick mental snapshot of the colorful room and immediately noticed that his clock was counting backward. She hoped he'd swiped it from a "Problem Saulvers" segment wherein he'd nailed the bastard who sold broken clocks, but by the looks of the office, she suspected that in Saul's world it was just a clock.

"Hold on, hold on, I'm in the middle of some research," he said as he took a shot first with the right hand, then with the left, concentrating so hard it looked painful. After each shot, he wrote something on a notepad.

His wardrobe betrayed his lack of fashion sense. Saul was stuck in the seventies—the eighteen seventies. He was dressed like Sherlock Holmes might've been, in a peaked hat, a well-fitted waistcoat with a visible pocket watch chain, and thick corduroy pants that were almost bell-bottoms. An ensemble trumped by the suggestion of—no, a feeble attempt at—a mustache. Coco thought, *A wisp of a mustache, a wisp of a man,* as she watched him try an over-the-shoulder shot. It ricocheted off the makeshift cardboard backboard positioned above the trash can and fell off the side, where it came to rest with a large pile of similarly crumpled paper balls. He turned back to his desk and made a note.

"Hi, Saul, thanks for seeing us. This is my friend Coco," Bailey said.

"What's up, toots?" Saul seemed enthusiastic.

Bailey continued. "We have a problem we hope you can help us solve."

"You mean *Saul-ve,* don'tcha, toots?"

"Yes, whatever. It's kind of a mystery. I know you love stuff like this," Bailey said.

"Ah, a mystery! Is it murder most foul? Or perhaps a jewel heist?" he asked, almost comically, stroking his nonexistent goatee.

"Well, it's actually the first one," Coco said.

"Really?" Saul immediately sat up in his chair, shocked. "I'm so used to cat groomers who missed a paw during a clipping." He started to rummage through his desk drawers. "I didn't realize you needed real sleuthing. Hang on, let me grab my index cards. I have to take notes."

"Can we trust him?" Coco asked Bailey.

"Oh, you can trust me. I've known Bailey since she was a little girl following her grandfather around with chocolate croissant all over her face," Saul said cheerfully.

"We haven't told this to anyone aside from the police, but we think we witnessed a murder, and we need help to get some solid evidence," Coco told him as he wrote furiously.

"Why are you coming to me if you already went to the police?" Saul seemed genuinely confused.

"They tried to convince us what we saw was a prank, but

we found out the police are in on it. So now we're on our own," Coco explained.

"A good old-fashioned hoodwinking! I like it," Saul said. "Who is your murder suspect?"

"The mayor of Greenwich," Bailey said. "But the head of the police, Chief Bruno, is involved somehow too. We just don't know what the connection is."

"Quilty, eh? Tsk, tsk," Saul said as he took a note on an index card. He was New York's version of Dominick Dunne and knew everyone of prominence in society, the mayor of Greenwich included.

"Yes," Coco replied.

"I never did trust that scallywag, but I never would've suspected murder. Tell me what you saw, tell me everything! I need details! Don't leave anything out." He was almost drooling.

Coco and Bailey told Saul every detail. The girl, the mayor's weird outfit, what they saw, smelled, heard—all of it. Saul wrote furiously on his index cards. He was an aggressively mediocre man, but he seemed to be their only hope at this point.

"I want to assure you, you came to the right guy. I'll get you dirt on these dirtbags, and together we'll nail them to the wall," Saul said confidently.

The girls thanked him and left.

"He's nutty but very well connected," Bailey said.

"I hope you're right. I mean, those index cards—what the hell?" Coco asked, shaking her head.

"Trust me," Bailey replied calmly.

As they left Saul's office, Bailey began to tell Coco a little about the tension at her job, but then her cell phone rang. Bailey's entire demeanor changed. She was suddenly energized.

"I have to take this, I'll be right back," she said hurriedly as she left Coco standing in the middle of the hall. Coco, not sure where to go, decided to just stay there and feign interest in the gallery of famous visitors that adorned the walls. Every type of celebrity was represented, from Jon Bon Jovi through Meryl Streep to crappy reality show contestants. It was quite a diverse group.

Bailey came back about fifteen minutes later, about the same amount of time some of the careers on the wall had lasted, but she was beaming. Coco had to know what was up, so she asked in the same straightforward manner as Bailey herself would have. Coco was already learning from her.

"Who was that, and why are you so happy all of a sudden?" Coco asked. "It's like you just got back on your meds. What's up?"

"Okay, I'll tell you, but you have to promise not to tell *anyone*."

"Of course," Coco agreed.

"Nobody!"

"I swear. C'mon, what the heck is going on?"

"I met someone. Someone amazing." Bailey could barely get the words out. "I've been seeing Graham Shore. That was him on the phone." She could hardly contain her enthusiasm.

"So, you're having an actual relationship with Graham Shore? *The* Graham Shore from *Chicago Counsel* and *Be My Spy*?"

"Yes, yes! We've been seeing each other on and off over the past year," Bailey replied.

"Don't you mean 'sleeping with'?" Coco asked.

"No, this is more serious than that. We weren't serious at first and were dating other people, but over the past two months he's been on this spiritual journey. He's so deep and complex, he's gone to Denali to climb Mt. McKinley! I think that's so sexy and manly."

When it comes to the celebrity adventure vacation, certain locales in the world go in and out of favor. Bora-Bora is passé, and the Wakaya Club in Fiji has become too conspicuous. For the celeb who needs to go "find himself," Alaska's Denali National Park is the hip new place to climb your cares away. Kilimanjaro is as dead as Hemingway.

"Very adventurous," Coco deadpanned.

"I suppose. Anyway, last weekend he decided that he wants to be exclusive . . . with me! He said he had been searching his whole life for his one true love and said that he had found her and it's *me.*" Bailey, normally reserved, was almost beside herself.

"That's fantastic, but is it what you want? You've been so independent for so long," Coco said.

"Well, dear, it's a slow boat to China patterns," Bailey said and played with her hair the way a child would. "Yes, it's what I want, and I've waited a long time. Gotta say, everything's so much better now that we're together," she insisted.

"So are you . . . in love?" Coco was hesitant even to say those words to her.

"I must be because I don't want to screw anyone new. Besides, I'm getting tired of all the junkets, the hotel rooms, the travel, the meaningless sex . . . Okay, maybe not the meaningless sex; some of that is a little hard to let go of. That life wasn't all that bad, and I haven't completely let go, but I'm just ready for a change. It's good timing all around, a full-life overhaul."

"Good for you then." Coco hugged her. "I'm happy for you."

"Thanks. Just don't tell anyone yet. I want to respect his privacy, you know? Besides, he has to have a publicist handle that kind of stuff."

"Sure. Listen, I'm gonna jump. Don't want to be late for my meeting. Oh, and I have a trade show tomorrow in Philly. Call me if you hear anything or if you need me. I'll be a train ride away, same time zone and all. I really think that's wonderful for you."

"Thanks, but I'll be with Graham, so I'm planning on being very, very busy." Bailey smiled as she danced away.

Back in Connecticut, Olivia was at Greenwich Country Day School, an eighty-acre campus founded by Florence Rockefeller. Olivia was putting Simon on the school's waiting list for prekindergarten, as was incumbent on her as a Greenwich mother. While there she was given a tour of the school, where she saw three- and four-year-olds learning Spanish, mastering computers, and choosing musical instruments to play for the semester. Since she herself was a biochemist, Olivia had chosen Greenwich Country Day because of its program in which the children learn sciences with a specialist in whatever field they are studying at the moment. Today they were learning all about forensic science, and, as luck would have it, Detective Casey was coming in to teach them about forensic fingerprinting. Unfortunately, every child in class was sure that they would be spending the afternoon finger *painting.* Someone was going to have to do some explaining to some very disappointed kids.

This was probably the worst day for Olivia to run into anyone, let alone this man whom she hadn't been able to stop thinking about since she met him, because, sadly, she was wearing a PMS outfit.

A PMS outfit is one that in the morning as you are dressing you are convinced is the height of chic and is innovatively fashionable. Then once you leave the house it occurs to you that you may be wearing the most hideous clothes you own, all at the same time. Today, this was Olivia. Once she went to a major dinner meeting with two potential female bosses wearing a turquoise jumpsuit with red cowboy boots and matching red beads. One of the women turned to her and said, "A week away from your period, huh?" which was when Olivia learned that her need for bright colors was hormone-induced. As a rational scientist, she could see it made perfect sense, yet she couldn't sidestep it. Despite being rather expensive and of good labels, all the outfits she wore through nine months of pregnancy were rejected out of hand by Goodwill shortly after Simon was born.

Today she did not disappoint. She wore a hormone-inspired bright yellow dress with red tights, brown booties, and a short brown fake fur that she'd bought on sale at Kate Spade. On its own, the fake fur was quite chic and beautiful, but today she wore it with colors appropriate only for a five-year-old. In fact, she may have been wearing it in the only appropriate venue. But the pièce de résistance was her Kate Spade owl handbag complete with metallic beak, suede feathers, and little leather dangling feet. The outfit screamed "Get me a chocolate donut and a cookies and cream sundae, stat!" There was no way to avoid Detective Casey once he'd spotted her—and how could he have missed her? He was coming her way.

"Olivia, you look . . . bright and sunny today."

"Oh! Detective Casey, how are you? What a nice surprise." She pretended she'd just noticed him standing there. "To what do we owe the pleasure? Has there been a juice box incident?"

"Ha! No, I'm here as an expert. Today the first-grade class is learning the science of fingerprinting in police work. We're starting with the ten-print system. You should stay and listen, it's fascinating stuff."

"I'm sure it is, and I certainly wish I could," she said earnestly. "But do you think they'll get it?"

"Well, I try not to go too deep. Come back next week, when we do DNA," Detective Casey said.

Olivia tried to stifle a giggle and prayed that it wouldn't lead to a brief fit of echolalia. "Oh, I'd love to," she managed.

She stopped and thought for a second. She didn't know whether she should say something about the fact that he'd called Bailey for fear it might seem obvious they'd discussed him. It would make it seem that she liked him, or worse, that they were furthering the investigation on their own. Either way, she realized mum was the word.

"You know, I called your friend Bailey," he said.

Okay, he'd opened the door, but she kept reminding herself to stay cool. "Oh, really? For a date? I don't think she is seeing anyone, in case you want me to put in a good word."

Damn, that wasn't at all what she wanted to say.

"Um . . . no. I called to make sure she was okay with me closing her case."

"Oh, right. Strange turn of events, huh?"

"Yes, as a matter of fact, it would really help me close the case and get my report together if we could talk about what was in your envelope. Just so that I have all the facts straight, you understand. I like to be thorough. Maybe we could grab a coffee?"

Olivia was totally confused now. She didn't know if this was a ploy to get a date with her or if he really just wanted information. Either way, she didn't care. He was cute, and it had been close to two years since she'd seen a naked man—and she really wanted to see Rob Casey naked.

"Yes. Coffee? Sure, when? You tell me." Gawd, did she have to seem so ridiculously eager?

"Well, how about tonight?"

"Tonight?"

"If you can't get a sitter, bring your boy along. I love kids," he said.

"Oh, okay," said Olivia, disappointed. It's not really a date when you bring an infant along, and there went the whole seeing Rob naked thing.

"Let's meet at Everyman Café. Do you know it?"

"Sure!"

"Oh, and can you bring that envelope you received? I just want to take a look at it to see if it matches another one. Just to be sure before I close the case, of course. Whaddya say to six?"

"Huh?" Olivia was so lost in his eyes she wasn't sure if he'd said "sex" or "six." Either way, she wasn't thinking about a meeting time.

"I asked if six o'clock was okay," he said again.

"Yes, yes, six, no problem. See you at six." Olivia blushed. She felt like a moron. "Bye, Detective Casey. Have a good class!"

"Rob," he said. "Call me Rob."

Olivia had a new color to clash with the rest of her outfit: bright red cheeks. "Right. Rob."

Coco returned home after her meeting to find both Sam and the dogs gone. She loved and hated the feeling of an empty house. On the one hand, she liked the quiet, something she wasn't entirely familiar with; but on the other hand, the high ceilings, vast rooms, and wood floors felt cold and lonely without Sam and the pups clattering through. Sam was probably out at the dog park, giving Coco an opportune time to collect the pillows and blankets from the couch where he had been sleeping for the past several nights. Sam had been in an even more depressed state because of the envelope and hadn't been functional. He would watch TV endlessly, pace, or stare out the window for hours.

Sam's melancholy tore Coco apart. She felt helpless to make things better, and she still had a business to run and couldn't afford to be immobilized by his erratic behavior. She could only tell him that he was entitled to be upset but that she was sure it would all be resolved soon enough.

"Sam, I want to make it all go away," she'd said to him. "But there's nothing we can do. Kornacki told us to just let him take care of everything. We need to trust him. For now, though, I've got to keep working. This is a big time for the company."

Sam opted to keep out of her way. The house was big enough for that. But she knew where he was and what he was doing, and it was shredding her insides. She needed a stiff drink or a long stretch. Maybe it was time for a yoga class with the Sarahs.

She decided she should make the bed upstairs for him. She would be out for the night, no need for him to sleep on the couch again tonight. It undoubtedly added to his anxiety and probably gave him a stiff neck.

She really should have a conversation with Sam before she left for Philly, if not to reconcile, then at least to tell him she thought things would be okay eventually, and they just needed time. But packing was first priority, and it would give her time to collect her thoughts. Sam had been so depressed since the whole business debacle, and she hadn't made it any easier on him since, on some level, she blamed him for not predicting his partner's injurious and careless behavior. This, coupled with her secrecy about Halloween night, made tension between them inevitable—but he was from Greenwich, so fighting wasn't an option. All of the underlying emotion that should have been openly expressed was stuffed deeper and deeper, until it ran the risk of being blurted out at the most inopportune moments. "Pass the butter. How did you *not* know your partners were crooked?" or "Would you like some more tea? Oh, by the way, I saw the mayor commit a murder and hide a body." That's just how it all goes down when you're a WASP.

She hadn't meant to be so furtive with him about what the Sarah Palins had seen, but telling him would be too dangerous. She didn't want to put him through another crisis, nor did she want him to be forced to reveal anything he knew. It would be easier for both of them if she controlled the information and managed the situation. It wasn't like she didn't trust him. No, she was protecting him. But then, why couldn't she share a vital secret with her boyfriend of ten years? Maybe there were other issues she wasn't acknowledging. Either way, right now wasn't the time to think about it. Right now was the time to think about Bags-B-Gone, the new product she would be announcing at the Philly trade show.

Coco's phone rang.

"Hey, it's CJ. I was going to go over to Malcolm's office to poke around, see if I could find anything useful. But what excuse should I use?" he asked.

"Well . . . the new relationship drop-by is always welcome, so I don't think you need an excuse. Just bring cookies," she suggested.

"Hmm, I'm not sure about that. Isn't it too early to do the drop-by? Won't it come off creepy and stalkerish?"

"No. You're only a stalker if he never told you where he worked and you had to Google him. But he's a public official. Sam's grandmother went by there last week to file a complaint because there were too many unattractive birds in the park. If she can do that, you can show up with cookies," Coco said.

"I'm not bringing cookies." CJ was adamant.

"Yes, you are. You are going by uninvited and unannounced. You have to bring a treat on the off chance that he is having the worst day of his life."

"Oh, okay, I guess you're right. By the way, what did Sam's grandmother expect them to do for her?"

"She wanted them to get more cardinals and blue jays," Coco said.

"And did they?"

"What do you think?"

After they hung up, CJ went to Good Boy Bakery, which had the best cookies in town. He also thought going there would give him some much needed symbolic redemption. He'd been anything but a good boy lately.

When Olivia walked into Everyman Café that evening, she couldn't help but notice it sounded like the *Rocky* theme was playing. An odd choice of music for a cool coffee dive, so she just had to ask the girl with the fuchsia hair and pierced lip about it.

"Can I have a large cappuccino, no cinnamon, and is this the theme from *Rocky*?" Olivia asked, wondering what else was pierced.

"Yep. We're already sick of all this Christmas music, so we thought we should go ahead and get a jump on Boxing Day," Pinkie answered in a dry monotone.

Olivia didn't quite understand what she meant but presumed it was a joke since the smart-aleck-looking hipster in line behind her guffawed in spite of himself, so she said, "Oh, ha ha!" and promptly knitted her brow and turned around with her cappuccino to look for a table. In a dark corner she managed to find a tiny, open table. No sooner had she put her bag down than Detective Casey walked in. He was even more handsome than she remembered. In the dim light of the café, his green eyes glistened olive, and his broad shoulders filled the doorway as he looked across the room for his date.

"Over here!" She waved like an idiot.

"Hi, have you been waiting long?" he asked.

"No, I just got here," she replied. He looked up as if he had just remembered something he wanted to say.

"Are they playing the theme from *Rocky*?" he asked her.

"Yes, they're getting a head start on Boxing Day, they said."

"Oh, ha! Very funny. This place . . . Can I get you anything?"

"No, thanks." She motioned toward her cappuccino.

"Okay, I'll be right back."

Olivia watched him walk away, his every move speaking directly to her, causing an abrupt flush of desire through her entire body that took her by surprise. She hadn't felt that for many years. It was one of the few things she missed about high school, when she'd get that feeling about a guy just about every month. She was attracted to Rob, yes, but this overwhelming feeling was unexpected. When she looked at him, she felt safe and warm inside. She was inspired by the same confidence and security that she felt around her father, but this was so much more. Rob made her feel like she had no greater desire in the world than to be enveloped by his body and arms all at once, head at his chest (for she couldn't reach any higher), nuzzling into those beautiful pecs, smelling both his cleanliness and the vague scent of his sweat after a long day of work. She was overwhelmed by an all-consuming desire to tell him everything about her life, to make him part of her everyday existence. She wanted to connect with him in the worst way, and suddenly she had to have him in every way she could—both in her life and in her bed.

But if she said anything even hinting at these thoughts, he would smell her desperation. Olivia, not known for playing it cool, decided to channel a person she thought would handle herself better. So she conjured a vision of Christina Hendricks's character from *Mad Men.* She loved how Joan was all woman but managed to stay discreet and in control even during the most calamitous moments. Joan could talk with the boys and drink with the boys, but she was a dynamo in the sack. She wasn't a woman who would lose control in front of a man—or a woman for that matter—she was a woman who waited for her moment. While she waited for Rob to return, Olivia's demeanor changed. She sat straight and prim in her chair, focused her gaze, and assumed control of her emotions. Elegantly sipping her cappuccino, she was Joan.

"Long line. Sorry I took so long," Rob said apologetically.

Olivia smiled easily and looked directly at him. "It wasn't long at all."

"So did you bring the envelope? I'm sorry, I don't mean to be pushy, I'd just like to get the business stuff out of the way." The truth was, he did seem a little too anxious to talk business.

But Olivia—as Joan—was unfazed. "Absolutely," she said, reaching into her bag. "Here you are."

She started to hand the envelope over, then realized she was about to give away her sole connection to him. If he was truly only interested in the case, then their transaction, and connection, would end right there.

"Hang on a second," she said. "Before I give this to you,

we should probably talk about what's in it. I think I should explain."

Olivia's explanation would do nothing to augment the detective's search for fingerprints, of course. He was only going to dust the envelope and then check the stamps and the seal for DNA. He didn't actually need to look at the contents. But a good detective always listens.

"Okay, sure, tell me," he said.

"Well, inside you'll see some legal documents. A case I'm fighting, of course, but you have to understand my family. My mother has some very serious problems, in life as well as directly with me. She has taken me to court several times in an attempt to take my father's money away. She squandered everything she had, and now she is trying to steal my dead father's house from me. It's an incredible mess, and she's totally in the wrong," she told him easily. Was he a good listener because that's what detectives do, or was he truly interested in her story?

"I'm so sorry, Olivia," he said. "Is there anything I can do to help?"

"Thank you, but I think it's up to the lawyers now. The only odd thing is that we had settled this particular issue years ago, so I have no idea where these documents could have come from. They say she's the beneficiary of my father's will, but he never, ever would have made her that. None of this makes any sense."

"Are they real documents, or have they been doctored?" Rob asked, suddenly interested in the actual contents of the envelope.

"I don't know. They *must* be doctored, but they look legitimate. Enough that they're going to cause me a lot of trouble," she said.

"Do you mind if I take the documents to the lab and look at them?"

Olivia had thought that was what he was going to do anyway. "I'm confused. Aren't you closing this case?" she asked.

"Well, I'm closing the alleged murder investigation, yes, and Bailey's case, but if you want me to look into the validity of these documents for you, I can do that. If these are forged documents, then this is a case in itself," he said. As he reached across the table, he touched her hand.

Olivia briefly lost her composure and fell back in her chair like a rag doll, though not losing eye contact with Rob for even a second. She felt herself flush again but kept repeating in her head, *Be cool like Joan, cool like Joan. You're in charge.*

"Okay, I'd like that. Thank you." Her words hung there as they looked into each other's eyes so long it started to feel corny and weird. But the moment was to be short-lived.

Out of nowhere the surly fuchsia barista yelled *"Latte."* But she rolled her tongue as she said it so it sounded more like *"Lrrratte,"* and the stress of the moment—of being with Rob and trying to control her emotions—overtook Olivia like a mule's kick. She couldn't suppress her echolalia. Out ripped *"Lrratte!"*

"Whoa, what was that? Ha, ha, ha!" Rob laughed somewhat uneasily.

Olivia's supercool Joan Harris was long gone.

"Shit" was all she could say, but then she felt it again. Out it came: *"Lrratte!* Shit!" And once more, *"Lrratte!"*

Olivia was completely humiliated. She'd blown it, and

right when everything seemed to be going so perfectly. The gorgeous hunk of man in front of her was staring, astonished, and Pinkie looked pissed, undoubtedly feeling like she was being mocked. Panicked and with her eyes stinging, Olivia didn't know what to do, so she grabbed her bag and ran out the door, all the way repeating, as if she had the hiccups, "Shit! I'm sorry, I'm so sorry. Shit."

The timing of CJ's visit to Malcolm was decidedly calculated. He had read that the mayor was out of town for the day, so there'd be no chance of bumping into him and possibly being recognized. Not that the mayor would necessarily know what he looked like without his Sarah Palin costume on, but he just didn't want to take that chance.

"Hi, handsome," CJ said, popping his head into Malcolm's office.

Malcolm looked jolted. "Oh, my god, what are you doing here!"

Uh-oh, maybe the drop-by wasn't the best idea.

"We're dark this week at *Rachael Ray,* so I thought I would stop by and say hello." CJ tried a big, sweet smile.

"My assistant didn't ring me. How did you get past her?" Malcolm said nervously as he looked both ways in the hall before closing the door.

"Bribery. I brought fresh-baked cookies," CJ said as he held up the box. "Want some?"

CJ moved closer. "They're from Good Boy, but don't let that stop you," he said jokingly.

Malcolm seemed to deliberately avoid kissing CJ hello or

showing any sort of affection. CJ didn't know what to make of the sudden coldness.

"Thank you, but I'm swamped today," Malcolm said as he motioned toward stacks and stacks of papers, magazines, and books on his desk.

"Whatcha working on?" CJ asked.

"The mayor has been under some pressure from environmental groups to form an initiative that would reduce carbon emissions and all of that saving-the-planet stuff, so he appointed me his 'climate control czar.' It's an ambitious sounding title, but I have to come up with a description of what that job actually entails. I'm going through stacks of research right now. Maybe I could use a cookie after all."

Malcolm was clearly in work mode—or, more accurately, asshole mode.

"Yes, cookies always help." CJ laughed uncomfortably. This wasn't smooth, vulnerable Malcolm, this was tense Malcolm; and CJ didn't know him well enough yet to figure out how to soften him up. One thing CJ did know was that there was no way he was going to get any information out of him right now.

"So, uh, why'd you close the door so quickly? Are you not out to everyone here?" CJ asked teasingly. He might not have been getting any information out of Malcolm today, but that didn't mean he wasn't going to have some fun. He loved poking the bear in more ways than one.

"Uh, *no*. No, I'm not. It's Greenwich, it's politics. Of course I'm not out." Malcolm sneered. "As a matter of fact, I'm trying to think of what to tell my secretary. Maybe I'll tell her you're my cousin." Malcolm was hot and hostile. He clearly didn't like being put in an awkward position. Not here, anyhow.

"So you're mad I stopped by?" CJ asked.

"Well, since you are asking, yes, a little bit. I don't expect you to understand since you're in the entertainment industry, where everyone's gay and okay with it, but politics is a totally different beast. Haven't you seen all of the scandals with politicians who get outed? I mean, didn't it occur to you that you showing up here could ruin my career? Fuck."

Crap. Malcolm was really pissed, and scared. CJ wasn't very happy either, at this point.

"Okay, fine, I'll go. Tell your secretary whatever the fuck you want. But two things before I leave: keep in mind there are *many* gay politicians who are respected for who they are—the mayor of Houston is gay, for chrissakes, and hel-lo? Ever hear of Barney Frank? How 'bout Harvey Fucking Milk? And, second, you know nothing about me or my background, so don't presume you do. Trust me, I know *all* about politics. Makes this crap look like student government."

CJ stopped himself at this point. If he revealed who his father was, the jig was up.

"Just go," Malcolm hissed.

"Bitch." CJ stood to leave.

Malcolm heard but made no response and started staring out the window. CJ wondered if it were a reflection or if Malcolm's eyes were actually watering up.

"Keep the cookies. You're welcome, faggot," CJ said snidely as he abruptly set them atop a stack of papers that were laid more precariously than they looked. The entire stack came tumbling down.

"Shit!" Malcolm yelled as he jumped toward the stack, trying to stop the avalanche. But it was too late, papers went everywhere.

CJ dropped to his knees to grab what he could. He started to help pick up the mess as he apologized profusely over and over.

"No, it's fine. Just go," Malcolm said angrily.

CJ rose to leave, looking back at the mess he had created and poor little, angry Malcolm, gathering papers on the floor. And as he was looking down, CJ noticed something with his proper name on it—Charlton Jeffre Skoda, right there in blue ink on a manila folder. In a flash he slid it into his bag and walked out the door.

ELEVEN

The Hubris of Power

Coco was on the train to Philly texting wildly with CJ for most of the trip.

- OMG, drop-by bad idea!
- Oh no! What?
- Closet case. 2 embarrassed to see me.
- Crp. Cookies didn't work?
- Sorta. He was bitchy, mad, tho. But, big score!
- What?!
- "Borrowed" a file.;) We've got info!

CJ seemed upset, though he kept denying his feelings for the angry little man from the mayor's office. Just as Coco was about to make a brilliant and astute point about the state of relationships today, a call buzzed in. She saw that it was Sam and debated picking it up. She knew they would argue, and she didn't think it was smart to have it out on the train in front of Rory, who was bundled up in a big seafoam green scarf. He probably wouldn't have heard a thing since he was wearing noise-canceling headphones and was thoroughly engrossed in *The Wall Street Journal*, but still, there are some things you don't do around the person who holds your purse strings.

Their main issue of late was this: Sam had decided he wanted to get married. It was as simple as that. He didn't want any kind of special ceremony or party, he just wanted the paper. It all tied in to his five-year Plan. And the fear and anxiety created by the arrival of the papers in the mail had brought him back to it.

"Why don't we just go down to City Hall and get it done?" he'd almost pleaded. "It'll just make me feel grounded and whole."

Coco simply didn't see any reason to. She didn't want children and they had a domestic partnership, so all of their legal and financial concerns were taken care of. Coco was a hey-if-it-ain't-broke-don't-fix-it kind of gal, but Sam was wearing her down. She cared deeply for him, but this issue felt petty, and she didn't want to concede. It simply wasn't her style.

Coco knew if she answered the phone this was where the conversation would end up. She screened Sam's call and went on texting with CJ, who couldn't seem to stop talking about Malcolm. Strange, considering how disparaging he was about him.

About a half hour later the train pulled into the other Penn Station, the one in Philadelphia, which actually had the right to the name. A limo was waiting to take Coco and Rory to the Pennsylvania Convention Center for the trade show, but as they got off the train Rory walked away from Coco, making a beeline for what she assumed was the men's room; instead, it turned out he was headed right to a particular man, an incredibly handsome man. Rory turned back to Coco, waving furiously. She could see his mouth moving but was too far away to make out his words. She shrugged.

"Coco, this is Jordan Ainsworth. Remember, I told you about him," Rory said enthusiastically when she finally joined them.

Rory *had* told her about him, but she'd tuned out the conversation. Jordan Ainsworth was Rory's new protégé, and, frankly, Coco wasn't crazy about the idea of sharing Rory's attentions. She liked having him all to herself. But had he told her how attractive Jordan Ainsworth was, she might have been okay with it much sooner.

What's more, it turned out Jordan was pretty smart, and he had a rather amazing invention, one so good that Coco wished it had been her idea. He'd invented hair dye that thickened the strands as it dyed them. You could cover your grays and end up with a thicker head of hair at the same time. He was going to sell millions of his product, no question, but he was also about to make enemies. In the way that her Butt-B-Gone had made personal trainers angry, Coco knew the backlash Jordan Ainsworth would endure from the sham baldness "cure" people. Even though Jordan was handsome, Coco took some solace in the fact that he was about to receive a beating he never could have expected.

"Hi, nice to meet you. I've heard so much about you," she lied.

Jordan's eyes suggested a hint of innocence, but he was far from a neophyte. He looked at her directly in a way that said he wasn't buying her bullshit.

"Really? What have you heard?" he asked. His sandy brown hair moved as he spoke, like he had a wind machine always blowing on him. And why was this guy tan? It was November, for chrissakes. Coco was beginning to get annoyed, and in an instant she changed her opinion about him. He was so perfect to look at, he was untouchable; and beneath his model good looks, she suspected he was kind of a shyster.

"That charm will serve you well in this business. It's ninety percent personality. Your product has to be good, of course, but what separates you from the other nincompoops is your savoir faire. And you appear to have it in spades, my friend," she said with the authority of an old pro.

"Well, thank you. That means a lot coming from you," Jordan said.

Coco couldn't tell if he was being sarcastic or not, so she just glanced at him sideways.

"Rory, we have to get going. Nice meeting you, Julius," she said. She always liked to pretend she didn't remember someone's name correctly when they were rude to her. Just to let them know how uninspiring and unimportant they were.

"Jordan," Rory said quickly.

Damn. Why did Rory have to be the one to correct her? Now it felt like he was taking Jordan's side and thus taking away some of her power.

"Yes, of course," she said as dismissively as possible. "Anyway, Rory, we should go."

"Yeah, we're gonna be late. Jordan, were you taking a cab to your hotel? Can I catch up with you later?" Rory said.

"Actually, I was going to head over to the convention center early," Jordan replied. "So I guess I'll just see you there. Unless you want to share a cab with me?"

Yep. Total shyster.

"No, no, we have a limo. Why don't you ride with us?" Rory insisted.

The hair on the back of Coco's neck stood straight up. "Well now, Rory, wait a second. I had some things I needed to discuss with you before we got to the booth. I'm sure Jayden would be bored with our business talk," she insisted.

"Nonsense. We can talk later. Jordan, you ride over with us," Rory said as he pinched Coco's arm.

"Ouch!" she said under her breath.

"Great, let me grab my bags," Jordan said as he pranced off to where he'd left his things.

Rory turned to Coco, put his hands on her shoulders, and said mockingly, "Now, sweetie, you are my first and my favorite business partner, and I am sorry your mother and I didn't tell you that you would be getting a new baby brother, but you two need to play nice."

"Yes, Daddy," Coco snarled.

The ride to the convention center was reasonably silent. Coco texted anybody who would text her back, all the while donning facial expressions to indicate she was very, very busy with work-related things. Every once in a while she threw in a deep sigh for good measure, as if some assistant somewhere just wasn't doing their job right and now she had to do it for them; but, in actuality, she was only texting Olivia, CJ, and a few old friends from high school. She even texted her mom, throwing in a well-placed "tsk" now and again. Rory went through his paperwork while Jordan answered a few e-mails. No one looked as busy as Coco, so she decided she'd won that round.

Entering the convention center, Coco kept a peripheral

eye out for her nemesis, Billy Blanks, hoping that their booths were not going to be right next to each other again. She walked in and immediately began to sweat, not at all up for yet another confrontation with Blanks.

As Coco's Butt-B-Gone had grown more successful, Blanks's Tae Bo began to take a hit. After all, why work out hard when all you had to do was rub a cream on your big fat rear to make the cellulite go away? Coco's success was immediate because her product gave results and required no work. For years companies had claimed to have creams that eliminated cellulite, but their studies were completely fabricated. When Coco and her team came across a compound that actually worked, they knew success was imminent. They just didn't consider the haters. It was at one of her first trade shows that Blanks let it be known how he felt about Coco and her "ephemeral shortcut," as he disparagingly referred to it. Later, he expressed himself more plainly to her: "That shit ain't gonna work."

There she was, a complete neophyte, excited to be at the coming out party for her new product, her partnership with Rory just starting, and all was right with the world. Then, even better, fate stepped in. When you are an exhibitor at a trade show, the location of your booth is rarely up to you; so, naturally, she was set up right next to Billy Blanks's Tae Bo team. At one point during the day, she decided to go check out the competition.

Billy was in the midst of his pitch and had grabbed a woman from the crowd, intending to excite and inspire her. There he was, working her out and, of course, showing off his amazing pitch skills to the onlookers, including reps from both Kmart and Home Shopping Network. Billy went right into his shtick:

"You need to get offa your ass, you need to change your lifestyle. Let me ask you: are you ready to work? Okay, bring your arms up, engage those abs, lean over to the right, give me a roundhouse kick! Yes! Where's your weight? Where's your weight? That's it, work it out! Technique! Where's your focus?"

Coco could see that the woman was embarrassed to be singled out in front of the waiting crowd. She was *so* not in shape, practically panting just standing there watching his demo. Coco waited until Billy was done and receiving applause for his pitch; she then quietly pulled the woman over to the side, not realizing that (a) Billy was still within earshot and (b) this woman was the rep for QVC.

"Listen, I can see that you're someone like me who doesn't have time for a big, long workout," Coco said. "And I don't know about you, but I don't care much for exercise. You're busy, but you want to look your best, right? Well, take this." Coco handed her a sample-size tub of Butt-B-Gone.

"It really works—you won't believe it," Coco assured her. "I have to show you my before picture." She dragged the woman to her booth.

Coco then went into *her* pitch, and the woman, rapt, called over her associates, saying, "Tell them what you told me." And Coco did, still not knowing that she was pitching the main decision makers at QVC. *Et voilà!* a career was launched. Rory moved in right away to get QVC signed, sealed, and delivered before walking around, gloating to his cohorts.

Coco had gone back to her booth to talk to some buyers who had just stopped by for a demonstration when Billy Blanks came marching over. “Hey, newbie, come over here,” he said as he beckoned Coco with a finger.

“You don’t poach, that’s all there is to it,” he said. “You get your gigs and I get mine. We’re selling two different products. Mine is a lifestyle that will keep you healthy and in shape your entire life; yours is some worthless snake oil. It’s cheating. Stay away from my buyers with your bullshit.” And as quickly as he’d marched over, he stormed away.

Coco didn’t get the chance to respond, but she knew he was right. Well, about the poaching anyway. Her product did what it said, so he was wrong about that part. She hadn’t intentionally poached and she didn’t mean to make an enemy, but the damage was done. Over the years she and Blanks had appeared together on panels about health, fitness, and weight loss, and even though he was cordial, Coco knew that his gaze was filled with disdain for her product and thus, by association, for her.

As if he had just read her mind, Rory turned to her and smiled. “Oh, by the way, Billy Blanks isn’t here. He’s in Vegas this week.”

“Who?” Coco acted cool, like it hadn’t even crossed her mind.

Rory looked at her with a wry smirk. He knew her too well, she feared.

“Our booth is this way. I think you’ll love it,” he said reassuringly.

Boy was he right. They got to the booth, and there was a cardboard cutout of Coco and a giant picture of her face next to the logo for Butt-B-Gone. In even larger letters was a banner that read "Now Introducing Bags-B-Gone." She was the star of the booth. *Take that, Jordan what's-yer-face,* she thought. Damn, too bad Blanks wasn't here to see this.

As Detective Casey sat in his office that evening, he was energized to finally do some real police work. Olivia's envelope could yield fascinating clues, he felt, but if he were being honest with himself, he was mostly excited about the prospect of helping this quirky little damsel in distress. He didn't exactly understand what had caused her to start blurting odd noises and bolt out of the café, but he had a pretty good idea that she had a mild problem that slightly resembled Tourette's—he'd had to study neurological maladies a bit at Quantico, of course. The abrupt departure he could only attribute to her absolute mortification. She was cute, and somehow the outburst endeared her to him even more. He felt like she was someone who needed to be cared for, and he thought he might be the right person for the job; maybe he was a little too blue-collar for this community, but it seemed as though she liked him. And, yeah, she was cute. Really cute, especially considering she'd just had a baby. He liked a woman who cared about her body. So, if working on her house issue would get him a little closer to her, and help her at the same time, then it was all good.

The call to his buddy Gary had put him right back in business. All of this Patriot Act legislation had given the feds a silent back door into just about anyone's network. He wasn't a computer security expert, but he knew enough, and he had a trusted colleague in the Justice Department who knew that Casey would never abuse his privilege . . . unless it was in pursuit of a real case.

With the software and the codes needed to gain access to computer files on the police station network, Casey would be able to read through his boss's files. Files that were proprietary, but absolutely necessary to see if he were going to investigate the chief of police. He suspected that Bruno was corrupted and in deep. And he suspected the chief had something to do with the forged documents that had so distressed Olivia. Up until now, Casey didn't have any hard evidence; he just knew that something about Bruno simply wasn't kosher.

In the meantime, Detective Casey dusted Olivia's envelope for fingerprints, but there were so many it would take him a while to decipher whose were whose. Ah, the perfect ruse to call Olivia. He could tell her he needed her fingerprints in order to rule her out, and he figured she was not in the federal database, unless she'd been arrested as a teen, which he truly doubted. He called but got her voice mail. The message he left was as businesslike as he could muster, since he didn't want to presume anything, especially after she'd run out of the café. He asked her to come down to the station to answer a few more questions. He hoped that would take care of it.

Back at the trade show, Coco was being shown off like a prize pig. Between Butt-B-Gone selling its five millionth unit and the product being accepted into Walmart stores across the country, Coco was Rory's hottest commodity, and he wanted to boast. They had almost two hours until the launch announcement of her new creation, so Rory took advantage of the time by parading Coco past all of his colleagues, detractors, anyone who had rejected them in the past, and anyone who didn't pick up Butt-B-Gone for their stores.

As they went by the CVS/Pharmacy sales team, he bragged, "She's my little workhorse, wait till you see the new invention!" The folks at HSN were told, "Butt-B-Gone sold its five millionth unit this week. Have you met my cash cow?" When he ran into the fellas from Costco, who were surprised to see him back at a trade show, he said, "Make sure to come by the booth, gentlemen. The chickens have come home to roost."

That was it. Coco couldn't take any more.

"Hey, farm boy, what's with all the animal analogies?" she asked.

"What? I'm proud of you," he said, surprised by her tone.

"Horse, cow, chickens—what are you, Old MacDonald all of a sudden? E-i-yi-yi."

"Okay, okay, I'll try to stop using animal analogies," he said. At that moment he saw the reps from Dillard's, who originally, albeit reluctantly, had put some of Coco's cream at a few of their makeup and skin counters. They congratulated Rory on the big news.

"They're selling like hotcakes, huh? Bet you'll want the whole enchilada now! Stop by the booth today, we'll get into the meat of it," Rory said, as he escorted Coco by the small of the back.

"Really?" she said, rolling her eyes.

"What? You said no more animals."

"Oh, for god's sake. I'm going to take a look around, I'll see you back at the booth in a few," Coco said, disappearing into the crowd before Rory could even respond.

Coco liked to look at the other products being introduced; it inspired her before a presentation. She especially loved the ones that were not in her category and bordered on ridiculous. She got a kick out of seeing pancake batter in a single-serve can, or the fishbowl toilet tank. She knew that this year wouldn't disappoint. Amid the bacon-flavored envelopes and pens that doubled as toothpicks, there was an LED doormat, which could be programmed to say anything from "Welcome" to "Go away!" There were costumes for your cat designed to look like characters from *The Lion King,* and a dieting mask that could only be described as looking like Hannibal Lecter teamed up with Jaws from 007. It came in fashion colors too, so one could wear it on a night out with the girls if she so desired. There were shoes with adjustable heel heights and bras with adjustable cups, to look bigger or smaller as the need warranted. She stopped to watch a demonstration of an automatic bed maker that had a giant toilet paper–like roll with disposable sheets. This one looked promising, she thought. She hated making the bed.

Just then, an arm grabbed her out of nowhere, causing her to start. She was even more surprised to see that it was Lois Thomson, Rory's wife.

"Well, hello, darling! Isn't this place just *precious*? All of these inventions are so lovely and so clever, aren't they?"

What the heck was she doing here?

Lois continued. "I came down for another event, and I ran into a very important person who's going to come to your presentation. It's a surprise, a lovely surprise. Oh, you will be just *thrilled*!" She beamed.

"Thank you for coming to support us, Lois. It means a

great deal," Coco said, cringing. A guest? What? How dare Rory allow this?

"Oh, of *course,* darling girl. Oh, and by the way, did you see those kitten Mona Lisa paintings, and the kitten Whistler's Mother? Aren't they wonderful? Just *precious*!" Lois was simply unbearable. *How could kitsch be so easily lost on someone?* Coco wondered.

"Yes, they are, Lois. Fabulous. Okay, well, I'll meet you back at the booth in a bit, all right?" Coco needed a few more minutes to Zen out. Why hadn't she worked harder in yoga this morning?

"Oh, of course, darling. Toodles!" Lois sang as she traipsed down the aisle.

Crap. Who the heck was Lois Thomson's surprise guest? This did not sound good at all.

When Olivia drove up to the police station, Detective Casey was waiting outside. Jeez, he didn't even give a girl a second to collect herself. She was going to have to face him right when she got out of the car. She was anxious after what had transpired at the coffeehouse and would have liked a minute to breathe and gather her thoughts before seeing him.

"Hi, Rob," she said, emerging from her car, overstuffed bag in tow, as usual. Years of therapy for her echolalia had helped her to manage these "morning after" situations. Still, she'd called her therapist to go over how to deal with this particular case. Olivia's rather long mantra was that this was part of who she was, and, if someone was not going to accept all of her right from the start, it was good to know that up front.

While getting ready to leave the house, she'd discussed the matter with Simon, which was perfect since it was like a rehearsal, and it made Simon coo and laugh to hear his mama talking to him like he was an adult. She presumed he too thought she was just some silly lady.

"So Mommy had another one of her verbal volcanoes, my little boy," she had said to Simon as she changed him. On cue, he burst out in giggles. When she didn't reply in kind, he adopted a more serious look, almost a scowl.

"But she did it in front of a very nice man, a man you would just love!" Well, she certainly hoped so; that was the fantasy she'd already concocted. "So Mommy's going to go and face this man. He's seen the worst Mommy has to offer, so he should be happy to get this out of the way. If he still likes us, then he's right for us, right? If not, then we didn't want him in our lives in the first place, right? Right, my little pumpkin?" She tickled Simon's bare, pink belly, and he screamed in laughter. He approved of this approach. Okay, she was safe to go.

Detective Casey helped her open the door and awkwardly held out his hand for a shake while she sort of leaned in for a cheek kiss. Both, realizing their miscues, switched. He went for the cheek kiss, and she held out her hand. Both laughed nervously before she went right for it:

"I have echolalia." The subtext was "Deal with it!"

"Oh, you mean the tiny little guitar they play in Hawaii?"

"Huh? No. I think that's a ukulele." She was now completely thrown off her game.

"Oh, okay. So, echolalia then."

God! He was so matter-of-fact about all of this. Maybe this

was a good sign. There didn't seem to be any judgment in his tone.

"Yes. In case you don't know," she began, "it's a sort of tic that I have where I have to repeat unusual sounds I hear. Like at the coffeehouse when the barista said 'latte' the way she did, I had to repeat it. Does that make sense?" she asked.

"Is that why you ran out?" he asked.

"Yes."

"Ah, I wondered what was going on. Okay, good to know. So, you want to go grab a bite to eat, and we can talk more about those papers?"

Olivia didn't know what kind of response she was expecting, but this certainly wasn't it. Did he not care because it wasn't a big deal, or because he didn't care about her and who she was? That's why it sucks being a girl. Girls think like that. Olivia was no exception.

"Wait. That's it? Don't you want to know more about my thing?" she asked.

He gave her a bit of a sideways glance and a knowing smile, turning her comment into a double entendre. Finally, an indication he might be attracted to her!

"Stop it," she said coyly while gently touching his arm. "I'm serious."

"Sure," he said, "tell me more about your 'thing.'" He smiled and chuckled.

"No, forget it. You're not interested," she flirted.

"No, that's not true, I'm interested. I just didn't want to pry. C'mon," he said as he touched her arm back, but higher up, by her elbow.

"I don't know why I'm making such a big deal. Most people don't see past it. I guess there isn't much more to tell. It was worse when I was a kid. I walked around the house all day saying, 'They're GRRRREAT!' and my father thought I was just a really annoying child." She laughed, a bit self-consciously. "But when I was twelve and in counseling because of my parents' troubles, I was diagnosed. They put me on a medication that doesn't always work, but it usually does."

"Why does it still happen then, if you are on medication?"

"Usually it happens if I've had too much to drink, or when I'm particularly stressed out. That's pretty much it."

Olivia had been waiting for the face—the one that men got when they learned she had this weird affliction. The one that was a combination of pity and "um, yeah, I won't be sleeping with you, thanks," but it didn't come. *Boy, that was easy,* she thought. She then realized that a cop's probably seen it all, and that there wasn't much that would surprise him about the human condition. *Wow, this could be better than expected,* she thought.

"You didn't seem drunk at Everyman, so I'm guessing all of this stuff with your mother is stressing you out. I don't want to talk here at the station since yours is kind of like a side project I'm doing," he told her. He looked over his shoulder, slyly pulled a small electronic device out of his pocket that slightly resembled her iPhone, and poked at it a couple of times. "Do me a favor and put your fingertips on this thing." She did. "Great, now the other hand." She did as he asked.

"What's this all about?" she said.

"I needed your fingerprints so I can eliminate yours from the ones I've taken off the envelope. Don't worry, they won't go into any kind of database. This is just for my use right now."

"Okay."

"So let's have dinner tonight, so we'll have more time to talk, okay? I'll come pick you up at eight thirty. And I wouldn't mind seeing this much coveted house I've been reading about." He chuckled.

"That sounds great," Olivia said. She allowed her gaze to linger, trying to read his face. Did he just ask her out? She didn't know which expression to have since she wasn't quite sure what had happened

"I want to help you. And I really think I *can* help you," he assured her.

He sounded confident. No, he *was* confident. She realized he also thought she was adorable, echolalia and all. He'd passed the test. Oh, god, he'd passed the test! She wanted to call her therapist immediately.

Coco was in the ladies' room fixing her hair just before her presentation, which basically entailed staring blankly at herself in the mirror making sure she didn't look like a five-year-old girl. It was possible she knew less about hair than she did about makeup. As she walked back to the booth, she could see Rory's snow-topped head above the crowd. He was both very tall and prematurely gray, so it was easy to spot him amid the multitudes. She drew closer and saw Lois Thomson talking to a man in a suit, whom she didn't recognize from behind. Lois spotted Coco approaching.

"Oh, don't you look marvelous!" Lois exclaimed.

Well, at least she didn't say "precious," Coco thought.

"Here is your surprise guest! Mayor Quilty was in town for a GOP fund-raiser, which is where I found him. So I dragged him along to show off some of Greenwich's finest. Isn't that lovely?" Lois was so proud of herself and so clueless.

"Ms. Guthrie, the Thomsons told me of your good fortune. You do Greenwich proud. It sounds like you have a big future in front of you if you keep doing what you're supposed to," the mayor said.

WTF? The son of a bitch! Boy did he have a pair. Figuratively only, from what she could recall of his ridiculous outfit.

Coco's experience as a top-notch saleswoman jumped right in to save her neck. "Mayor Quilty! What an honor! I'm so flattered to have you here. It's such a pleasure to meet you," she said loudly enough to be heard over the thudding sound in her chest.

"Oh, I didn't realize the two of you had never met," Rory said.

"No, I haven't had the pleasure until now," the mayor said charmingly.

Just then Lois took the mayor by the arm. "I have one more quick introduction to make before the presentation, Your Honor. You absolutely must meet John O'Hurley, he's just darling. He's the emcee for tonight's event. Come along," she sang.

Rory pulled Coco aside. "I thought you met the mayor at the Halloween party."

"Nope. He wasn't there when I was, as far as I know."

"Ah, right, he had to leave early, so you probably missed him. He had a pipe break in his house that night. It flooded the entire living room. Poor bastard. Those old Greenwich houses, eh?" Rory said.

"Yep, the upkeep can be murder." Coco laughed to herself. The presence of the mayor was disconcerting and was about to make the rest of her weekend and that night's awards ceremony tenuous at best. Coco knew she wouldn't be able to handle it alone, so in desperation she ducked behind the booth to call CJ. After his disastrous visit to Malcolm's office, he'd surely be needing some camaraderie, and so was she. She begged him to get his butt down to Philly, even offered to pay for his train ticket, though he would have to share her room since the convention had the town booked up. None of this was remotely enticing to a wealthy, fashion-forward producer of the *Rachael Ray* show, yet CJ, her savior, was on the next train.

A few hours later Coco was back at her hotel, in the lobby awaiting CJ's arrival. He phoned from the taxi to say that he was just blocks away and rather nervous that they were going to be in the same town—nay, at the same event—as the mayor. Why was *he* in Philly anyway?

CJ wafted in like he was on the red carpet trying to avoid the paparazzi. He was the type of gay man who always made an entrance, no matter where he went.

"Don't panic, but if I act a little weird it's because I may have taken my Prozac twice tonight. I'm gonna be eighty milligrams of fun," he declared.

"God, I'm just so glad you're here! There's no way I can face that jerk-off by myself tonight. Rory and Lois think he hung the moon."

"Did you say 'hung the moon' or 'hung *like* the moon'?"

"I see the pills are already starting to take effect. C'mon, I have to go get dressed. The awards ceremony starts in just a couple of hours."

"Oh, girl, we'll need way more than a couple of hours to get this mess cleaned up," he said, circling her face with his finger. "Don't worry, though, the Virgo is on the case."

TWELVE

The Hideous Color Purple

Bailey was at home waiting for Graham Shore to call. He'd said he was going to call at 7:00 P.M. sharp, and it was 6:55. As much as she hated being one of those girls who waited by the phone, he *was* on a mountain in Alaska, so this was an exception. Plus, he was always very punctual. She looked at her cell to make sure it was on Ring and not Silent, but just as she picked it up to check, it rang, showing an unknown number. Wow, Graham was early. Maybe he was as excited to talk to her as she was to talk to him, she thought.

"Hello, lovah," she started.

"Ummm . . . Miss Warfield?" the voice said.

"Oy! Yes." *Oh, god.* Bailey was mortified. It wasn't Graham.

"This is Detective Rob Casey. Did I catch you at a bad time?"

"Well, I *am* waiting for another call," she said, cringing.

"Oh, so you don't answer your phone like that all the time," he said jokingly.

"Yes . . . I mean no. What can I do for you, Detective?"

"I need to close your case, and I had a few follow-up questions—"

She interrupted him. "Yes, I got your message. Listen, I

have to get off the line, so why don't you come over here in about an hour and we can fill out whatever paperwork and you can ask me whatever questions you have, okay?"

"Tonight?" he asked.

"Yes, is that okay? I'm leaving for L.A. in the morning, so if not tonight it'll have to wait until the end of next week."

"Okay, I can swing by," he said, purposefully. Code for "I can't stay too long."

"I have to go." She had call waiting, of course, but she was just too anxious to stay on the phone with someone who wasn't Graham, so she hung up. It was 6:59.

By 7:50 she was in shambles. She was not good at relationships, and this was a great example of why. The truth was, Bailey may have been magnificent to look at, wildly successful, from an amazing, charitable family, and she was exceedingly good at her job—*but* she was terrible with men.

Sure, to an outsider she appeared to be a skilled puppeteer who controlled every aspect of her life with poise. Yet she just couldn't transfer that confidence into her relationships. She was a ball of insecurity who still, at age thirty-seven, analyzed every little aspect of her relations.

A typical call to a friend went like this: "Jennifer, listen, it's me, Bailey. Do me a favor, listen to this message . . . What? . . . No, it's Zander. He left me that today, then he didn't call by four when he said he would. . . . No, no, listen again. There, where he says he needs some rest. What's up with that? Should I call him?"

Other times she would describe a date in full detail for diagnostic purposes. Her friends were disturbed by this characteristic of hers.

"Bailey, listen. Maybe you should just relax and let some time pass. Not every single thing a guy says has meaning. You're probably driving the guy nuts."

"Driving him nuts? How? He should be fucking *overjoyed* to have me. Fuck him!" It didn't take many of these calls before her "friends" would stop answering the phone.

Bailey focused so much on her relationships with men that she really didn't actually develop her relationships with women; they ended up being just sounding boards. In fact, she had only one woman whom she called a friend, her roommate from college, who now lived in Seattle.

When asked about her intense insecurity, Bailey would dismiss it, saying it was merely "an occupational hazard," which might have been the case were she an investigative reporter, but she wasn't. The truth was that she *did* have an occupational hazard that affected her in a much more tangible way. Since she had spent so much time in the world of celebrity and entertainment, she was all too familiar with the desultory nature of celebrity relationships, narcissistic personalities, the lack of loyalty, and, in many cases, the complete lack of character. Her prolonged exposure to this lifestyle was more of a problem than she realized.

Not only did she report on affairs but she had them. So why on earth would she trust a man she was with to be loyal? She'd learned her lesson early. When she was eighteen, she met Matt Damon at Harvard, the only school anyone in her family was allowed to attend, especially after the library's Warfield wing had been erected. She had an all-consuming relationship with the handsome young English major, who spent most of the school year jetting off to L.A. to make movies. His parents had divorced early on in his life, prompting him to say rather often how much he liked her family's stability and how he longed to be a part of it; they frequently talked of their future together. But when Hollywood began to become his, he called less frequently, saying he was too busy; and he stopped making plans for their future, rightfully provoking her paranoia. She finally decided to fly out to California to surprise him, only to discover that he had been having a torrid affair with the actress Annabeth Gish, whom he'd met on the set of *Mystic Pizza*. Bailey was crushed. At that moment she decided she was never again going to let a powerful man overpower her—well, emotionally anyway. Sexually, she didn't mind at all. So began her career as paramour to the stars, in which she never actually became attached to any particular one.

Eight P.M. rolled around, and she still hadn't heard from Graham. Because most of her acquaintances were sick of hearing her go on about yet another man who didn't do the right thing, she grabbed her phone and decided to call Coco, a fresh ear. Just then, the doorbell rang. Her parents were out for the night, and there was nobody to greet the guest at the door, so she moped her way downstairs wearing an oversize man's shirt, not really caring whether she was presentable. Being Bailey, she actually looked pretty hot, but she didn't care.

"Of course! Detective Casey," she said in sudden realization as she approached the door.

Rob Casey stood on the front step looking as handsome as ever, wearing slim-fit, dark denim jeans that made his waist look small yet gathered in all the right places, with a steel blue, nicely fitted utility shirt that showed off his perfectly defined pecs, under a double-breasted twill peacoat, which revealed a pair of robust and ready shoulders. When Bailey opened the door, she exhaled softly. He was as beautiful as she was.

Bailey didn't know that he was dressed for Olivia, not her; it simply didn't occur to her. All she could think about was him standing there in front of her. She was sad about Graham, feeling lonely and abandoned, and it was as if the gods of heartbreak had sent her this hunk of man meat as a consolation prize. Not one to waste any time, Bailey dashed through the art of seduction by pulling him inside with one hand while unbuttoning her shirt to the navel with the other. Then she sidled up to him, grabbed his face, and kissed him wildly.

•

Rob was completely taken by surprise, just as any man would have been upon being ravaged by a seemingly untouchable, hot-as-hell, half-naked woman. His immediate reaction was to pull her to him, feeling her incredible, pert breasts rubbing along his shirt as she kissed his neck and rubbed her hand along his immediately rock-hard visitor through his jeans. It had been so long since he'd had any sex, let alone with a woman who looked like this. And, though he wasn't bound to anyone in particular, he recovered his senses momentarily and held her by the shoulders, pushing her back a step and examining her delicious body.

"Good lord, Ms. Warfield. I, uh. Wow, you're amazing. You're beautiful, and you feel incredible, but I'm really sorry. I can't."

Bailey stopped, stunned.

"What." She didn't say it as a question. What. What the fuck? No man had ever done that to her. She was flabbergasted.

"I just . . . I'm here on official business. I'm afraid it would be completely inappropriate, as nice as I'm sure it would be. Please. Pardon me."

Quick to recover and regain her pride, Bailey countered, "No, no. Pardon me. I don't know what came over me. I was just dozing. I thought—I guess I thought you were someone else. I'd been expecting . . . Never mind. Forget it ever happened."

"Okay, good. I, I almost forgot the reason I came here to begin with." He reached into his coat pocket. "Would you mind signing this for me?"

"Oh, sure," she said as she reached for the pen he was handing her. She felt like an ass, and now they had nothing more to say to each other. She wanted him to leave as fast as he could so she could go inside and cry.

Just then, Bailey's phone rang. *Thank god,* she thought. She signed, handed the paper to Rob, and waved as she closed the door while answering her phone.

"Hi, baby," the soft, sexy, yet masculine voice on the phone said. "We were in a place on the mountain where the satellite phones weren't working. I'm so sorry I'm late calling you. You good?"

It was Graham. *Damn,* why had she been so fucking insecure?

Coco stared into the mirror, watching CJ trying to make up her face. He was a terrible gay, knew nothing about makeup. He hesitantly dusted her cheeks with blush but was timid with the eye shadow, and he looked blankly at a pencil of some kind that was flesh-colored. "I don't know what this is," he said. Then, addressing the pencil, "What are you? Where do you go?"

He knew she looked ghastly, but he just didn't know how to fix her.

"Hang on a second. You looked amazing at the Halloween party. You can do Sarah Palin but you can't do anything else?" Coco asked.

"I didn't do that," he admitted. "They put me together at work. I'm one of the few gays you'll meet who never did drag, and I know nothing about makeup. I just know what looks good. I'm good with men's fashion, but that's where I draw the line."

"You have amazing style!" Coco said, comforting him.

"I can put an outfit together for me, I'm just not a cliché gay."

"Well, thank the lord for that," she said. "It's not all *Will and Grace*, you know."

"True. Oh, but let me call Dajuan," he said, reaching for his phone.

Dajuan was an amazing makeup artist at the *Rachael Ray* show, and CJ realized he might be able to save the day.

"Baby doll, we have got one serious fashion emergency here," CJ said when Dajuan finally picked up. Knowing full well that CJ's strengths were in other areas, Dajuan took over immediately. He suggested they photograph Coco's face, all the makeup, and all possible outfit combinations, and text the photos to him. Coco had brought only a few outfits, so they had to be creative.

"Damn, I wish we had Skype," CJ said as he snapped away. Once the photos were sent, they put Dajuan on speakerphone.

"What on earth did you try to do with that pencil, CJ?" he admonished. "Uh-uh. We're starting all over here. That's not makeup, that's throw-up."

Dajuan had incredible style and had been working in fashion for a long time. He and CJ worked on her for the next hour, and, in the end, Coco looked stunning. CJ was so proud of himself that he took photos of her from every possible angle so that Dajuan could see his work.

"That's it, baby! Dajuan can work his magic in-ter-state!" crowed his voice on the speaker.

"Let's open up some champagne," CJ suggested, walking to the minibar. "We'll need a social lubricant for tonight's activities."

"Good idea," Coco replied.

"Oh, I've *had* mine. I got started as soon as I got on the call," said Dajuan.

They thanked their savior of the evening, promised a night out when they got back to town, and hung up.

Champagne in hand, CJ turned to Coco. "Honey, I have to ask why your man isn't here with you. When you left, I assumed that because it was a business trip you couldn't bring him along. So on the way here I was wondering why you called me and not him."

"Because I never told him about the mayor or what we saw. I didn't want to get him involved, whereas you already are. It seemed like the right move."

"Well, if that's all it is, I won't pry. Okay, who am I kidding? I have to know, what's the deal with the two of you? Why aren't you married?"

"Really? From a gay man in Greenwich of all places, I'm getting the Speech?"

"Well, that's the point, isn't it? Nobody in Greenwich society would be unmarried for this long. I'm sure everyone wonders about you two. I mean . . . you are a pretty butch girl. If he's a beard, just say so."

"Ha, ha, very funny. But since you asked, the marriage issue has been a sticking point. He proposes every year, and every year I say no because I never understood the meeting, dating, getting married thing. A wedding should be a celebration of a couple's real bond, something you can't actually have with someone until you've been together for a while. I think a couple shouldn't get married until they've been together ten years. That's when they can legitimately celebrate a connection and a life together. I don't think a wedding should celebrate some haphazard, lustful romantic notion that usually happens when two people barely know each other's names. I've never understood that."

"Okay. So, how long have you been with Sam then?" CJ asked.

"Almost ten years."

"So?"

"Well, that's why we're having issues. He knows how I feel—and basically agrees—so he wants to get married this year, and I'm . . . thinking it over."

"Why just 'thinking it over' and not jumping right into it after all these years?" CJ asked, looking into her eyes. "Oh no, it's sex, isn't it?"

"No, it's not sex. It's the fact that he's glumming around because he was forced out of his company. Which is being made worse by those goddamned phony documents," Coco said flatly. "But now that you mention it, our sex life could be better. Whose couldn't? I can't even talk to him about it. I asked him 'Why is it all we ever do is missionary and girl on top? Don't you want to be adventurous?' And he said no, that's who he was, a boring sex guy, take it or leave it."

"Yikes. Nothing worse than going to Disneyland and only one ride is working, honey."

"Exactly. But he's happy with the way things are. Sam's idea of experimenting is seeing if he can get it up while Nancy Grace is on."

"Oooh. Oh, honey, you two definitely need to start experimenting. Just try one new thing and see how it goes."

"I don't know. We've been together a long, long time. After a while sex just stops being adventurous, I suppose. I should probably just get over it."

"No it doesn't, not for everyone."

"For most people," she said, hoping that was true and she wasn't missing out.

"Not for my grandparents or Nanny. They *all* still have wild sex."

She looked at him with a worried expression. "I'm afraid to ask. Do you mean together?"

"Oh, god, no . . . no! No, no, no. But they might. My grandparents are pretty out there." He laughed. "And before you ask, I know because I visit them and stay the night all the time. So, trust me. I know."

"So sex in your golden years, huh? Must be nice. What are they into?"

"I don't know what they're into, I just know they do it and that my grandma wears a diaper, but those ideas aren't related. No golden showers in the golden years, I guess."

"That's gross."

"Anyway, I say get married so I can buy a hat."

"Oh, crap, look at the time. I was supposed to call Rory twenty minutes ago."

CJ looked at her with wide eyes and said, "You know who knows everything about everybody? My aunt Lois. We have a huge resource there that we need to tap into tonight. She practically runs Greenwich."

"Can I put you in charge of that? You're better at getting information out of people. You're like the gay Gestapo." She dialed the phone, but before it rang through she put her hand over the receiver and said, "And you are calling Malcolm and apologizing. We need him, too. . . . Rory! Hi."

As she spoke to Rory, there was a knock on the door. Coco motioned to CJ to answer it, thinking it was room service, she hoped with more champagne. Instead, it was the handsome, windswept Jordan Ainsworth with the champagne.

"I intercepted the guy on the way up. May I come in?" He was so smug.

"Oh, yes!" CJ was suckered in right away. "C'mon in, gorgeous."

For Olivia, eagerness turned to acrimony with every minute Rob was late. She started thinking that maybe this wasn't a date since he hadn't shown up on time. Then he nonchalantly called to say he had a late-running case, something no date of hers had ever done. She was under the impression that hers was his biggest case at the moment and the reason he was coming over. Nothing made sense, but it was made even worse because she didn't know if this was a date or not. If it wasn't a date, fine. She would just hear what he'd found about her mother and the forged documents. If it *was* a date, then, she wondered, should she give him the lameness-of-lateness speech? Olivia didn't believe in being fashionably late for anything, since she was neither fashionable nor late. Ever.

But when Rob finally arrived, Olivia was just so happy to see his handsome face she forgot completely that she might be angry. Instinctually, she wanted to run up and hug him, but she channeled Joan Harris again and kept cool, as if she hadn't even noticed the time.

"Oh, hi," she said.

"Sorry I'm so late. I was closing another case and had some unexpected issues arise," he said, without a glimmer of self-consciousness.

"No problem. I have so much work to do that I didn't actually notice the time."

"Oh, really? What are you working on?" He was in a particularly jovial mood.

"I worked on a study last year, and we just got the results back, so I'm writing it up for my colleagues. I'm still publishing academically," she said reluctantly, since she didn't think he could possibly be interested in her life outside his police work.

"Wow, that's really wonderful. How exciting! You'll have to tell me all about it," he said, sounding oddly giddy.

"Ooookay," she said mockingly.

She hadn't known him to be this effusive but thought that it might have been because it had been an especially long day. Usually, he was pretty low-key and businesslike. She started to hope he really, really liked her and this was how he was showing interest.

"I'm also working on a blog," she said proudly. "It's kind of a mommy blog, but it's more about criticizing other mommy blogs that give terrible advice, coupled with observations of all of the bad parenting I see in the playgrounds."

"Interesting. What's it called?" he asked

"*Colicky in Connecticut.* Clever, right?" She smiled.

"Very." He smiled back, and their eyes locked for so long it became uncomfortable, even awkward. Someone had to break the tension, so of course it was Olivia.

"You want to see the house?" she asked, semiseductively.

He was giving off an unusually potent sex vibe. She couldn't help but pick up on it.

"Sure. Where's the little one? Sleeping?"

"He's at the babysitter's tonight. I needed to concentrate on my work, so she has him for the night." Oh, lord. She hoped he'd buy the fib. Was it obvious that she was hoping he'd spend the night?

"Great," he said, grinning with all the subtext of a pouncing lion. Olivia didn't realize how much trouble she was in, but Bailey had unleashed the animal, and Olivia would never know enough about it to thank her.

Olivia started in the safe zones: the kitchen, the living

room, the family room, and then she led him upstairs. She deadpanned her way through the house history as she climbed the most elaborate freestanding, curved staircase Rob had ever seen. She was giving an Oscar-winning performance as the girl who plays hard to get, channeling her best austere Greenwich lady of society. She didn't want to give him the idea that she was easy or that she would do anything untoward, or that she herself was nearly ready to attack *him.* They stopped at the top of the stairs, at the threshold of her father's study. She opened the door to show him the room and began laughing.

"What's so funny?" he said, leaning against the wall, looking her over from head to toe.

"Look at the color of the room."

"It's . . . well, it's certainly regal."

It was. The room was a shockingly bright shade of purple.

"Oddly enough, this is the most important room in the house to me."

"Why is it so vivid? I'm no interior decorator, but isn't it a rather odd color for a study?" Rob asked.

"Oh yeah, but there's a great story behind it. My brother, Finn, came to stay with us a few years back after his wife kicked him out. He was so grateful to my dad for letting him stay here rent-free while they reconciled that he thought he would surprise him by giving the room a much-needed paint job. So Finn goes to the paint store, grabs a bunch of cans of paint, then spends an entire day painting. He's so excited when my dad gets home that he can't wait to rush him upstairs to show him. He has my dad close his eyes, has music playing—the great unveiling, you know. My dad opens the door and bursts out laughing. 'Finn,' he says, 'what color do you think this room is?' 'Light blue,' my brother replies. By now my father is laughing so hard there are tears rolling down his face. He says, 'No, Finn, it's bright purple. But I love you so much for doing it, I'm keeping it like this,' and he hugged him and thanked him. That's the kind of guy my dad was. So in that spirit, I keep the room as is."

"Why didn't Finn realize what color he'd chosen?" Rob asked.

"Oh, did I leave that part out? He's color-blind," she said, laughing.

"And your dad left the study this color for all these years?"

"Yep, hideous, isn't it? But I wouldn't change it for the world."

Rob was so moved by the story and her sweetness that he leaned in and gave Olivia a gentle kiss. She let him for a second, then stopped him, took half a step back, and smiled. She didn't want to give him the wrong idea.

"I'm hungry. You hungry?" she asked before he could say anything.

"Actually, I'm *very* hungry," he replied.

"Great, let's go out and have dinner. You can tell me what you've learned about those documents, okay?" she said.

All of Rob's interactions with Olivia up until this point had been sweet and tender. He listened to her, was interested in everything she had to say, laughed at her stories, and seemed to care about her opinion. When she stopped his kiss and suggested dinner and he didn't show any frustration or anger, she surrendered to him completely. It was at that moment she decided that over dinner she would tell him all about what she and the Scooby-Doo team were up to. She knew she needed a competent, trustworthy ally who had some juice, and she realized Rob was all that and more. Plus, she hadn't been given any assignments by the group; this was her chance to show that a thirty-six-year-old mom had some value.

"Incidentally," he said, "there are fingerprints on your envelope that belong to a government employee named Malcolm Marconi. Does that name mean anything to you?"

THIRTEEN

When Bailey Met Gertie

Olivia wasn't accustomed to going out on dates, most certainly not on Tuesday nights. Who ate dinner this late on a Tuesday, anyway? But there she was, out with Rob. Despite the kiss, the purpose of their night was still undefined. Was it some muddled-up version of a date, or was this part of the investigation? She wasn't sure. Either way, she vowed to channel her inner Joan. The hostess sat them next to two men who were heavily engaged in a heated conversation about work. Something unjust had happened to one of them at the office that day. She could tell because after every statement he whined, "Man, that is just *messed* up!" in incongruous "street" lingo, and the other man's agreement fed his anxiety. Olivia wasn't sure if the man had actually been wronged or if he was just a crybaby who'd had one too many scotch and sodas.

Across from them in an intimate corner sat a pretty young thing in her late twenties or perhaps early thirties, looking too sexy for this early in the week. She was leaning forward in her seat, smiling at her companion, a handsome, well-dressed man in his fifties with perfect teeth who laughed at everything she said. They both wore wedding bands, but they didn't match. Olivia noticed stuff like that.

The only other people in the restaurant were several barflies who didn't know each other but would comment to the air about the game on the bar TV, which, from what Olivia could tell, was professional soccer but may very well have been rugby.

And then, of course, there were she and Rob, who were . . . well, they were the only people in the bar she didn't know how to categorize, but it didn't matter. Olivia was excited. She felt like they were bonding—something she didn't know she'd be able to do with another man after the twenty-car pileup that had been her last relationship.

After they ordered their food, Olivia told Rob the entire story, starting with when Chief Bruno tried to convince them that what they had seen was an aberration, and how she had been satisfied with that explanation at the time. But her innate paranoia had kicked in the next morning, giving her pause, and a few days later, when CJ summoned the troops, she was relieved that he too had been suspicious. Collectively, they could not doubt what they'd seen. She told Rob what their plan was, explained CJ's relationship with Malcolm, how Bailey had enlisted her TV friend Saul King, and that they were now thoroughly convinced they had witnessed a murder, and they were going to do something about it.

She waited for a reaction. Rob was quiet. Was he shocked or angry? She couldn't tell. *God, what a cool customer,* she thought. A great trait for a detective, but a shitty one for a boyfriend.

"Thoughts?" she said uncomfortably.

"So the four of you are trying to solve this on your own with no help from law enforcement? Is that what you are telling me?" He seemed insulted.

"Well, yeah. It didn't seem like anyone there believed us, present company included. What else were we supposed to do?"

"So, what was the plan?" he asked sarcastically. "To enlist the help of all of these outside people and then do what with your information?"

Rob stopped, folded his arms across his chest, then propped one arm up and began rubbing his hand across his lips, practically squeezing them. "Okay, so say you and your team of sleuths get to the bottom of this. What then? If the man is a murderer, as it appears he is, and he has the power to blackmail you less than twenty-four hours after the fact, what else do you suppose he's capable of?"

"Oh. Yeah, I guess . . ." Olivia was crestfallen because Rob seemed so angry.

"Look, I get it, I get it. I'm not angry with you. I'm upset because if something had happened to you guys—and you, especially—it would have been my fault, since it seemed like I caved so easily to my boss. But, look, I *had* to act that way so he wouldn't suspect anything. It just never occurred to me that you guys would go after him on your own. My god. I'm so sorry."

Olivia felt a pang in her chest when Rob said he worried for her. But she also felt stupid. "You're right," she said. "We didn't think this through. I guess we were going to go back to the police once we had hard evidence that couldn't be ignored?"

"You *guess*? And what if the police *were* corrupt? Then what? I'll tell you what! Never mind the extortion, your lives would have been in jeopardy." He paused. Olivia was just about to burst into tears; her heart was ripping open because Rob thought she was foolish.

"But no, you didn't. So that's fine. You didn't do anything wrong—you spoke with me before anything bad happened to any of you. I don't know what I would have done if someone had hurt you." Rob reached across the table and caressed her hand, bringing a slight smile back to her face.

"So you're on our side? You believe we saw a murder?"

"Yes, I think you did. I always have."

"You have?" Olivia had been sure he would need more convincing.

"Yes. I knew that Chief Bruno was lying, but I couldn't prove it. So I called a friend in the Justice Department, who found this," Rob said as he reached into his messenger bag and pulled out a document.

"Before I show you this, I want you to understand that I never closed the case. At all."

"But isn't that why you called Bailey? To close the case?" Olivia was confused.

"Well, that's what I told her, but I was hoping to get her fingerprints and DNA so I could eliminate them from those already on the envelope. I was looking for DNA on the envelope seal or on the stamps. I sent them to the lab at the Justice Department, and I'm still waiting for results."

"What are you looking for?" Olivia asked.

"Well, the test results should be very revealing. The DNA

will be matched with a massive criminal database, but guess who else's DNA is on file. Every city, state, and government employee nationwide," Rob said, with a sly grin.

"Ohhh, I see where you're going with this."

"Well, maybe. That's why I asked about this Malcolm Marconi character. I think there could be something more to this, and if city employees are involved, it's not them I'm concerned about so much as their associates."

"I'm not sure I understand after all."

"See, that was my point, Olivia. You guys could get yourselves into some serious trouble. Please let me handle things from here on in, okay? If there is any connection to organized crime here, you really are at great risk."

"Oh, my god. The mafia?" Olivia suddenly felt ill.

"I don't know, but I'm looking at it from every possible angle. I'm trying to protect you, Olivia," he assured her. "That's what's most important to me."

"Okay, I know. I know," she demurred. "So what was it you were going to show me?" She was still amped with the thrill of the chase, in spite of his attempt to discourage her.

"Here you go," he said, handing a folder over to her. "I think you should know about this now, though it may not mean anything yet."

The folder contained page after page of information on Chief Bruno, from when he was the police chief of the wealthy community of Kennebunkport, Maine. According to what Olivia was reading, Bruno had been brought up on drug-related corruption and bribery charges, but in exchange for selling out the local mayor and two judges, his charges were dismissed. Now relocated to Greenwich, he remained under investigation by the Justice Department for a heck of a lot more ongoing crime.

Olivia flipped to the last page of the report.

> Suspect regularly accepted bribes from citizens who habitually violated noncriminal statutes or ordinances (i.e., traffic laws); accepted bribes by those who violate the law in order to make money (i.e., prostitution); accepted money in exchange for police services or protection. Other charges of his alleged corruption in both Greenwich and Kennebunkport included fraud, nepotism, extortion, and the actual commission of felony crimes.

Her face was frozen. Not only was she surprised that their chief of police was so dirty but she now realized that they weren't dealing with some garden-variety bureaucrat. This guy was a dangerous thug.

"I-I didn't realize," she said, almost shaking.

"Mm-hmm. Now you understand why I believe you and your friends really did see a crime that night?"

"Undoubtedly. But how is Bruno involved with the mayor?"

"I'm not sure yet. I'm trying to make the connection now. But I'm pretty sure the chief helped the mayor cover up the murder. I just don't know why he would put himself in that position if he's trying to stay out of trouble."

"Wait, that's it! That's what the mayor has on him. He must know about Kennebunkport," Olivia said proudly.

"You don't think he's known about that all along?" Casey asked.

"I'm guessing not, because Greenwich politicians don't generally like to get involved with lower-class criminals. The people here would immediately disown a politician associated with any sort of riffraff. Greenwich is a lot of things, but organized crime kinds of violence, well, that's beneath us. They go Enron when they go bad," she said.

Olivia suddenly realized Rob could have construed that as a dig at him, which it wasn't. It was just one of those things that happened pretty regularly in Greenwich. The distinction between the haves and the have-nots was so substantial that even if the haves were benevolent, generous, and down-to-earth, their vast fortunes and excessive lifestyles made the most secure blue-collar men feel inadequate. It was one of the reasons folks in Greenwich kept to their own. It wasn't snobbery so much as adaptive, learned behavior. Many Greenwichites had had friendships ruined when their hometown, and therefore wealth and status, were discovered. Unfortunately, Olivia knew it all too well. Even when she was at her Ivy League college, she tried to keep her origins a secret because she'd learned early of the social disadvantage. People simply couldn't relate, and no one was about to pity or sympathize with her.

It had started when Olivia was twelve. She spent a summer at a camp in Massachusetts. Her best friend at the camp was a girl named Allison, whom she had invited to visit her in Connecticut over the winter, since she'd been invited to visit Allison's family in Silver Spring, Maryland, a few months before. Olivia hadn't realized that during the course of their friendship she'd never said she was from Greenwich, only Connecticut. When Allison finally came to visit, her mother couldn't stop talking about it.

"Allison never told me you were from *Greenwich.* I had no idea you lived in *Greenwich,* oh my!" She was pathologically, and annoyingly, impressed.

From then on, Allison and her mother began to treat Olivia differently. Allison's visits became miserable for Olivia, because it felt like Allison was trying to get things from her. For example, Allison would ask if Olivia's dad could take them shopping—expecting him to pay. Olivia suspected Allison's mother had encouraged her. When they got back to camp the following summer, it was widespread knowledge that Olivia was wealthy beyond belief. The magic of the summer camp was gone forever. Campers and even some counselors were hostile, while others were overly friendly, appearing almost out of nowhere. Olivia had the worst summer of her life. For her, the Greenwich curse started that summer, and now she worried it would haunt her relationship with Rob.

"I see you feel like we may have jeopardized your case by playing amateur detective, but we really need you. I really need you. Will you help us?" Olivia asked in her most seductive Joan Harris voice.

"Of course." Rob would have said yes to anything Olivia asked in that voice.

"Great. Can I make a phone call?" she asked.

"You should, yes."

Olivia called Coco but got her voice mail. She left a long message.

"Who is that?" Coco yelled to CJ from the other room when she heard him speaking to whoever had knocked on the door.

Coco's hotel suite was exactly that, sweet. It was her one indulgence in life. She wasn't one to spend money in general, and she was not excessive by any means. So she afforded herself one luxury—tax-deductible—when she traveled for work: she stayed in the best rooms of the finest hotel of whatever city she traveled to. Once, in Santa Monica, her favorite hotel, Shutters, was booked every night she would be there except one. So she booked a suite for that one night even though her meeting ran until 11:00 P.M. and her flight left at 8:00 the next morning. Those few hours, even asleep, were luxurious and *so* worth it.

When Coco walked to the door, her stomach dropped. Jordan was standing there talking to CJ, holding the champagne that she and CJ had ordered. Jordan was certainly not invited, and after his little performance earlier that day, he was also unwelcome.

"What are *you* doing here? Is that our champagne?" she asked in a nasty tone.

"Yes, I hope it's okay that I brought it to you. I ran into the room service guy in the hallway. I tipped him well, don't worry."

"I'm not concerned that you didn't tip well. I'm quite sure

that you overdid it, if anything, but what exactly are you doing *here*?" she asked adamantly.

"I felt like we got off on the wrong foot, so I wanted to come up and start over, maybe even escort you to the awards ceremony since your husband couldn't make it," Jordan said.

"First of all, I have a date," she said, motioning to CJ, who was now curled up like a cat in a big comfy chair. CJ waved a sarcastic little wave at the handsome young man. "Second of all," she continued, "it's really none of your business, but my *boyfriend* was going to be here, except he had an important business deal he was closing. Thanks for asking." She looked at CJ, who rolled his eyes.

"C'mon, let's have one glass of champagne together; it's on me. I had them charge it to my room," Jordan said.

Before Coco could answer, CJ flew out of his comfy perch, grabbed the bottle from Jordan's hands, and chirped, "You don't have to ask me twice. Drink up, honey."

And they did. Bottle after bottle after bottle. They "drank up" many times over and well into the night.

At 7:00 the next morning Coco's room phone rang in such a way that she was sure someone had brought a jackhammer into the room. Hotel room phones have a special way of being unpleasant. She reached over with her eyes still pasted shut and held the receiver to her ear.

"Hmmgph. *Cough.* Hello." She was near inaudible as words squeezed out of her painfully dry mouth.

"Hi, it's Rory!" he said, incredibly loudly and as if it was just one word, "HiitsRory!"

"What?" she said. She couldn't understand why the lights were on when the sun was shining through the window.

"Whatcha doin'?" He sounded chipper. Too chipper, in fact.

"Ummmm, sleeping?" she said.

"Just making sure you're okay. You missed the awards ceremony last night. I have your trophy and plaque," Rory said.

"What? Oh, god! Right, yeah, I guess I did," Coco said as she put her hand to her forehead and moved her hair off her face in one motion. "Shit!" This woke up the warm body next to her, which in turn woke up the warm body next to the first warm body. She heard soft groans, painful ones.

She continued, "Rory, let me call you back. I think I drank too much last night."

"Okay, but don't worry about it, you didn't miss anything. Just a bunch of suits congratulating themselves on a job adequately done. John O'Hurley bombed. They hated him. You missed nothing," he reassured her.

"Let me call you later," she begged before hanging up.

"We missed the whole event last night," she whispered to CJ's big head lying next to her.

"Yeah, I know. You grabbed the fourth bottle of champagne, aimed the cork at that lamp," he said as he pointed to the broken porcelain on the floor, "and said we should boycott the event on behalf of the Aborigines. You said something about giving 'North Korea back to them because they canceled *Arrested Development.*' We drank to that too," CJ said.

"Looks like we drank to a lot of things," Coco said as she surveyed all the empty champagne bottles and airline bottles of booze on the floor. "How are you feeling?" she asked him.

"CJ's been derailed and is off the tracks, honey. She's nothing but a train wreck."

"Oh, my god, are you naked?" Coco gasped.

"Of course! I have to be unencumbered, especially when I've been boozing it up. The skin has to breathe, you know!" CJ said it loudly enough that the body next to him stirred again.

"Wow, I feel like crap. What time is it?" the raspy voice said.

"Jordan?" Coco asked.

"Yeah, hi . . . Did you catch the license plate number on that eighteen-wheeler that ran me over?" Coco couldn't believe he'd actually used that hacky old line.

"You're not naked too, are you?" She was afraid to know the answer.

"What do you mean 'too'? Who's naked? Is everyone naked except me?" Jordan asked.

"*No! I* am fully clothed," Coco said as she peeked under the covers to be sure. "Fully. I still have my shoes on even," she said, seeing her high heels peeking out from the other end of the bed.

"Huh? Me too," Jordan replied as he stuck his loafers out from the bottom of the covers on the king-size bed.

"God, you guys are making such a big deal. Me, okay? I'm naked," CJ said.

"We missed the awards ceremony," Coco told them.

"Well, you were pretty adamant last night about not going. Your misaligned political views are obviously a strong platform for you. Something about your favorite TV shows and foreign despots. I thought that's why we didn't go," Jordan said.

"Huh, wish I could remember. I really must remember to

eat before I drink. Well, Rory said we didn't miss anything," Coco said.

"That's good," Jordan replied, suddenly becoming conscious of the naked man next to him.

"Yeah," she said, sensing his discomfort.

"I'm gonna get out of bed now," Jordan said awkwardly.

"Oh yeah, so am—" CJ said, but before he could finish that sentence he was interrupted.

"No, no, that's okay!" both Jordan and Coco yelled as she reached down on the floor and grabbed CJ's pants.

"Here, put these on," she insisted.

"Let's meet down in the fourth-floor restaurant. They have the best omelets," Coco said.

The mere mention of food made Jordan gag and hurry to the bathroom. Apparently omelets were not going to be in his immediate future.

Coco watched as he closed the door to her bathroom. *Why the fuck is he here?* She dropped her head into her hands and felt the remnants of last night's beautiful makeup.

Bailey found herself once again driving down Sunset Boulevard looking for an address. There had been so many restaurant and club openings and closings she could no longer keep track of whether the place she was going was the old Forty Deuce or the old Halo. Tonight was a launch party for the much-hyped remake of the TV version of *Fast Times at Ridgemont High,* produced by Gertie Whitmore's production company and marking Jennifer Garner's big return to television. Bailey had never met Gertie before, nor had she ever interviewed Jen Garner. For the first time in a long while, she was actually excited about a Hollywood event—if she could just find the damn place. That her GPS kept "recalculating" was of no help whatsoever. Shouldn't it have been searching rather than calculating? She decided she would just drive around until she saw the red carpet, the fan pit, and the klieg lights shining all over the sky like a damn Bat-Signal calling all the wannabes, has-beens, and never-weres.

After finally finding the place, Bailey went in a back entrance designated for press since she wasn't covering the red carpet, only the party itself. Normally, members of the press are led to either a pressroom or a special holding area so that they can see the party but not actually be a part of it; it's like they're at some flamboyant aquarium watching the big fish swimming in their big pond. But tonight was different. It was just a party with everyone mulling about. No VIP area, no pressroom, just men dressed like pirates serving hors d'oeuvres and cocktails, in homage to Judge Reinhold's job at the seafood restaurant.

Bailey was standing at the raw bar collecting shrimp and oysters when someone came up behind her and put their hands over her eyes.

"Guess who!" the voice said.

Bailey had no idea who the mystery guest was, but by the feel of the little, delicate, moisturized hands she could tell it was a female.

"C'mon, I hate this game!" Bailey pleaded.

"Oh, you're no fun," said the hands' owner as they fell away from Bailey's eyes. She turned around to see her dear old friend Christina Applegate.

Before Bailey's mom moved the family back to the manse in Greenwich, they'd lived in Hollywood, next door to the Applegates. Christina's mom, Nancy, was best friends with Bailey's mom, so the girls went shopping together, went out for lunch on Saturday afternoons, and the four even took a mother-daughter trip to Paris once. Bailey had fallen out of regular contact with Christina, which she'd always regretted. She suspected that had she not been such a lazy correspondent, Christina would have remained a close, constant friend.

"What are you doing here? How are you? How's your mom, your grandfather . . . everyone? Do you still see Christian? Tell me absolutely everything! Oh, it's so good to see you!" Christina squealed as she hugged and kissed Bailey.

Bailey was so accustomed to women not liking her, Christina's greeting unexpectedly lifted her spirits.

"Well, let's see. I'm here covering the party for my news show in New York, Mom is her usual pathological self, Grandpa is doing great . . . and no, Christian and I stopped talking after you guys broke up." Bailey had cut Christian Slater out of her life after his rather ugly, far too public breakup with Christina.

"Didn't you date one of his friends?" Christina asked.

"No, no, he tried to introduce me to Emilio, but we were never able to hook it up." Truth be told, Bailey didn't want to work her way through the cast of *Young Guns.* She'd already slept with Kiefer Sutherland while the movie was being filmed. It really would have been too awkward.

"Gosh, I haven't seen you since I was in New York doing *Sweet Charity,* and that was years ago," Christina said.

"I want you to know how sorry I am. I feel terrible that we lost touch and I wasn't there for you."

"No, no, you were. I got your cards and flowers, I know you were thinking of me. Believe me, that's a heck of a lot more than a lot of people did at the time. People get really freaked out by the C-word, but I'm fine, I'm fine. Oh, look, there's Gertie," Christina said as she waved at Gertie Whitmore. "Have you ever met her? She's an *amazing* woman. A total angel."

When Christina said "amazing," she closed her eyes for emphasis so that Bailey would understand that she wasn't being all Hollywood about it, that Gertie was the genuine article.

If Hollywood is America's Camelot, then Gertie was the heir apparent. She came from a long line of not just stars but superstars. Her grandfather, Edwin, was the absolute monarch of Hollywood practically from its beginnings and starred in the most memorable and award-winning films of the 1930s. Her aunts and uncles, parents and siblings were littered through American film history. There wasn't an era in which a Whitmore didn't figure prominently. And now was Gertie's time: She'd shown élan as one of the greatest child stars film has ever seen. By fourteen she was a tired old pro, already a rehab grad, and by eighteen she'd made her totally unexpected comeback in the biggest blockbuster of that summer. She'd been going strong ever since. She was a wonder.

"We did a film together . . . Gertie! Gertie! Come here." Christina waved again, now more frantically. "I want you to meet someone," she yelled above the music.

Gertie came over and gave big hellos and cheek kisses to Christina before noticing Bailey's plate of seafood.

"Don't eat that shrimp. I saw the waiter picking his nose before he put it out," Gertie joked.

"So that's what that extra seasoning was," Bailey fired back with a twinkle in her eye. "Delicious." Gertie was sharp, witty, and familiar. She was as likable as Bailey had heard.

"Well, if you like that, you'll adore the oysters. You can't *begin* to imagine where they were," Gertie replied. She looked at Bailey as if she were trying to figure out if she knew her.

"Yummy," Bailey said, meeting her gaze. She felt an instant camaraderie . . . and an odd surge of energy.

"You must be important," Gertie said flatly.

"What makes you say that?" Bailey asked.

"Because Christina never introduces me to anyone."

"Have you guys met before?" Christina seemed puzzled at their familiarity.

"No. Gertie," she said, holding out her hand to Bailey.

"Bailey."

"Now we have. I have a secret for you, Christina, but can I trust Bailey to keep it?"

"Oh, I don't have loose lips. Had my plastic surgeon take care of that years ago," Bailey teased.

Gertie did a spit-take of a laugh and grinned widely.

"Well, Sam Rockwell is here, and he just asked what your 'story' was!" Gertie told Christina.

"I have a 'story'? What's my story?"

"You know, he's interested in you, silly," Gertie said, throwing an elbow into her side.

"That's sweet, but no. I'm married, so don't even ask. Rockwell obviously doesn't read *People*. We're done here," Christina replied.

"Jeez. Okay, okay. Lighten up, Bundy. So, how do you two know each other?" Gertie asked Bailey.

Christina chimed in. "Bailey and her family lived next door to us growing up. Her grandfather is Mark Warfield from *Eye Investigate.*"

"Get out! He's one of my favorite journalists. I own a kinescope copy of an interview he did with my aunt Diana," Gertie said.

"Really?" Bailey felt as though she needed to say something.

"I'm having a brunch at my house tomorrow, you should come. I'll show you the reel," Gertie said, looking directly at Bailey as if there were no other person in the room. But then she noticed Christina and said, "You should bring her tomorrow."

"I would, except *I* wasn't invited," Christina said, rolling her eyes.

"Shut up, of course you are." Gertie punched Christina in the arm.

"You know, I'm interviewing you on Friday," Bailey said to Gertie.

"Are you now? Well, that oughta be fun." Gertie started to step away from them just as a man walked over, got her attention, and told her that she needed to greet a few more people. After all, she was the woman of the hour.

"It was nice meeting you," Gertie said to Bailey. Then she yelled over her shoulder as she was being dragged away, "See you both tomorrow."

"Boy, you two really hit it off," Christina said.

"Yeah, she seemed pretty cool. She calls you Bundy?" Bailey remarked.

"Yeah, and I call her Toxie."

Bailey looked at her, puzzled.

"You know . . . from all of those Toxic Tonya movies she made?"

"Right. Clever."

"Come get me on your way over there tomorrow. We can make an entrance together," Christina said.

After the party, Bailey went back to her hotel room. The light was blinking on the room phone, which was odd since she had her BlackBerry with her. She wondered who on earth would call her room. She dialed up the voice mail and discovered it was Saul King. He obviously knew where she was staying since they worked together, but why wouldn't he have called her cell? He was a peculiar little man. The voice mail said, "Call me immediately. I have some very important information for you."

It was 3:00 A.M. Pacific time, which meant that Saul would be in his office in an hour. He was always there by 7:00. Bailey considered going to bed and waiting until she woke in the morning, but she knew, having heard his ominous message, there was no way she'd be able to sleep.

FOURTEEN

Yoga for Breakfast

Hiya, toots, howya doin'?" Saul King asked.

"I'm exhausted, Saul, it's four A.M.," Bailey replied.

"Whaaa?" Saul said as he dropped the phone. "I'm back. Jeez, I'm sorry. These darned clocks."

"No, Saul, it's four A.M. in Los Angeles. That's where I am."

"Oh, for pete's sake, of course, of course you are!"

"I got your message, Saul. What did you find out for me?" Bailey was impatient.

"Okay, now wait a minute . . ." Saul sounded like he was all of a sudden across the room. "Let me get my index cards together. Yes, okay, here they are. That Bruno guy, the police chief? He's dirty."

"Dirty? How so?"

"Well, I did some digging, and though the records I found were sealed, I was able to learn that when he was in Kennebunkport he was some kind of informant. I'm thinking mafia. What other kind of rat could there be? Doncha think?" Saul asked rhetorically. "My guess is witness protection. He's posing as Bruno, but his real name and identity might be something else."

"Get out. Really?"

"Well, it's just one theory."

"What would be another theory?"

"That I'm totally wrong, and I'm barking up the wrong tree."

"What are the odds of that?"

"About fifty-fifty, I'm guessing. But I surprise even myself sometimes."

"Oh, *Saul.* Did you find anything that could help us?" Bailey was a bit disheartened. This wasn't going to help at all.

"Well, this might be something. There are some documents that contain information on someone the Kennebunkport police are calling Blackbeard. This must be the person who knows all of the *real* information. I'm going to get to the bottom of it, toots, I promise you that. Just as soon as I sort out the orange cone caper I'm working on here. I'm so close."

"Oh, are you still working on the 'Uncivil Servants' feature?"

"Yes, yes, I am, and I'm very close to *Saul*ving the question of who has been stealing the orange cones for their own personal use."

"Okay, Saul, good luck with that. Call me again if you find out anything else . . . even if it seems like nothing. You never know."

"Oh, toots, I taught you well. Say hi to your lovely mother for me."

"Will do."

No sooner had she hung up the phone than Bailey picked it right back up to call Detective Casey. She hesitated for a moment because she felt both a little embarrassed by her behavior the other night and a little incredulous that he'd had the *nerve*—and the willpower—to reject her. *Maybe CJ's more his type?* she wondered, still stinging from his rebuke.

"Hi, Rob, it's Bailey. I need to talk to you about the case."

"Ms. Warfield. Hi. Thank you for calling." Detective Casey sounded relieved. "I've been wanting to speak with you."

"Listen, this isn't about the other night . . ."

"I'm sorry. I—"

"No, no. There are more important matters at hand. Let's put that away. It didn't happen." Bailey was happy to save face for herself and for him. If she hadn't needed an ally, however, she would've made him the sorriest man on earth.

"Okay. Good . . . good. What's up, then?"

"Do you know anything about Chief Bruno's life when he was police chief in Kennebunkport?"

Detective Casey was silent.

"Rob?"

"Wow. You've done some good detective work, Bailey," he said, this time stunning Bailey into silence.

When she didn't reply, Casey went on. "It's okay, I know everything. I know you guys didn't buy Bruno's story about what you saw, and I know you've been doing your own investigation. Olivia told me the whole story. And it sounds like you've done great work. I didn't buy his story either, and I've been conducting my own inquiry. It sounds like we both got to the same information."

Olivia?

Bailey had, as they say, a moment of clarity. It all made sense now. And, suddenly, she was even extremely happy that he had pushed her away.

Casey continued. "So, you know then that Blackbeard is Bruno, and you know that he's willing to cross anyone for the right price. He's dangerous. I'd rather you all let me do the police work from here."

"*Bruno* is Blackbeard?" Bailey realized Saul had only skimmed the surface, and that they were indeed way over their heads. *That self-serving, narcissistic, evil bastard,* she thought.

Bailey agreed to back off and let Casey investigate the chief. None of them were equipped to handle Bruno or the mayor, she realized.

"Could you do me a favor, though, Bailey?" Casey asked. She thought he was going to ask for her silence about their little encounter, which she'd understood as a given. But he wasn't going there.

"If your guy—Saul was it?—gets anything on Blackbeard, let me know. He must have some decent contacts to have gotten that much. We need all the good detective work we can get. Just promise you'll pass everything on to me and let me handle it from now on."

Bailey agreed. Her next call was to Olivia. She had never phoned her before, but now she felt like she needed to connect with her. Maybe it was guilt, maybe there was a grudging respect—she felt certain that Rob had refused her because he was smitten with Olivia.

Olivia suggested they get together for yoga and have brunch afterward at Early Girl. They set the date for Saturday morning. After hanging up the phone, Bailey worried that she and Olivia alone could get awkward. She might blurt out something inappropriate or, worse, be unable to hide her guilt. Best to invite Coco and CJ as well. Fortunately, Olivia thought that was a great idea, so it was settled. They'd reconvene and catch up. And decompress with some much-needed yoga.

Yoga, like long-distance running, is about a thousand times easier when it's done with friends. So, even though Bailey, Coco, CJ, and Olivia had taken dozens of classes at Asmita Yoga together, they'd only just started doing so as friends. Suddenly they were stronger and more flexible than they'd ever felt in their lives. They finally understood the "energy flow" their too new-agey and slightly loony instructor couldn't stop talking about, and, for once, in their warrior poses they felt like actual warriors. The only shred of self-consciousness they had was about what they wore, all having deliberately tried to outdo the others while they were getting dressed.

CJ, as expected, was better put together than them all; Bailey's outfit was the most expensive, of course; Olivia looked cute and doll-like but unremarkable; and Coco made sure nothing she wore looked remotely like it could've been purchased in the eighties. But they put such energy and intensity into the class and they were all so drenched in sweat and feeling gross by the end that it didn't really matter. While working on inversions—when students are told to pair off and do headstands against the wall—the four grouped together, held each other up, and encouraged each other enthusiastically. Neither Coco nor Olivia had ever had much luck holding a headstand for more than a second, and had always kicked up awkwardly, but with CJ and Bailey's assistance and reassurance, they were flawless. All four were euphoric and starving after they showered and changed. So it was a good thing that Early Girl was close by.

Brunch in Greenwich was like brunch anywhere else except it was white. White people, white tablecloths, white napkins, white servers, white omelets, and the whole thing made Coco very nervous. She grew up in an ethnically diverse neighborhood, but it was at brunch that she was always reminded of her color since it was *everywhere*, as if she'd stumbled onto a sinister secret society.

The restaurant was a mélange of rustic bookshop meets twee cake shop. It felt more like Vermont than like Connecticut, especially on this, the first really cold day of the season. Coco wasn't sure if the mismatched chairs were actual antiques or modern furniture distressed to look old. The furnishings didn't fit with the stark white, so it was clearly an effect the restaurant's owners were going for. The man sitting outside holding a dachshund on his lap seemed rather out of place as well. Coco didn't think the pairing of the man and his dog was odd so much as the fact that man and dog were wearing matching gingham scarves. The way the man handled the shaking dog's anxiety was also peculiar. He reached over to the kiosk in front of him, took out a brochure that had MASSAGE written on it in large letters, and began rubbing the dog's back with the brochure, saying "there, there." Coco looked on in amusement until her gaze was broken by a tap on the shoulder.

"Hey," Bailey said as she air-kissed Coco's cheeks hello. Coco, always the fast dresser, had gone ahead of the others to reserve a table while CJ and Olivia, sharing Olivia's car, had stopped at Starbucks because Olivia absolutely had to have a venti caramel macchiato. CJ had scolded her for being so gauche as to bring her own coffee to brunch.

"As soon as they start serving caramel macchiatos, I won't need to. In the meantime, I just did yoga, so I deserve one," Olivia declared. So off they went, telling the others they'd arrive shortly.

Coco was surprised to see Bailey already. "I figured the others would've gotten here long before you," she said. They were seated by the hostess who, not liking that their whole party hadn't arrived, refused to smile and practically threw menus at them as they took off their coats.

"Oh no, I'm never late for anything. In my business you can't be, yet everyone is. I'm convinced it's why I get all the good interviews: I show up. Also, my bosses know they can count on me, so I always get sent out on the important jobs," Bailey replied.

"Ah, makes sense now. I think you and I are probably a lot alike. We're both so driven. People like us would never even dream of being late; it's not in our nature," Coco said.

"Even as a kid I was always on time for stuff." Bailey read her menu as she spoke.

"So, are we going to talk about Graham in front of Olivia and CJ, or am I still keeping this to myself?" Coco asked.

"No, I want to talk about him, definitely, but I thought I would wait until everyone is here. Oh, but did I tell you I met Gertie Whitmore this week?" Bailey said, suddenly animated as she tossed her menu on the table setting next to her.

"Really? I'm surprised you didn't already know her. What's she like?" Coco asked.

"The best! I like her so much. I met her at an event, and she invited me to her house for brunch the next day."

"Ooh, exciting. I loved all of those Toxic Tonya movies . . . Oh, and I loved her in that Woody Allen film. . . . I bet she's got one of those L.A. pads people out here always dream about, swimming pool overlooking the valley, right?"

"Not overlooking the valley, but it was a cool place with a sixties vibe. She's simply one of the nicest, funniest, most wonderful people you'll ever meet. She's really smart, has such great people around her. She said she'd be coming to New York in the next few weeks, so we're planning on getting together. You'll meet her, she's amazing. We totally hit it off. I felt like I've known her my whole life," Bailey gushed.

Coco didn't know what to make of Bailey's sudden adoration for Gertie Whitmore, or why she'd brought it up after Coco had asked about Graham, but Coco chalked it up to that thing that happens sometimes between women. It's like you've been best friends your whole lives even though you just met. Coco understood—it was what had happened to her when she met her college roommate, Winnie. They were so close, people assumed they were lovers. They weren't, but they remained friends, sisters almost, to this day.

"Yep, sometimes it just happens in an instant," Coco said.

"Yes. Yes, it does," Bailey replied, seeming a little lost in her thoughts. She snapped back to attention when she saw Coco looking over her shoulder at the café's entrance.

"Sorry. There's CJ," Coco said as she waved toward the door, making sure he saw them.

"Honey, have some decorum. You're waving like you're hailing a taxi," CJ said as he kissed them both hello and whipped his hat off his head. "Whew, it's getting cold out there. Feel my fingers, aren't they frostbitten?"

"Where's Olivia?" Bailey asked.

"Oh, I told her she wasn't allowed to bring that mocho-choco-lata-yaya thing in here. I said they didn't allow outside food or drink, but the truth is I hate Starbucks. I can't even stand to look at those cups, so I didn't want her to bring it in." He suddenly turned to Bailey. "I know you just came from yoga, girl, but you have a glow like you just got laid."

"Oh, I could say the same about you, darling. We all have that post-yoga flush. It's better than sex sometimes." Bailey laughed.

"Oh, you *must* be out of your mind!" CJ said. "Or you seriously need better lovers."

Coco laughed. "I think the key is a combination. Good sex with someone who does a lot of yoga."

"True that," CJ agreed as he looked at the menu. "What's good here?"

"Speaking of . . . Did you call Malcolm?" Coco asked him.

"Nooo-ah," CJ replied like a child whose mother has asked him for the fifth time to clean his room.

"CJ! C'mon!" Coco replied.

"Oh yeah, little Malcolm. How's that relationship going?" Bailey said as she made air quotes around "relationship."

"Ugh, don't *ask*! It's a disaster."

"Oh, you didn't hear?" Coco said.

"No! Tell me," Bailey insisted.

"I almost outed him at work when I so nicely brought him cookies from Good Boy Bakery. Now he isn't talking to me," CJ said. "How was I supposed to know he was still in the closet?"

"Mmm, Good Boy. I love that place," Bailey said.

"It's not serious, he's just a guy," CJ said.

"Oh, so now he's *just a guy*?" Coco asked.

"Yes, dear," CJ said. "Sometimes a girl just likes to go for a ride."

"I don't care, we need him. Call him, make up, and pretend you like him."

"Well, on that front, I've got some news for you two," Bailey said. "This thing has gotten complicated. Rob, uh, Detective Casey, is back on the case. He actually never left it but didn't want to tip his hand to his colleagues, so he didn't let us know either. Chief Bruno is up to his eyeballs in this."

Coco's and CJ's mouths dropped open.

"Get the fuck out." CJ looked worried now.

"No joke. But look, Casey wants us to lay low. He thinks it could be dangerous if we start poking around. Olivia and I told him we'd draw back."

"Wow, okay. Well . . . look, Casey may not want us involved, but CJ can't just drop Malcolm," Coco insisted. "That might be suspicious too, if we're being watched. And you never know if Malcolm might accidentally provide some information even if CJ isn't digging for it.

"Besides, I think there's a little more than just information gathering and humping going on," Coco said slyly. "Call him and apologize, damn you."

"*Fine.* I'll call him tonight. Are you happy now, Miss Cranky Pants?" CJ said.

"I'm not cranky," Coco rebutted.

"Oh, you have on a big ole pair today," CJ insisted. "I saw you smirking when the instructor was reading her little prayer-poem thingee."

Coco rolled her eyes. "Sorry, I hate that shit. I go to yoga to stretch, not for church."

"Amen to that," said Bailey, without a hint of irony. "I guess you guys missed my shirt," at which she pulled the buttons of her chemise apart to reveal a baby-doll tank top that read KEEP YOUR DOGMA OUT OF MY YOGA!

Coco shrieked with laughter. "Awesome."

Just then CJ looked up from the table. "Here comes Mother Earth," he cracked.

And sure enough, walking toward them was Olivia, looking like a hippie Eskimo. She wore an oversize parka with an enormous hood that was part embroidery, part Arctic fox, and 100 percent excruciating. But on her head things got worse. She wore a baby pink woolen earflap hat with what looked like fake braids coming down the sides.

"I can't tell if she's incredibly chic or homeless," Bailey scoffed.

"What's with the getup, Nanook of Nantucket?" Coco asked.

"Ugh, this? I'm such an idiot. All of my really warm winter stuff is still in storage. This was the only thing in the closet that wasn't garden wear or golf clubs. I think it was my aunt Toby's from the sixties. It's the warmest thing I could find in the house," Olivia replied.

"Shame she was a flower child and not a mod; that could have been a really sharp outfit," Bailey said.

"Right!" Olivia laughed. "Sorry I took so long out there. I had to talk to the nanny. Simon was fussy today, so she put me on the phone with him. We're not eating yet, right?" she said as she glanced at the table.

"This isn't brunch conversation," she said as she nibbled a mini muffin from a basket the busboy had just set down, "but I got him all dressed and was running out the door and saying good-bye when he poops in his diaper, so I had to change him *again*—she'd just arrived and I didn't think it was fair to start her day with that. Then as I was trying to get him dressed, he kept crawling away like a madman—he's fast, that little guy. So I put on Barney to distract him, but when I got up to leave, he threw a tantrum because he wanted me to watch with him, and then I felt guilty the entire way over to yoga. Ah, kids. Don't have them," she said.

"I don't know how anyone has more than one," CJ said.

"Sam's mom had six!" Coco said.

"Oh my!" Olivia gasped. "That just seems . . . unbearable. Where is he in the family? Oldest, middle . . . ?"

"Youngest," Coco said. "His mother is a saint, six kids and she fucked up none of them."

"Speaking of Sam, if you don't mind my asking, what's the deal with you two? You're married, right? Are you thinking about kids?" Olivia asked.

"Not married, actually. But we've been together for about ten years. Funny you should mention it, because Sam really wants to get married, and has been bugging me a lot about it lately. I've been fighting it, though. I may give in, but I really hate that ceremony and party stuff, so that's my big sticking point," Coco said to a table full of rolling eyes. *"What?"*

"I told you in Philly, girl, you're just using that as an excuse—a lame one, at that—to not get married. If he was the one for you, it wouldn't matter how you do it," CJ said.

"I agree," Olivia declared.

"Me too," Bailey said as she fidgeted in her seat. It seemed like the subject of marriage made her uncomfortable too. "When I get married, I won't care how it's done."

"Now *you're* thinking about getting married?" Coco asked.

"I don't know, I'm just saying. I have to start thinking about it—at thirty-seven I'm becoming extinct," Bailey told her.

"Wait! Stop the presses. Is there a man attached to all of this?" CJ said.

"Well . . . I might as well tell you. Yes." Bailey confessed. "I've been seeing someone off and on for a while, and it's just started getting more serious."

"Is it someone famous? I bet it's someone famous. Am I right?" Olivia asked.

Bailey smirked imperceptibly, more of a cringe. "I've been seeing Graham Shore for about a year, and it's been getting pretty intense. I think he could be the one." She beamed.

"Holy Brat Pack, lady!" CJ exclaimed.

Bailey continued. "I know it's weird. I met him when I was doing a TV story on David E. Kelley. Graham was one of the interviews I had lined up. He was *so* funny, told me some great stories and some touching personal stuff—he was terrific. I could tell he was a guy who saw what he wanted and took it."

"How do you mean?" Coco asked her.

"Well, he asked me out as he was walking out the door.

Usually they get your number from a publicist or someone. The fact that he asked me before he even left the room and in front of everyone was so different and so *bold.* It was really sexy," Bailey said.

"Sounds like it," said Olivia, clearly someone in love with love.

"Well, he didn't try anything that night. But over dinner we just *knew.* We had this mad, crazy connection and just stared into each other's eyes; he held my hand, and we both knew. He said that since his divorce he hadn't met anyone like me and hadn't connected this way with anyone, ever. Every time he talks about the future it's always what 'we' will be doing. He even started to clean out his house anticipating my moving in with him. Then 'we' went shopping at Williams-Sonoma, and he told me to pick out what I liked since I will be the one using everything," Bailey said. "Either he's in love with me or I'm his new chef."

"When did it get more serious?" Olivia asked.

"Last week. He's in Alaska right now, climbing Mt. McKinley. Before he left he said that when he came back he wanted me to move in with him. I've already met his kids, Sebastian and Elijah, and I adore them!" Bailey smiled big.

"Oh, lord, you'll probably get married before I do!" Coco laughed.

CJ's phone rang. He looked at the caller ID and said, "I'm not answering it."

"Why, who is it?" Coco asked him.

"My father. I'll call him back later," CJ said with a hint of insolence.

"What's that about?" Bailey asked.

"We don't really get along," CJ said. "He doesn't like that I'm gay, and he wants me to keep it a secret. He's a big politician, running for governor, and he's afraid it will ruin his career if anyone finds out about his fag son."

"When did you come out to him?" Coco asked.

"Well, I didn't really. An evil ex outed me. He called my father and said, 'Your son is gay and he sucks dicks.' Nice, right? My conservative, right-wing father! So he calls me into the living room, tells me about the call, and asks if it's true. I couldn't bring myself to deny it. I said, 'Yes, it's true, especially the dicks part,' and his response was 'Whatever you do, don't tell anybody, including your mother.' I don't know why, but I agreed to those rules. As I was leaving the room he added, 'And by the way, *never* under my roof.' So I moved out shortly after that. I took his checkbook and got a place in the city with some friends," CJ told them.

"Isn't your father also incredibly religious? Weren't you?" Bailey asked. The Warfields and the Skodas had attended the same church for forty years. Well, at least their parents had.

"Sorta. I mean he is, but it's mostly for show, like a lot of Catholics and *all* politicians. I never really connected to that church—although a couple priests sure wanted to connect to me."

"Ooh! I bet! Father Bruce, right?" Bailey chuckled.

"Oh, at the very least, sister." CJ smirked.

"Did you ever tell your mother?" Olivia asked him.

"Eventually. She was upset and thought I became gay because my father was away a lot. So she tried to blame that, then asked me what *she* did wrong. She kept apologizing for raising me 'wrong.' It was interesting that she put it on herself, like she'd screwed up somehow."

"And now?" Coco said.

"We still pretend that I'm not, I think. We never spoke about it again. But one day I want to reassure her that she didn't screw up. My father used to take me hunting, golfing, to baseball games. I was on the wrestling team, the whole straight-boy thing."

"Ummm . . . wrestling is the gayest sport," Bailey pointed out.

They all laughed.

Just then a very handsome older man with auburn hair and a nice smile was seated across from them. The waitress brought him coffee as soon as he sat. He was by himself and read *The New York Times,* seeming quite engaged in the business section.

"He's cute," Bailey said, motioning toward CJ. "Go talk to him."

"I'm not just going to walk over and say 'hi.' I don't even know him."

"What's to know?" Coco agreed. "Not a lot of available guys in this part of the world, and he's really cute."

Coco waved at him but then realized he might think she was hitting on him, so to be sure, she began pointing at CJ and mouthing "my friend."

The guy laughed.

Bailey walked over and said, "I'm Bailey, that's CJ," pointing at a completely crimson and mortified CJ.

"Ted," said the man.

"Ted, what do you do?" Bailey asked.

"I'm a dentist." Ted smiled, slightly uncomfortable but playing along.

Bailey turned, looked CJ square in the eye, and said, "CJ, give me your card." CJ sighed and handed her his card.

Bailey handed CJ's card to Ted, and continued talking with him, out of earshot.

CJ turned to Coco and Olivia and said, "I just had Botox, so I can't express how truly angry I am with her right now."

Bailey came back and announced, "He's single, forty-seven, works in Pound Ridge. Martha Stewart is one of his patients. You can date Martha Stewart's dentist! Won't that be fun?"

"I'm going to kill you," CJ hissed. "See this face? Imagine it scowling."

FIFTEEN

Threesomes with the Foursome

CJ sat on his couch rehearsing in his head what he would say to Malcolm—something that didn't sound too corny or too contrived. But every time he mustered up the courage to call, his phone would ring and it would be someone from work. Weekend calls from his junior associate producers were a matter of course regardless of where he was or what he was doing. His was the kind of business that could only be described as "chaotic" in its calmest moments when they were in the midst of a season. Once he'd had to hide in the bathroom during a friend's wedding in order to frantically book a last-minute guest for a show. CJ never complained since he was grateful to be working in the television industry with people he adored. For as many backbreaking hours as he and the crew labored through together, they still missed each other when they went on hiatus.

The other distraction CJ had was his parents' looming homecoming. He was there to care for Nanny while they were gone, and he enjoyed doing so as she had done for him his whole life, of course, but their return in a few days made him incredibly anxious, not to mention the fact that he hadn't been home to his own apartment in over a month. This little sojourn had turned into a horror show—he never would've gone to that godforsaken party and witnessed a murder if he'd been at his place in the city. But then he never would have met the girls, whom he was coming to love more and more each time he saw them.

He felt another Nelly coming on. He didn't like being alone in this enormous house that held so many memories, good and bad—though mostly bad, of late. Nanny was spending the night at her cardiologist's house, which was the safest place she could be, considering her condition and the trouble CJ and his friends had gotten into.

The phone rang yet again.

"What fresh hell is this?" CJ said aloud as he picked it up. "Oh, it's you, hi," he said to Coco.

"I haven't spoken to you yet today. We have to fill our daily quota," she said with a laugh. "I'm now to the point where if I don't talk to you and the day is over, I feel like I've missed something." After Philadelphia and the yoga and the brunch, they talked constantly, like high school lovers. "So, what'd I miss?"

"Ugh, nothing. Just the usual drama at work. This one can't do her job because that one isn't answering her e-mails. The usual hell that is my life."

"You love it."

"I do."

"So any news from Malcolm? When are you seeing him?" Coco asked.

"I think I'm glad my mother isn't interested in my gay life," he said, "if this is what it would be like."

"Okay, okay. I'm sorry."

"I appreciate your concern for my love life. But it's probably I who should be badgering you about yours," he said.

All of a sudden the doorbell rang.

"That's the door, stay on the phone with me. The kind of day I'm having, it's probably a process server."

CJ went to the door. It was the local florist delivering the most incredible bouquet he had ever seen.

"Someone must really like you. This is our most expensive arrangement," the delivery guy said with a wink as he handed CJ the floral treasure. CJ took it inside as he held the phone between his shoulder and cheek.

"Someone sent absolutely gorgeous flowers. Probably for Nanny. She's banging her cardiologist. He has more money than God, who he is actually older than," CJ said.

"Wonderful. Your seventy-year-old Nanny has a better sex life than me," Coco said bitterly.

"Oh, honey, you still didn't talk to Sam about a three-way or something to spice it up a bit?" he asked.

"Well, a three-way isn't my idea of fun, necessarily," she replied.

"Girrrrl! *Do not* knock it till you've tried it!" CJ said.

"I don't feel like talking about me. I want to hear what happened with Malcolm."

"I chickened out. I still haven't called him. I'm kind of waiting for him to make the first move. I don't know."

"CJ, this isn't *The Bachelor,* and you aren't looking for your perfect fit. We need this guy to help us, and, besides, I thought you didn't really like him."

"I don't! I'm just a girl who likes to be wooed, that's all," CJ said.

"CJ!" she said sternly. He knew what she meant.

"Fine! I'll call him. God, you're so pushy." He laughed. "I'll call you after I talk to him," he said.

"That's all I'm asking," Coco replied.

They hung up. CJ fixed his hair in the mirror of the front hall bureau, where the flowers were. He noticed a card that had his name on it and that it had originally been slated for delivery to *him* at the *Rachael Ray* show. One of the secretaries must've given them his home address. Surprised, he opened it and read:

> I wanted these flowers to see how beautiful you were.—M

CJ choked up, almost to tears.

"Oh, girl, don't do it, your eyes will puff right up," he said to his reflection.

Bailey was so excited that Graham was coming home she didn't know what to do first: prepare herself or prepare her bedroom. She still hadn't unpacked her stuff from L.A., which included lots of shopping bags—her room looked as if Rodeo Drive had thrown up on it. She also had this *thing*, this ritual, before seeing men she really liked, men she enjoyed having sex with. Actually, it was three things. First she would shower, then she would groom her nether regions so that they were smooth, stubble-free, and ready for action. Second, she would dab perfume on all of her erogenous zones; and third, she would watch the Marx Brothers classic *A Day at the Races,* to put her in a jovial mood. She hadn't done any of this for a man in a long time.

Tonight Graham was coming straight from LaGuardia (only half an hour away without traffic, but he wouldn't dream of simply meeting her in the city) to pick up Bailey at her house and take her back to the city to the suddenly hot again Balthazar restaurant in SoHo, where even *he* had had to make a reservation earlier in the week. As an avid list maker, she ran through her date night checklist:

1. Cute new outfit bought in Beverly Hills: new Zac Posen flirty dress, DVF clutch, and YSL shoes . . . *check.*
2. New toothbrush for boyfriend to use when he stays over, to help him feel welcome . . . *check.*
3. Groomed, fresh, and ready for action . . . *check.*

She was ready to move in for the kill.

Graham's car showed up on time, a miracle on a Sunday night. He greeted her warmly and was excited to tell her about Denali, and climbing Mt. McKinley, regaling her with stories about everything he and his sons had done on the trip, grizzly bears sighted and a couple new Sarah Palin jokes from the locals. The boys were on their way back to their mother's house, and Graham already missed them.

When they got to Balthazar, they had to wait for their table, much to his chagrin. They sat at the bar and had a drink; everything seemed fine. Graham caressed her hand, then touched the small of her back as he led her to her seat. Even at the table when they ordered food and talked more about his trip and when he had to be back on the set of *Chicago Counsel,* it was all good. Then dessert came. Graham leaned in to speak more intimately to Bailey, or so she thought. The background noise faded into the distance. They could've been the only two people in the restaurant; heck, they could've been the only two people in the world at that point. He took her hand and spoke gently.

This was it. Bailey shook nervously but imperceptibly. Moving in seemed a fait accompli so . . . *Was he about to propose?* she wondered.

"I had an epiphany on the mountain," he began.

Here it comes.

"Bailey, I came to realize that you're not the one for me," he said.

And that was all he said. He let it hang there, thick in the air like syrup. Bailey had no idea how to respond. She had two possibilities, she thought. No, three actually. She could yell about the fact that he had waited until they finished dinner, that he should have told her at her house instead of making her come all the way into New York and sit through a three-hour meal, only to have it completely spoiled at the end. She could also have made a scene, enraged that she'd been blindsided by his news, since before his trip he had pledged his undying love for her and asked her to move in with him. Her third option was to say nothing, just take the sucker punch and be devastated later. She chose number three.

He might as well have slipped a Mickey into her drink. From that moment, the night went black. The next morning

Bailey called in sick to work. She didn't answer the phone for anyone, not even Gertie Whitmore.

"I left two messages for Bailey and one for Malcolm. I haven't heard from either one today," CJ said. "She was supposed to find out about this Blackbeard character from the problem-solving guy at her station. Olivia says that even Detective Casey was interested. Where the heck is everyone?"

"Oh, I spoke with Olivia. She's probably in the middle of a happy baby pose about now. I have a conference call, and then we're meeting up to go shopping for clothes. If that brunch ensemble taught us anything, it's that the woman obviously needs a shopping partner," Coco said. "I may not have the world's best sense of style, but I know when to say no."

"Well, you'll be proud of me. I haven't heard from Malcolm yet, but I'm going to his place after work. When I called him last night to thank him for the flowers, we made a date for tonight." CJ had been so excited about the flowers that he'd immediately called Coco back to tell her about them. It had also gotten him off the hook with her, since she'd been needling him about contacting Malcolm.

"That's great news. How are you going to tell him about the mayor?" Coco asked.

"I need to gauge his loyalty to the man before I do. It could be tricky," CJ replied.

"So your plan is no plan?"

"Basically."

"Oy."

"Coco, don't worry. I get stuff out of people for a living. If you knew how much we prepped those guests for the show back when I worked for *Tyra,* you'd flip. They come on camera and spill it! Don't you worry."

"Why is it that actually *does* worry me?" Coco said with a laugh.

"Look, what I do is like a well-choreographed tennis match. I serve it up, but they rarely hit it back where *they* want to. I'm like Serena and Venus rolled into one."

"Just don't lose your balls." Coco couldn't resist the pun.

"Gotta get back to work. Call ya later," CJ said and hung up.

Sam walked into the kitchen, where Coco was having her afternoon jolt of caffeine.

"Hi." He was relatively cold and didn't look her way.

"Mmm. Hi." Coco sipped her coffee, speaking with no affect while looking at him over the top of her mug. "It's not as good when I make it. You do it so much better. What's your secret?"

"Just have the touch, I guess." He looked toward her when he knew she was looking down at the paper.

Something was slightly amiss in their relationship for sure, but all of this tension, ill-timed travel, and secrecy had brought it to the surface.

Coco wanted to say, "Look, all this stuff with the envelope and the forged documents . . . it's, uh, because I witnessed the murder of a young girl in the mayor's mansion, and now he's extorting us. I need your love and support because I'm scared." What came out instead was "Are you hungry?"

"Nope, I'm fine." The big problem was that every time

they talked about it, either they fought or he turned it into an indictment of her ring-a-phobia, as he liked to call her fear of marriage. "You waiting for that conference call?" he asked.

"Yep." She didn't mean to be cold, it just came out that way. This whole situation was frustrating, and if she engaged him, she knew where it would end up.

Then out of nowhere Sam said in an accusatory tone, "Who is Jordan Ainsworth?"

"One of Rory's new clients. He's kind of a tool. Why?"

"So he was in Philly *with you* at the awards ceremony?"

"Yes . . . but I don't like the implication of 'with me.' He was there. I was there, but by no means was he *with me*," she replied.

"Then can you explain this?" he said, and he threw down the Philly paper, revealing a photograph of Coco passed out and Jordan Ainsworth with his arm around her giving the camera the thumbs-up. Clearly he'd taken the photo himself, since his reflection could be seen in the mirror as he held the camera out in front of them.

"That *asshole*!" Coco screamed as she grabbed the paper and held it up to get a closer look. "That fucking social-climbing bootlicker!"

"Whoa," Sam said. "A little defensive? Maybe you should be explaining this instead of going off on him. Who's the injured party here? Why the fuck is there a picture of the two of you in a hotel room, and why are you passed out?"

She barely heard Sam, she was so engaged in the tabloid.

"'My torrid night of passion'? I'm passed out! Can't they tell?" she screamed. "Do I look engaged in passion here to you?"

Sam took the paper and looked at it closely. "Hard to tell. You do always look tired. Maybe this is afterward," he said snidely. "Is there something you need to tell me? I think I'm starting to understand why you don't want to get married."

"Sam. Oh, c'mon, Sam." She looked at him pityingly. "You know that's not my style. CJ was there too, and they don't mention *that* anywhere! Assholes!" She was really pissed now. Goddamn, these local newspapers kept getting her into trouble.

"Can you just tell me who this guy is?" Sam said.

"I told you, he's Jordan Ainsworth, he . . . No, I guess I *don't* know who he is. I don't know him at all!"

"You look pretty chummy in this shot," he said as he held up the paper.

She ripped it out of his hand.

"Damn it, Sam, this isn't funny. This guy's a dead man. How soon can we train Farnsworth and Milo to be attack dogs?"

"Not in this lifetime. That'll teach you to love esoteric, gentle breeds, although the puppy really let his rubber hedgehog have it the other day. You should've heard it screeching. You're gonna have to find a different route. How 'bout reaching into your bag of Brooklyn?"

It's true. You can't take Brooklyn out of the girl, and she was about to go all Bensonhurst on Jordan Ainsworth.

To his credit, for having discovered his girlfriend in bed with another man, Sam was remarkably calm. But then, he really did know Coco. And this wasn't her style; he knew she was being set up.

"I'm really losing my touch. I can't believe I was hoodwinked."

"I can't believe you just used the word *hoodwinked.*"

"Where's my fucking phone? Rory's going to rue the day he brought that guy on. Damn it!"

Sam stopped her. "Wait. I think you owe me an explanation before you call Rory. Why were you in a hotel room passed out with some guy you barely know? You were supposed to be there for an awards ceremony. And why was this CJ guy there?"

"An explanation?" she said. "Okay, here's your explanation. There was a sexual revolution going on over the past ten years, and I totally missed it. Do you even know what a rabbit is? Did you know that everyone is having butt sex now? And I'm not even talking about the gays. Women are more sexually liberated than ever before, people are having one-night stands but are calling them 'hookups,' and nobody is mad at you the next day if you don't call them. And this isn't just in New York, it's all over the country. Sam, we are missing all of this!" Coco didn't know this was all pent up inside her, but it came tumbling out.

"What. The. Fuck? What the fuck *are* you talking about?" Sam asked, astonished. He looked at her closely, as if checking on her health.

"Just . . . just forget it."

"No, no. You can't just let that out and let it drop. No way. I want to know what you're talking about and what this has to do with your being passed out in a hotel room with, apparently, *two* men. Did you fuck them?" Sam was getting testy now.

"I'm talking about a decade, a whole generation that we missed because you and I are stuck in the nineties sexually.

Nothing happened with Jordan Asshole, period; and CJ was there as my friend and stylist, okay? And he's really, really gay, and even if he weren't, I'm pretty sure I wouldn't sleep with him. But if you want to marry me, you are gonna need to step up your game, mister."

"Let me get this straight. You won't marry me unless I have a threesome with you and some, I don't know, random third person?"

"God, no! Nobody said threesomes. Have you been talking to CJ? No! I just mean that while the whole world is out there doing god knows what and loving it, we nearly have bed death. I would like us to have some sexual exploration. CJ and I have discussed it, and we agree that this is what you and I need most. Okay? Can we?"

"Oh . . . so . . . you talked to your new gay best friend about *my* sex life? Thank you for your respect and privacy."

"No, it's not like that." Coco knew she'd really stepped in it.

"And you made decisions for me?"

"No, for us. I just needed someone to . . . Forget it. Forget I ever brought it up."

"No, you tell me. Why is our sex life a discussion point between you and CJ?"

"Honey, girls talk more about sex together than you'll ever know." She was calm now.

"But he's . . . Never mind. Okay, fine. I am willing to talk about our sex life," he relented.

"Thank you. That's all I'm asking."

"You're not going to try to pee on me or anything weird like that, are you?"

"Eww."

"Okay, I guess if that's what you feel like you need, then that's what we have to do. So where do we start?"

"Good question, I'm not sure because I don't know what we're into. Let's go to one of those feminist, professionally run sex shops, like Toys in Babeland, and look at things. See what jumps out."

"Okay, fine. If that's going to make you happy. Just as long as there's nothing, you know, weird." He still wore a perplexed look, but also one of relief. Considering Sam's blue state, Coco was relieved to see that he was at least game for some change. She didn't expect much discussion. She knew he wanted to do what he could to make her happy so she wouldn't belabor the point.

"I'm sorry, I have to call Rory."

"Go get 'em, tiger."

That night couldn't come soon enough for CJ. He needed to find out if Malcolm had any useful information for them or if he knew anything about the case at all. He had to tread lightly.

CJ showed up at Malcolm's apartment with a bottle of wine and some snacks from Citarella. He'd had an intern make a special trip between tapings; he wanted to have every advantage to get Malcolm to talk. After the usual pleasantries, CJ started to produce the conversation.

"You don't talk about work all that much, but I'm very curious about what you do. Do you mind?" He knew that a narcissist like Malcolm would enjoy talking about himself, especially because he vaguely remembered him referring to himself in the third person once or twice.

“Sure. What do you want to know?” Malcolm said.

“How do you become something as important as a mayor’s aide?” CJ was smooth. Of course he knew all this, but he had to play the naïf to draw Malcolm out.

“I worked with the press team on the mayor’s first campaign, in 2001. He saw how dedicated and hardworking I was, even more than the people who were getting paid.”

“You didn’t get paid?”

“Oh no, I was a volunteer. I needed it for my résumé, of course,” Malcolm said, as if CJ should know that. He was such a dick sometimes.

“Then, even though we lost,” Malcolm continued, “he offered me a job as a paralegal at his law firm. I took it, made myself invaluable, worked my ass off until he made me his campaign manager on his next run for office. And, naturally, that’s why we won.”

CJ tried to contain his amazement that this guy had the balls to take credit for the mayor’s win. But he sucked up and pressed on.

“And how is the mayor? You know . . . as a person?” CJ asked, as smooth as Oprah.

“Oh, he is such a vulgarian. He thinks Bach is something a terrier does,” Malcolm said, prompting CJ to wonder if he’d been schtupping Henny Youngman. “When I said I run his office, I meant it. I force-feed every bit of information to him; and sometimes I have to do it several times. The guy has a mind like an Etch-A-Sketch.”

“I take it you don’t like him much,” CJ said.

Malcolm thought for a second and drank a sip of wine. "It isn't about that. It's about whether he's the right man for the job and the man who can help me get to the next level. Get me to where I want to be. Don't get me wrong, I'd sell the fucker out on a moment's notice if I thought anything he was doing would get out and ruin *my* reputation. In this business all you have is your reputation, and as you well know—and experienced, sorry—I protect mine like it's Tiffany glass."

CJ knew this was his opening. Malcolm didn't care about the mayor, just about himself. Good narcissist, good boy.

"You may want to finish that glass of wine, because I'm guessing you'll want another. I have something to tell you," said CJ confidently, since now he had the upper hand.

"You're scaring me. What?" Malcolm said as he did what CJ suggested.

"You haven't met my friends yet, but we witnessed your boss kill someone on Halloween." CJ waited a second before he continued. He knew he had to let the thought sink in.

"*What?* No, no, c'mon, you're putting me on. No way is that possible. You have to be mistaken." Malcolm sounded sure of himself.

"It's true. We were at a party next door and went wandering around the property. We saw the whole thing, all four of us."

"There were four eyewitnesses to the mayor murdering someone? Wait, is this the—"

"Yes."

"But if this were true, why wouldn't you go to the police? Why wouldn't there be an investigation? You don't witness a murder and just ignore it," Malcolm said. He liked to win arguments. He thought he had with that point, so he sat back in his chair and folded his arms.

"We did go to the police. Of course we did. But Chief Bruno convinced us that what we saw was a prank," CJ said.

"Ah, well, there ya go." Malcolm was relieved.

"We don't believe for a second that it was a prank. Besides there being no reason to pull a prank like that since there was no intended audience, we have evidence. Trust me, it really happened," CJ assured him.

"Proof? What kind of proof?" Malcolm was curious again.

"First off, there was DNA on an envelope my friend received. Yours. It was a letter blackmailing her so she would never tell what she saw. We all received letters like this."

"An . . . envelope?" CJ could see Malcolm's mind working. "Holy shit. Are you—Is CJ short for Charlton Jeffre?"

"Yes."

"Oh, my god," Malcolm said as he dropped his head into his hands. "How much trouble am I in? Who else knows? I swear I didn't really think he'd *actually* killed someone. I thought he was just worried about the S and M stuff." CJ had played his cards correctly. Clearly, Malcolm really didn't give a shit about the mayor.

"Just the four of us . . . and Detective Rob Casey. But don't worry, he's on our side," CJ reassured him. "Oh, and possibly Saul from that 'Problem Saulving' TV show."

"Huh?"

"Never mind. As long as you cooperate, everything should be fine for you."

"Please believe me when I tell you that I had no idea what was in those envelopes. The mayor told me they were going to degenerates who were trying to threaten him. I typed up the letters for him. I thought he was being a bully to get some annoying people to shut up about a petty white-collar crime." Malcolm was certainly covering all his bases. "Part of doing my job well sometimes is not asking questions. I had no idea, I'm so sorry. Tell me what I can do to help," he pleaded, since now it was clear his own aspirations could be on the line.

CJ looked sympathetically at the wounded Malcolm. Inside, though, he was grinning like that cat that ate every canary in the pet shop.

Game. Set. Match.

SIXTEEN

The Gert Locker

Coco was excited about her shopping excursion with Olivia. Truth be told, she'd let her friendships go over the years. The more successful she became, the fewer friends she had. She resented the fact that her level of success seemed commensurate with a dearth of female companionship. Nothing had happened per se between her and her old friends, it was just that when you are a woman in a male-dominated business, you have to dedicate yourself to your work in a way men never have to. Often Coco would be the only woman at a table full of male buyers and decision makers, and she'd become a chameleon. If they expected a sultry seductress, she was not above using her feminine charms; if they were looking for one of the boys, she was always ready with a dirty story; when they would go out on a bender, she'd use whatever trick she could to make them think she could drink them under the table.

When you live in a world like that, you have to sacrifice something. It wasn't going to be her relationship with Sam, and it wasn't going to be the pups; so it was her female friendships, and in the long run she'd suffered for it. A woman without her girls is like a dress without Spanx. You don't *need* a pair of Spanx in order to wear *that* dress, but the support is everlasting, you feel much more secure, and you hold your head just a little higher knowing you have them.

Olivia suggested they shop in SoHo. Neither of them had been there for some time, but from what they could remember from their twenties, it was a place where fashion was eternally au courant. Certainly, it was the place to go if you were a person, like Olivia, who needed to step up her outfit game now that she was back in the dating pool.

What you wear while you shop is almost as important as what you buy when you shop. Since it was nearly wintertime in trendville, Coco wore a simple but chic, long black Burberry coat; because of where she was, she wore it as if it were armor. It wasn't until they walked into the Catherine Malandrino store that Olivia got a peek at what was lurking underneath Coco's cashmere. For some reason Coco was wearing the most dazzling Diane Von Furstenberg chiffon kimono dress with bell sleeves that Olivia had ever seen. It was as if she were at a movie premiere. Olivia stared at Coco as if she had just revealed a clown costume.

"My god, that's beautiful. But why on earth are you so dressed up?" Olivia asked.

"Honey, I used to live around here. What if I run into someone I know? I don't want them going back and telling the rest of the neighbors that I moved out of the city and let myself go. They're already judging me for moving to the burbs," she said.

"But you live in Greenwich. It's not like you moved to New Jersey!"

"You don't understand, sweetie," Coco explained. "When

you're out of the city, people who stayed here make you feel like you lost the war. Like you couldn't hack it, so you retreated. That isn't a white picket fence around your house, it's a white flag. It screams, I give up! Uncle! You win!"

"That isn't true!" Olivia was practically pleading, like a child who'd been told there is no Santa Claus. But then she thought about it and doubt crept in. "It's not true, is it?" she half whimpered.

"Yes, and it's our fault. We give our friends who didn't leave Manhattan power every time we see them. We always say that we would like to come back here one day, or we vow to get a pied-à-terre to keep a foot in New York's door. We just can't sever that tie. Manhattan is like that guy you just had really bad timing with, or maybe it's a codependent, unhealthy relationship. Either way, we miss it and just can't get over it," Coco said.

"Not me. I'm happy to be out of a big city. Besides, you can't be single in New York after the age of thirty. It's just not possible," Olivia concluded.

"Really? Why is that?" Coco asked.

"Well, it's an awkward age. The men your age want younger women, and the older men want still younger women. Let's face it, unless you're willing to be a trophy wife to some eighty-year-old, you've got no shot."

"Oh, honey," Coco said patronizingly, "that's pitiful."

As they left Malandrino, Coco noticed Alessi, the designer Italian housewares store, across the street.

"Oh, can we run in there for a sec? I have a cousin who just got engaged, and she's registered there," Coco said.

"Sure. What were you thinking about getting for her?" Olivia said.

"Dunno, a gravy boat perhaps? Something weddingy."

The girls walked in and began looking at some of the bizarre, novel items. They took turns picking up things they did not readily recognize and mouthing, "What's this?" across the aisles, which was repetitively met with a big shoulder shrug.

"This place is turning objects back into *objets*, isn't it?" Olivia said. "Look at these wacky spoons!"

"They aren't just spoons, dear. It's a *'collection.'* Aren't they just *precious*?" Coco said mockingly, sounding suspiciously like Lois Thomson.

Then she stopped a well-dressed salesperson midswagger. "Excuse me, where is your bridal registry?" she asked, and the woman pointed toward the back of the store. Coco went to a computer in the last aisle and looked up her cousin's name, then began poking around the vases. She carefully scrutinized the four the bride-to-be had chosen.

"Just pick one. What's the difference, she wants all of them," Olivia said.

"I'm trying to decide which one will look best smashing up against her wall," Coco replied.

"Why, is she hot-blooded?"

"Oh, that's an understatement. She once took out an entire stack of dishes over a guy she caught kissing another girl at a bar. Next day, turned out, it was some other guy she mistook for her boyfriend. She only likes volatile relationships. She does it for the makeup sex, you know. Says it's the hottest sex you'll ever have."

"Ah," Olivia replied.

Coco held the vase up to the light, thoroughly analyzing every inch and angle.

"I want to get her a vase, but I don't have the heart to tell her that it's a stupid gift since she'll never get flowers again," Coco said.

Olivia thought for a moment. "Yeah, that's true, isn't it?"

Coco continued. "And you know, everybody makes the biggest deal out of you when you are first engaged. But then as soon as the wedding is over, you're just some married lady nobody invites to parties anymore."

"Same thing happens when you have a baby. At the baby shower you're the hero having the child, but as soon as he turns one, you're just some annoying mother who can't keep her kid quiet on the bus," Olivia told her. "You get all those onesies that first year, then by age three you've got nothing for the kid to wear and no time to go out and buy it."

"I really don't know why Sam is so eager to get married," Coco said.

"Oh, you should do it! Marriage is great. You have that one person you'll be with the rest of your life! It's so romantic, you're a team, and it's the two of you against the world. All of that," Olivia said dreamily.

"But we *have* all of that. Why ruin things with legalities? And if CJ can't, why should I be able to?" Coco's voice trailed off as she put the vase back on the shelf and noticed other customers staring and pointing subtly just over her shoulder. SoHo was known for celebrities, so she was sure there was some major star standing behind her. It had just been in the papers that Beyoncé and Jay-Z were shopping in the area;

Leonardo DiCaprio sightings were almost de rigueur there. But when she turned around to see Graham Shore, she was doubly surprised. First, because she assumed he was with Bailey that day, and second because he was playing tonsil hockey with some hot little redhead in a micromini.

Coco grabbed Olivia by the arm. “Don’t look! . . . Wait . . . Okay now, look, look! Is that Graham Shore behind me?” she asked out of one side of her mouth, as if Graham Shore might read her lips if he were watching.

“Oh, my god!” Olivia said aloud. Coco put her hand over Olivia’s mouth as Graham Shore looked over at them and smiled politely.

“Shit,” Olivia said.

“Don’t worry, he doesn’t know us. He probably thinks we’re just fans who recognized him. He doesn’t know we know Bailey,” Coco said.

“Right, okay. But we do know Bailey, and we have to tell her,” Olivia insisted.

“No way. You’re on your own, little sister. I’m Switzerland as far as this situation is concerned,” Coco said.

“Bailey needs to know! She thinks this guy is the One. We have to tell her he *isn’t,*” Olivia hissed.

“They always shoot the messenger, don’t you know that? It’s never a good idea.”

“Let’s just call her, take her pulse on the whole Graham Shore exclusivity thing.”

“Good luck. I’ve been trying to call her for days. I keep getting no answer, and I’ve left, like, five messages. She hasn’t called back,” Coco said.

“Maybe she’s fallen off a ladder or is trapped under something heavy. We should go over there." Olivia was close to panic now.

"Well, if by 'trapped under something heavy' you mean Jack Black or Anthony Anderson, then I say we leave her be. Now c'mon, we still haven't bought you anything but a cookie. You're gonna need a lot more than that if you're going to start dating again. You'll at least need bigger pants."

Bailey's room looked like the scene of a terrible accident, and in a way it was. A heart had been totaled beyond repair. She lay under the covers, unable to speak or feel, just staring at the TV. Not watching any program in particular since she had the sound off, but the motion on-screen was a comfort, making it feel like she wasn't alone in her room. She knew she would get over this, she just didn't know when; and it wasn't going to be any time soon. That's the thing about breakups; you can get past them eventually—it's just that no one knows exactly when *eventually* is going to be. The last bad breakup Bailey had was in college, and here was that post-Damon misery all over again.

She rolled over to see that her cell phone message count was now at eleven. Not one call from Graham. Maybe it was better that way. She grabbed a pen and paper and decided to make a list. Her list making was epic, going far beyond the pedestrian to-do list. Bailey would make lists of men she still wanted to fuck, plus where and how; things never to say while doing an interview; the contents of a proper medicine cabinet; and things she would and wouldn't eat for breakfast. Today she decided to make a list of qualities in a potential mate that would never be okay with her. Yet all she could think of was

1. Must not be named Graham.
2. Must not have been in the movie *Hole Lotta Love* or *L.A. Existential.*
3. Must not smell like Frederic Malle musk (he did, it was scrumptious).
4. Must not ever climb Mt. McKinley (as if the mountain were responsible for his change of heart).

Maybe she wasn't ready for a list yet. She picked up her BlackBerry again. As she perused her call log, she saw that Saul King had called. She knew she had to call him back since she had this responsibility to CJ, Olivia, and Coco weighing on her. Somehow the doctored tape she was being blackmailed with didn't seem like such a big deal anymore. Not now. But she still had an obligation to the others. Maybe that could wait one more day. Then she saw one number she didn't recognize, so she decided to see who it was. Secretly, she hoped it was Graham calling from a pay phone or some other number saying he had made a mistake. But it wasn't Graham.

"Hey, pretty lady! It's Gert. Had so much fun with you in L.A., and I'm back in New York, and calling you as promised. Dinner Wednesday? Say yes. No, wait, you don't have to. I'm not giving you a choice. Call and let me know when and where we're meeting!"

Surprisingly, this perked Bailey right up, and she started wondering how she could get rid of her puffy eyes by then.

New list: things to do and people to see while getting over a bad breakup.

1. Have dinner with Gertie Whitmore.

When Detective Casey received the package from his colleague in the Justice Department at his mother's apartment, he knew exactly what he was going to see. The mayor's DNA was all over the envelopes he'd tested, as was the DNA of this Malcolm Marconi character, who was apparently now CJ's lover. That was a good angle, as far as Casey was concerned. He knew now that he had someone who might flip on Mayor Quilty if he were charged with a crime and wanted to plead out. Not only that but Bruno's fingerprints were all over the sex DVD that Bailey had been sent.

Casey had slyly obtained Bruno's coffee mug to acquire his actual fingerprints. He knew he had Bruno dead to rights, and Quilty too. All he had to do was build the murder case, figure out who the dead girl was . . . and find her body.

So, the case was progressing as well as could be expected. As far as the mayor and Bruno knew, there was no official investigation—the whole thing had been dismissed as a prank—and the four Sarah Palins appeared to have been hushed by the potentially damaging blackmail packages. Under the guise of taking time off to care for his mother during her chemotherapy sessions—though in fact she was faring quite well—Casey was conducting the investigation from home, making all his calls on a prepaid, untraceable cell phone. He left nothing to chance. He was immensely satisfied for the first time since he had begun working in Greenwich. Nothing pleased him more than being able to work a big case.

All that was bothering the detective was something he could do nothing about. While the investigation was in full force, he couldn't be seen talking to any of the four witnesses, though he desperately wanted to see Olivia. He simply couldn't get his mind off her, and couldn't shake the memory of her hand touching his arm, or her lips awkwardly brushing his.

Bailey was excited to see Gertie again. She liked that when they talked she had to be sharp, clever, and the best version of herself she could be. She suggested they meet at Gramercy Park. Bailey got there first; Gertie was twenty minutes late.

"It's always the person who lives the closest who keeps you waiting the longest, right? I am *so* sorry!" Gertie said as she walked toward a very cold Bailey, who for some reason was not angry. She was happy to be out in the cold night air with such a big star, and even though Gertie was becoming her friend, she felt awestruck when she was with her. Bailey wasn't like that around celebrities ordinarily. She didn't know why she felt the way she did now.

"That's perfectly okay. Welcome back to New York," Bailey said as she kissed her hello and handed her a little gift she'd picked up at the Mario Badescu spa. She'd seen Gertie's picture on their wall last time she was there for a facial.

"Oh, are you the welcoming committee? I didn't realize. Thank you, sweetie."

"Yes, we had a vote, and I was elected. I was going to

run for a second year, but we have term limits on that sort of thing."

"Repeal them! You are *quite* welcoming," Gertie joked.

"Where would you like to eat?" Bailey asked.

"I made us a reservation at Union Square Cafe, I hope that's all right. Their winter menu is the best, and they get all their locally grown greens from the farmers' market, right across the street in Union Square," Gertie said. "I love the banana tart with the macadamia brittle."

"For dinner?"

"When you are a grown-up, you can have dessert for dinner," Gertie said.

They laughed.

As they walked toward Union Square, they noticed a billboard with a larger-than-life image of Gertie's face promoting a new movie.

"My nose looks so wide. Is it that wide?" she said as she touched her nose.

"Well, from here it looks to be about eight feet. I dunno. Do you consider that wide?" Bailey said.

"God, it's so humiliating that they force you to see yourself that big. Even with retouching, nobody's self-worth is that good."

"It just takes some getting used to," Bailey replied. "For example, I have a fifty-foot billboard of myself at my house. I'm pretty okay with it now."

Gertie laughed.

"Sorry. I haven't seen that movie yet," Bailey said.

"It's okay, nobody has," Gertie joked.

"Well then, I guess dinner is on me," Bailey said as she

opened the door to the restaurant and stepped aside like a gentleman, beckoning for Gertie to pass through first.

"Don't be afraid of how much I eat, Hollywood," Bailey joked.

"I'm not afraid of anything." Gertie looked her square in the eye, making Bailey momentarily self-conscious. Bailey shivered slightly as the open door sucked the cold air in behind them.

After an amazing dinner—including the banana tart—Gertie suggested they go to Mercury Lounge to hear a friend's band play. Mercury Lounge was the record label promoters' favorite venue to bring their nascent bands; in fact, it was traditionally known to be a good-luck charm. Bands would perform there just before they broke big. Everyone from the Strokes to the Killers to Lady Gaga played there right before they went global. Tonight it was a new band called Lather, Rinse, Repeat, who, as friends of Gertie Whitmore, were probably going to be huge.

Bailey loved that Gertie seemed to know good music, so she was willing to forget the fact that Mercury Lounge held some bad memories.

"Oh, god," Bailey said as the cab crossed Houston Street and deposited them on the corner of Essex. "Last time I was here I had a pretty ugly breakup. Haven't been back since."

"Oh shit, are you going to be okay?"

"Nah, it's cool. It was ages ago. Christina set me up with Adam Duritz. You know, the Counting Crows guy with the Sideshow Bob hair?"

Gertie cracked up.

"The whole thing was a disaster from the very beginning.

He was working his way through Hollywood." *As was I,* Bailey thought to herself. "And, well, he forgot that he'd invited another girlfriend that night. But I was the one he kept off to the side, and he tried to play it cool all night, running back and forth between us."

"What a dick. What did you do?"

"Yeah. Well, suffice it to say that after a few shots of Maker's things turned pretty ugly."

"Ooh! Maker's. Love it." Gertie grinned.

"No way. Not tonight . . . Let's make it tequila."

Tequila it was, and another wild night at the Mercury it was. Gertie moved right up to the front of the stage and began dancing with Bailey almost impulsively. Since the club didn't have a backstage area, everyone seeing the band knew that Gertie Whitmore was there. But in case they didn't, halfway through the second set, her drummer friend Lance called her up onstage during the song that was going to be their hit. Gertie danced and sang along and was introduced to the swaying crowd as they went wild. If Gertie was there, it was the place to be—her presence reaffirmed everyone's confidence in their social choices that night. But what they didn't expect was what happened when Gertie got off the stage. Truth be told, Bailey didn't expect it either. Gertie, caught up in the moment, leapt off the stage—practically knocking Bailey over—leaned in, and planted a kiss firmly on her mouth. The fact that it didn't make the papers the next day, or YouTube for that matter, was astonishing. But the Lower East Side wasn't the Meatpacking District, and down there people were usually cool about that sort of thing.

Gertie and Bailey had a great night. Bailey couldn't tell if they were two girls caught in a moment, hanging out starting a wonderful friendship, or if they were on some kind of date. All she knew was that she was having a blast. The one thing the girls did agree upon was that they were both sick of all of their relationships ending in these not so private, hideous breakups. So maybe it was time to just focus on an exciting, new friendship.

SEVENTEEN

As Far as the Gay Crow Flies

Since the beginning of the whole fiasco, Olivia had remained completely dedicated to her yoga practice, not missing a day, and sometimes going in the evening as well as to the 8:30 A.M. class. As a practicing yogini, she really enjoyed having dharma buddies—yoga was not only easier with friends but so much more fulfilling and enjoyable. Olivia sent out an e-mail to everyone insisting they come to 8:30 yoga Saturday morning. She said, "No excuses, no regrets. Just be there," and one by one she got her responses.

8:30?? Fuck you. I'll be there.—CJ

What a great idea! My karma runneth over.—Coco

C U Saturday—B

On Saturday, Olivia got there by 8:00, excited to see her friends. She was bright-eyed, energetic, and waiting by the front desk, as if she were the one hosting yoga that morning. Her hair was in a perfect ponytail, and she was wearing the new yoga clothes that she'd bought in SoHo with Coco.

"My, don't *you* look like you are ready to take on the world? Or at least a really good warrior pose," CJ said as he walked in and kissed Olivia hello.

"Thanks! Oh, here comes Coco," she said.

"Holy crap, it's freezing out there. What happened to global warming?" Coco said as she took off her ski gloves to rummage around her bag for her yoga card. "Anyone hear from Bailey?"

"She e-mailed me back saying she would be here today, but that's about it. You guys?" Olivia said.

"Nope," CJ and Coco said, almost in unison.

Coco disappeared into the dressing room.

"Oh, my god, did Coco tell you what we saw in SoHo the other day? Or rather, *who* we saw and what he was doing?" Olivia asked.

"Yeah, she called me that night. So, are you going to tell Bailey?"

"I haven't decided yet. I thought I would wait to see how things were going."

"I wouldn't tell her if I were you. They always shoot the messenger."

"So I've heard."

Just then Bailey bounced in. She was obviously happy—no, *ecstatic*.

"Hey, everyone!" she said as she fervently kissed each one of them, including Coco, who'd reappeared out of the dressing room. "It's a gorgeous day, isn't it?"

"Um . . . I guess," Coco said. "It's kinda cold."

"Nonsense, it's exhilarating. C'mon, let's go salute the sun!" Bailey said as she skipped into the yoga room.

"Well, I guess everything is okay," said Coco, eyebrows arched, to Olivia and CJ as they followed Bailey, yoga mats in tow.

After yoga the foursome decided to do brunch again, but this time at the less formal, less white diner across the street. Hot dish was the main course. Since Coco was never all that hungry after exercise, she was always more engrossed in the gossip. Today she was mostly interested in Bailey's gossip—she was really curious to know where things were with Graham, considering what she'd seen—but CJ got started by holding up his pinkie.

"See this?" He waved it around. "This is where I have Malcolm. Completely wrapped around this little finger."

Coco grabbed it. "It's kinda bony, are you sure it will hold him? He's pretty big," she joked.

"What do you mean?" Olivia asked. "Why is he wrapped around your finger. What happened?"

"I told him what his boss did, what we saw, and that we had his DNA on those envelopes. He caved immediately and is going to give us access to anything we need. I'm going to put Detective Casey in touch with him. Let him take over from here. Isn't that what he wants anyway, Olivia?" CJ asked.

"Yep. He doesn't want us involved. My adventure gene was thrown out with my placenta. I just want this taken care of," Olivia said. "Rob told me on the phone that as long as we don't appear to be talking to any law enforcement, it'll look like we're complying with the blackmail and we should be safe for now."

"That reminds me, Saul King called. He has something for us on that Blackbeard character, but I haven't had a chance to catch up with him," Bailey said.

"Saul has more information? Why didn't you tell us? When did he call?" Coco asked.

"I don't know, Monday?" Bailey said.

"*Monday?* It's Saturday. Why haven't you called him back yet?" CJ asked.

"Well . . ." Bailey was being coy, almost at full blush. "I have been a bit preoccupied this week. Every night, as a matter of fact."

"Didn't you see Saul at work this week?" Olivia asked.

"Well, I didn't go in on Monday or Tuesday, then he was out on assignment for two days, and yesterday I took a very, very long lunch." She giggled.

"Okay, spill it. What's going on with you and Graham? Did you elope? Why all the secrecy?" Coco said.

"I'm glad you guys are sitting, because you would not believe the week I had. Graham broke up with me on Sunday. I crawled into bed right after and didn't get out until Tuesday afternoon, which is good because I was planning on taking the week, but midweek my life changed," Bailey told them.

"You and Graham broke up? *Why?*" Olivia asked.

"Get this, he had an 'epiphany' on the mountain. I'm not the one for him. That's what he said. It's ridiculous, I know," Bailey said, almost laughing at the absurdity.

"I'm so sorry, sweetie," said Coco as she reached out to touch Bailey's arm.

"Thanks," Bailey said.

"I see he doesn't just play a prick in the movies," CJ said.

"No, I'm not gonna do that. I don't want to be with someone who doesn't want me," Bailey said.

"You're being awfully strong about this. I mean, the guy just broke your heart!" Olivia exclaimed.

"I'm okay. I promise. Well, I wasn't, but now I am," Bailey said.

"You actually sound like you're doing good. What gives, girl?" CJ asked.

"It's the strangest thing. When it happened I was devastated. I really thought I would be comatose for weeks, but two days later someone else came into my life unexpectedly. The best part is, you know that incredible feeling when you are first falling for someone? I have been feeling that, and it trumped my breakup sadness. Between the breakup and this new person, I am one raw emotional nerve these days, though, and completely inappropriate too. I bawled my eyes out yesterday when the Starbucks guy put regular milk in my latte instead of soy. I've become a total nut job," Bailey said.

"Okay, so when do we meet this amazing new guy?" CJ demanded.

"Well, that's the surprising thing . . ." Bailey hesitated and was interrupted by an overly caffeinated Coco.

"Surprising? Why surprising?" Coco asked suspiciously.

"Because it happened so fast, I'm sure," Olivia said.

"Well, I guess it's the timing too, but the bigger surprise is that she's a she," Bailey said and then waited for a reaction.

They all just sat there and stared at her.

CJ spoke first. "Let me get this straight. You no longer are?"

"One minute you're moving in with Graham Shore and the next you're a lesbian?" Coco said sarcastically. "Oh, honey, you must be very upset. This is all a little hasty."

"I'm not a lesbian. Nothing's actually happened. Gertie and I have just been spending an incredible amount of time together. We have this really intense connection. Something I've never experienced before," Bailey said.

"A girl named Gertie? Like Gertie Whitmore?" Olivia said.

"*Exactly* like Gertie Whitmore," Bailey said as she gave them a knowing look.

"Oh, my god, you're fucking Gertie Whitmore?" CJ exclaimed.

"*Shh!* I'm not fucking her! Nothing's really happened. I'm just . . . attracted to her," Bailey said, smiling.

"Attracted?" Coco asked.

"Yeah, it's a bit confusing for me," Bailey said as she looked at the table of gaping mouths.

Olivia turned to CJ. "So what is she?"

"I'm gay, so I'm the expert?" CJ said.

"Well, yeah. More than anyone at this table at least," Olivia replied.

"Slow down, you guys. She isn't a lesbian and neither am I. We're just exploring a friendship right now," Bailey said.

"Okay, sure. Well, I can tell you this," CJ said. "Female sexuality is fluid. They call it 'flexisexual' these days. So it isn't so unusual for a woman to all of a sudden be attracted to another woman. It's why you'll see a woman who has been with a man for years up and leave him for another woman," CJ said.

"I'm not rushing into anything. It just feels right for now," Bailey said. "We've been inseparable all week, and she is just amazing. She is really involved with charity work. She's been to Kenya twice with the World Food Programme. I'm in awe. I can't wait for you guys to meet her."

"You sound smitten," Coco said. "Good for you, sweetheart. Love's love. It's all good."

"So, you and Gertie Whitmore." Olivia was still in shock.

"Never mind all that. I think our bigger issue now is getting Malcolm and Saul to talk to Detective Casey and . . . Oh, god, did you tell Gertie Whitmore?" Coco asked.

"No way!"

"Okay, good, let's keep it on a need-to-know basis. You have to call Saul," Coco said to Bailey.

"I'm seeing him Monday."

"Not good enough. Call him now," Coco insisted.

"Yes, you must. I'm going to get a Nelly again, and it's going to *ruin* my weekend! I have to know what he needs to tell you. Please, do it for the children," CJ said.

"What children?" Coco asked. "What the hell are you talking about?"

"I don't know. People are always doing things for 'the children.' She's a Hollywood type, so maybe it will motivate her."

"Stop it. You two are pathetic. I'll call him, sheesh," Bailey conceded.

Normally Bailey wouldn't bother a co-worker on a Saturday, but Saul was always on the job. He told her that after some digging and calling in a few favors, he had a cell phone number that he believed belonged to Blackbeard, the one at the center of the Chief Bruno mystery. He had learned that someone had ratted out almost the entire Kennebunkport government, and everyone went to jail, everyone, including, apparently, Chief Bruno. But Blackbeard was still out there, and the mayor must've known about it. Saul was sure this was what the mayor had over the chief of police. He suspected, in fact, that the mayor was Blackbeard. Or maybe Bruno was. He was still working on it.

As Bailey listened to Saul tell her this story, the other three could see on her face that it was juicy. When Bailey got off the phone, she explained that it might be the mayor, and not Bruno, who was Blackbeard. Knowing that they were getting similar information from two sources, they realized they might be close to an answer. They felt a bit of hope that they had a shot at justice for whoever that poor girl rolled up in the rug was. They agreed to call Detective Casey immediately to tell him what Bailey had just learned. Casey, paranoid their phones could have been bugged, insisted they meet him in a parking lot, the municipal lot behind Tiffany's off Lewis Street. Of course they knew where that was.

Olivia, who hadn't really spoken since she heard the news about Bailey's impending lesbianism, perked up when she heard they would be meeting with Rob.

Coco pulled her aside on the way out. "Are you okay, sweetie?" she asked.

"I've never had a gay friend before, and now I have one of each," Olivia said.

"This isn't a state quarter collection, hon."

When they arrived at Detective Casey's meeting spot, he was dressed as he had been at the party: bad suit jacket, terrible shoes, but very cool Wayfarers.

"Well, at least his shades are trendy," CJ said snidely. "But I wonder if he's just had the same pair since the eighties. What goes around comes around . . . except the rest of that getup."

"Stop it, you snot," Bailey scolded. Fortunately, she was the only one who'd heard.

When Olivia saw him again, she thought that he was incredibly handsome, maybe even more than the last time she saw him, and she bolted out of CJ's car the moment it stopped.

"Way to keep your cool, girl," CJ yelled after her.

But Olivia just ignored him and ran up to Rob, unsure if she should kiss him hello or shake his hand. She may not have known how to act, but she knew she was extremely happy to see him. Rob leaned in for an it's-in-front-of-an-audience-but-I-like-you hug-kiss combo.

"I could never get away with that," Coco said, referring to Olivia's blatant tail wagging.

"Me neither, it reads too desperate from me," Bailey said.

"She can pull it off," CJ replied. "She has that small-fragile-kitten thing going on."

When Coco caught up to Detective Casey and his retro sunglasses, she had a vision that it was 1950 and Olivia was a bobby-soxer, ogling the dreamboat captain of the football team. She suspected he had the same vision as she noticed him trying not to be distracted by Olivia's gaze, yet leaning in slightly to smell her perfume.

"Tell me what you've got." Casey directed this statement to Bailey, staring at Olivia all the while.

Bailey told the detective everything she had heard from Saul, then handed him a piece of paper with the mysterious Blackbeard's alleged cell phone number scrawled on it.

"What are you going to do with it?" Coco wanted to know.

"I'm not sure yet. We'll see what happens," Casey said, as noncommittal as a detective should be to interlopers.

"We have some more information for you. It's about those envelopes," CJ said.

"Great, let's hear it," Detective Casey said in his best FBI voice.

"You told Olivia that the DNA on the seals of those envelopes belonged to Malcolm Marconi, is that right?" CJ said.

"Yes."

"And the way you matched it to him was that all government employees have their DNA, fingerprints, all of that crap on file, is that right?" CJ said.

"Yes."

"I just want to make sure that's how you know, and that Malcolm doesn't have a criminal record," CJ said.

"Even if he did, I couldn't disclose that information to you," Detective Casey said.

"Don't worry, I'll ask him myself," CJ replied insolently.

"So, I take it you know him? Did you ask him about the envelopes?"

"I did, and he said that he had no idea why the mayor wanted him to gather that information on all of us. He was told that *we* were the corrupt ones and that it was some great heroic gesture on the mayor's part. But I set him straight."

"He knows the mayor was trying to blackmail you? How do you know he's loyal to you?"

"Oh, I know, trust me. I'm a thousand percent certain he's on our side. Here," CJ said as he reached into his man purse and handed Detective Casey copies of all of the original documents the mayor had made as well as the ones he'd doctored.

"Impressive," said Casey as he looked over the documents, which were encased in plastic. "Should I ask what you had to do to get these, or should I just be happy you did?"

"The second one," CJ said, giving a knowing smile. "Unless you want a demonstration, hot stuff."

"Some other time."

"Hang on a second. Are all of our papers in there? Mine too?" Coco asked.

"Yeah, this is everything," CJ said.

"You didn't tell me you got *my* stuff too," Coco said as she ripped the documents from Detective Casey's hands and furiously thumbed through them until she got to the ones with Sam's name on them.

"That asshole!" she screamed.

"Who's the asshole? What's wrong?" CJ asked.

"These *were* totally changed. I knew Sam had no idea that his partners were doing any of this. That asshole changed all of the dates. Here's the original!" she said as she held a piece of paper two inches from CJ's face.

He backed up a bit. "Yeah, that's what forgery is. It's a crime, Mary. So's blackmail. This is just another to add to the list."

"I just wanted to see for myself. I'm going to have to tell Sam. He thinks I don't believe him. I mean, I did believe him . . . but on some level I wasn't exactly sure. Oh, god. I feel horrible," Coco said.

"Oh no, no. You can't tell him yet! The fewer people who know, the better. Give it another day or two. Please." Detective Casey was practically begging.

"Okay, okay." Coco understood his point. A day or two wouldn't matter in the long run as far as Sam was concerned. The detective needed to crack this.

"So is that it?" Bailey said.

"That's all we have for now," Casey said. "Leave the rest up to me. Olivia, I think you and I need to take these to your attorney so you can get your mother's case against you dismissed."

"Thank you, Rob." Olivia's big saucer eyes were moist as she looked up at him. "You saved my house. I don't know what I would have done without you."

"And your hideously purple room." He smiled.

"Yes, and my hideous purple room." She laughed.

CJ, Bailey, and Coco looked at each other quizzically.

As they said their good-byes and turned to walk away, Olivia felt sad that this meet-up with Rob had been socially fruitless, especially after she'd bought new date clothes and everything. But just as she had lost hope, she felt a hand grab her arm. It was Rob. He leaned in and whispered in her ear, "How about dinner at Lupe's tomorrow night?"

"I have the perfect dress," she replied in her most demure tone.

"That's a yes, right?" he said.

"Yes, it's a yes," Olivia said as she was whisked away by CJ.

"Pick you up at eight," Rob shouted to the back of her head. She waved.

"Honey, you really have to play it cooler than that." CJ sighed.

"Why? If he's my soul mate, it will just work out. The right guy is the right guy, and you can't screw that up," Olivia said.

"Oh, honey, what turnip truck did you fall off of? Back in the eighties I would have six soul mates a night, girl. It's about who wants to be honest and stick it out, who wants to be around long enough. Take it from me, it's who you can learn to disagree with, argue with, go through it all with. Life is full of bullshit. Your partner in life isn't perfect. You take the good with the bad, sweetie, and that's my advice as far as the gay crow flies," CJ chirped.

"Coco, what do you think?" Olivia asked her.

"You wanna know what I think?" Bailey interrupted. "Love is like an amusement park. You can get on either the teacup ride or the megamonster roller coaster. But if you choose the coaster, you'd better hold on for dear life, because if you fall off there's a whole line of women behind you waiting to get on."

"Uh, thanks. Coco?" Olivia said.

"Well," she began, "the way I see it, relationships aren't just about always having a date on a Saturday night, getting laid, and not being alone on your birthday. They're also about waiting for the person to get ready when you're in a hurry;

doing the dishes when he's cooked; dealing with his friends or your parents; having a fat day or a bad hair day, or just waiting for you to pick the right tomato at the supermarket. It's more than just the good stuff at the beginning. You have to be ready for all of it."

"I think I am," Olivia said.

"Just be sure *he* is," Bailey said.

"My best piece of advice? Take out your wisdom teeth and your back molars. Make room, girl," CJ said.

"Jesus. You are *vile*," Coco said as she smacked him.

EIGHTEEN

And the Dogs Came Running

Coco came home with a peace offering. She knew that her sex talk with Sam was a fantastic start, particularly since he had agreed to go along with whatever she wanted to try. But she also knew that she needed to keep talking, to open up more; she worried that keeping him in the dark about what the four friends saw on Halloween night would only keep them at a stalemate, yet she had promised Detective Casey that mouths would stay closed for now. So she went with what worked with dissatisfied customers when shipments were late: bribery.

Into the house she waltzed, overflowing with big bags of McDonald's. For her, nothing fast was really food, but it was Sam's favorite indulgence; she knew it was what he secretly ate while she was away on business trips. He did a shitty job at hiding the wrappers. So she showed up with tons of the stuff. That's how bribery works.

"Hello, it's your McWife. I'm McHome!" she chirped.

Sam walked in from the living room, where he'd been fully engrossed in a repeat of the World Series of Poker finals. He didn't really play poker, except for occasionally on his iPad, but for some reason he enjoyed watching it. It was the ultimate in no risk gambling.

"I wasn't expecting you. What's all this?" Sam said.

"Now don't play coy with me, I know that you, Mayor McCheese, Grimace, and the McNugget Buddies have regular orgies while I'm away," she joked.

"Thank you. That's a nice treat, but I feel totally outed now. How can I enjoy it anymore if it's not a secret?" Sam asked as he dug into the fries.

"And that's not all. Say hello to a couple of our mutual friends, Monsieurs Ben et Jerry," she said as she held up Chunky Monkey and Chubby Hubby.

"Is this your passive-aggressive way of telling me I'm fat?" he scoffed.

"No, it's not, silly boy," she said as she ruffled his hair. "It's just my way of saying I'm sorry for being such a McShit lately. And to tell you that I really do love you."

"So you're finally going to tell me what's been going on?"

"Well, I can't. Really. Give me a few more days."

"A few more days? What is so secretive and so important that you can't share it with me!" Sam was starting to get upset.

"I'm sorry," she said.

"Of course you are. You always are. But that's not good enough. If we're to be husband and wife, you're going to have to start trusting me with everything; otherwise this is never going to work." Sam was finally losing his cool, double cheeseburger or no. "So are you going to tell me or not?"

"Not. I'm really sor——" she started to say it again.

"Don't! Just don't say another fucking word. Good-bye,

Coco. You call me when you figure this out, and maybe, just maybe, I'll be there. But I doubt it," he said as he stormed out the door sans Big Mac.

Coco sat there for a second in disbelief. Had Sam really just walked out? What the hell was she doing? In an effort to protect him she'd sacrificed him. It no longer made sense. She knew who was to blame. Not her, not Sam. No, it was that goddamned mayor—Quilty, not McCheese. She picked up the container of fries and threw them against the wall. The dogs, who'd been cowering from all the yelling, were elated. They hadn't had McDonald's in a while either.

Later, as Coco drove to Olivia's house, it all began to sink in. She was almost in hysterics by the time she got to the door. Neither Detective Casey—who'd stopped by—nor Olivia could console her.

"Just a few months ago everything was great, all was right in my world. My career was going well, my life with Sam was good, and our relationship was stable. Sure, his business had collapsed, but I was making more than enough money; we were going to be just fine. Yet now, ever since that stupid goddamned party . . . I wasn't even going to go. Rory insisted because of that scarf woman and the rumors of my death. Argh!" She was exasperated.

"Have a tissue," Olivia said as she held out a box of Puffs.

Coco hardly noticed but took one anyway. "No, no, I didn't ask to witness a murder. Why did he have to do that, the asshole? Why did we have to go over there? This was all inflicted on *us*. He's the one who killed someone, and we're paying the price. Besides that poor girl, of course. Damn it! I can't, I can't . . . I simply *cannot* do this anymore. He's going to pay for what he did. I'm not sitting idly by waiting for you to gather evidence against him," she said as she pushed Detective Casey in the chest, sending him back a foot or two.

"Please, Coco. Please calm down. I'm incredibly close to wrapping this up. *Please.* I need your patience," he begged.

"No! You've ruined my life. *He* ruined my life," Coco sobbed as she pointed toward the mayor's house. "If you're just going to sit there, I'm going to do something about it. No more patience. I'm done!" She turned and headed for the door.

NINETEEN

Dial BDS-M for Murder

Coco wasn't usually this hotheaded, but her anger propelled her toward the mayor's house to confront him. When you grow up in the tough streets of Brooklyn, you acquire a certain amount of fearlessness and a willingness to fight that come out at both opportune and inopportune times. She wasn't sure which one this was. Her street sense had kicked in, overriding her normal calm and rationalizing self; she no longer cared about consequences. Every once in a while, a woman just can't take it anymore.

Grabbing her keys, bag, and coat in one fell swoop, she stormed out the door. Olivia and Detective Casey knew that if Coco challenged this devious creep on her own she would be no match for him; but her blind rage couldn't be reasoned with. Rob turned to Olivia and said, "Let's go."

They ran after Coco, but she was already speeding out the driveway.

"Let's take my car," he said. "Get in."

Olivia felt the tension building within her. She knew that this was one of those times her echolalia would betray and embarrass her; she could feel it coming. Even though Rob seemed understanding about it, she prayed she didn't hear any loud noise that would suddenly make this moment about her.

Coco careened mindlessly down the mayor's block. Even though she was propelled by rage, a pang of fear hit her as she realized she had not been at the mayor's house since the night it all went down. What a cliché that it would end where it began. That part seemed, irrelevantly, to jump out at her. When she got to the guard booth, she saw nobody was there. "Is there anybody ever in there or is it just for show, like this whole fucking façade?" she wondered aloud. No time to be philosophical. She had to put the little big man in his place. How dare he screw with their lives? How dare he ruin her relationship? Sam had left because of *him*, not because of her. For Coco, rage was the order of the day.

When she got to the door, she didn't just bang on it, she practically beat it up. "Open this goddamned door, motherfucker!" she screamed.

Then she began a diatribe in full Brooklynese, with versions of "fuckhead" and "scumbag" creatively thrown into the mix until it occurred to her that no one was likely to open the door to a raving lunatic. Wouldn't you just hide inside and pretend you weren't home? Or call the police? She decided on another approach and politely rang the doorbell once. And it felt so good she pressed it again and again and realized that she was too angry to stop. In the midst of her realizing how much she was enjoying pressing the button and that it was relieving her hostility, the mayor himself opened the door.

In the meantime, Olivia and Detective Casey caught up to Coco and were right behind her by the time the door opened.

"Ah, Detective Casey, little Olivia from down the street, and . . . well, I don't think we've had the pleasure, who are you?" the mayor said, reaching his hand out to Coco. He knew who she was, the faker, they'd met in Philly. She still refused to shake his hand.

Olivia stared at her neighbor the mayor and didn't speak a word, her lips firmly clenched.

The mayor continued. "I think we have a little misunderstanding. I guess you'd better come in so we can clear things up." He led them inside. "I'm just as concerned about all of this as you are, so I was only trying to look out for all the parties involved, but I see we'll need to resolve this face-to-face."

"Damn right. You ruined my life, you blackmailing piece of shit!" Coco wasn't buying his politician act; she'd come for some satisfaction and wasn't leaving without it. Didn't that idiot realize she was standing there with a police officer?

The mayor led them into his living room. *Either,* Coco thought, *this is the epitome of chutzpah or we're about to be killed.* He was taking them, literally, to the scene of the crime.

"I have to apologize," the mayor began. Olivia wondered if he was about to confess to the envelopes, the murder, or something else they didn't know about. Her mind raced, and it took her out of the moment. When she rejoined the conversation, he was saying something about Malcolm.

"I'm sorry, what about Malcolm?" Olivia asked.

"Well, you know how those queers are, especially the

little ones. Napoleon complex, you know," he almost stage-whispered. "When they don't get what they want, they'll stop at nothing. I have discovered that he's been trying to blackmail you and your two friends. This is a very grave problem, and I'm so glad I uncovered it before he could do anything to harm you. I didn't realize I was working with such a dangerous psychopath. My attorney is drawing up a settlement so he will be discharged. My office will support you fully if you wish to press charges."

"Charges? Against Malcolm?" Olivia was dumbfounded. "Why would we do that?" The mayor had certainly made the most unexpected play possible.

"Is this guy for real?" Coco asked. Then, turning to her cohorts she asked, "Is he joking?"

"No, no. You shouldn't be shocked. I am happy to be of service. After all, I'm a servant of the people. Whatever you decide to do moving forward, I will be at your disposal," the mayor said.

"Yes, that's very kind of you to be so understanding and helpful," Detective Casey said firmly. He clearly wanted the mayor to keep talking.

"Detective, I understand Malcolm's DNA was on those envelopes, so I realize it should be rather easy to prosecute. I was a district attorney after all," the mayor said.

"Will you excuse me one second?" Detective Casey asked, holding up his cell phone, even though nobody had heard it ring. "I need to take this," he pretended.

"By all means," the mayor said graciously.

"I'll watch him," Coco said to Casey, her eyes never leaving Quilty.

Detective Casey ducked into the next room to call CJ, who was with Malcolm and Bailey on their way to the police station. Casey had called them from the car to let them know what was going on at Chez Quilty.

"Question. How would the mayor know Malcolm's DNA was on those envelopes?" Detective Casey asked CJ.

Hold on, let me ask him. Detective Casey heard muffled voices and CJ speaking to someone, presumably Malcolm.

CJ came back in a matter of seconds. "He says the mayor insisted he use old envelopes and old stamps without the self-adhesive, and now that he thinks about it, the mayor refused to touch them. Sounds like he was trying to frame him from the beginning."

"Gotcha, okay, gotta run. See you over there in a bit."

"Detective? Before you go, I would like an acknowledgment that I did not make a dirty joke about Malcolm licking things," CJ said proudly.

"Now's not the time, CJ. But duly noted," Casey said as he folded his phone shut and went back into the living room.

"Everything okay, Detective?" the mayor asked.

"Peachy," Casey replied and then said, "So let me ask you, how did you know that we found Malcolm's DNA?"

"I am just assuming. I mean he did have to lick those stamps and envelopes. That's why it's nice to have someone who does all that stuff for you, you know?" The mayor chuckled.

"You think this is funny?" Coco said.

"Not at all! All I am saying is that Malcolm committed several crimes and blackmailed you to keep his crimes hidden. Those faggots have no morals," the mayor said sternly.

"I'm not going to sit here and listen to this. *You* committed a murder. You! Not Malcolm, we all saw *you*," Coco said, pointing to Olivia and around the room as if they were all there. "We saw you from that window," she said, motioning furiously.

"You must be mistaken. I lent the house that weekend to Malcolm. I was away! You couldn't have seen me," the mayor insisted.

"No, I'm pretty sure it was you," Coco maintained. She said "pretty sure" facetiously, but it was lost on Quilty.

"Pretty sure? That wouldn't hold up in court, young lady." The mayor laughed again, looking suddenly relieved. "Besides, Malcolm confessed the whole thing to me. He said he had a mask on. He said that's why he didn't think he'd get caught. It was Halloween after all. Well, I guess he was wrong."

That was the last straw. Olivia couldn't take it anymore. The laughing, the lying, the condescension, the homophobia, and the way he was trying to manipulate her, making her feel as if her own eyes had betrayed her. This was the same crap her ex always pulled, making her, the victim, feel like she was responsible for her own misery. And it was exactly what her mother had tried to do—both to her and to her father. The mayor was aware of her mommy issues, and he was taking advantage of them. Damn him.

Olivia felt *that thing* inside her about to burst, and she didn't know what it would do. She just knew she couldn't stop it.

Coco looked over at Olivia, and her eyes widened. She could see that her friend was transforming. Into what, Coco didn't know. A fire emerged from somewhere deep inside Olivia, the glint in her eye telling Coco she was about to witness something they had never seen before. Then, it seemed as if Olivia's insides burst and the venom came spewing out.

"You little worm! No, you are lower than a worm. You are a lowly, lifeless piece of shit. I wouldn't spit on you if you were on fire! You disgusting scourge of humanity!" She was possessed and screaming at the mayor, mere inches from his face, like a cute, prim, totally insane drill sergeant. *"You insignificant, awful little man, you pathetic creature. You disgust me. You disgust everyone. How ashamed your parents must be of you. How do you look at yourself in the mirror? How can you possibly sleep? How can you live with yourself? You represent everything that's wrong with this country and with our society. I'm so glad I'm not you, so thankful I'm not you. What you need is to be put over someone's knee and spanked like the insolent, bratty, awful child that you are!"* Olivia's voice was ferocious and dripping with loathing.

There was a moment of silence as her explosion was absorbed. Detective Casey stood stunned, witnessing the second meltdown of the day. And as Olivia went on her rant, Coco watched the mayor. She couldn't take her eyes off him actually. Coco saw the mayor transform. He, who had known sweet little Olivia from around the neighborhood since she was a child, was in shock. Something had clicked in *him* this time. His head dropped, his body almost collapsed within itself, his shoulders caving in, his face suddenly sallow. It was like the evil Mr. Hyde crumpling into the meager, weak-willed Dr. Jekyll. He whimpered almost imperceptibly, like a scolded child who had disappointed his mother. His lip quivered, and then, as if out of nowhere, the mayor, who only moments before had been arrogant, overconfident, and smug, dropped to his knees.

"Oh, god, oh, god, you're right. I'm so sorry. I'm worthless and repulsive. I'm so sorry I've let everyone down," he said as he bowed his head.

The silence of profound shock filled the room.

Standing in front of them was a new person. The contemptuous swagger of the conniving politician dissolved, making way for this fawning, dejected wretch. Coco saw immediately what was going on and took over the interrogation. Olivia stood dazed but still in a rage, as shocked by her outburst as everyone else.

"Tell us everything. *Now.*" Coco knew this was the moment to strike, while he was vulnerable. They needed to get the whole story out of him in front of Casey.

Detective Casey was completely out of his element. In all his years of police work, including that with the FBI, he had never seen such an exchange. Yet intuitively he knew to let Coco and Olivia step in. If his years of experience had taught him anything, it was when to be silent.

"I didn't mean it. It was an accident. I killed that woman, it was me. But I swear it was an accident. I deserve to be punished." The mayor groveled, still on his knees and almost in tears. As he spoke, he reached out toward Olivia. Not knowing what he was going for, and glad she'd worn hard-toed leather shoes, she stepped back so she could kick him if she needed to.

Detective Casey couldn't believe what he was witnessing and motioned to Coco to continue. She shrugged, as if she didn't know what to say next, so Olivia stepped back in.

"You're going to tell us every single detail. You're going to tell us who helped you blackmail us, you're going to write it all down and sign it, and then you'll turn yourself in," she said with power and disdain.

"Okay, okay. I'll do it. Whatever you want. I can't live with it anymore. It'll help if I show you this," he said as he led them out to the guesthouse and unlocked the several locks on the door that Coco had noticed on the night of the event.

Once they got inside, they discovered that the walls were lined with black padded vinyl, the smell of pomegranates—the nectar of the underworld, it is said—wafted throughout, and the floor was a thick shag. On the walls hung medieval looking switches, latex garments, leather masks, and handcuffs; a cage and something that looked like a swing was suspended from the ceiling. *Holy crap,* Coco thought, *the mayor has a dungeon in his guesthouse.*

The hypocrisy of it all did not escape her. She was filled with a curiosity that disgusted her, but she knew that once he was in his element, he would tell them everything.

Coco decided to make sure that happened and played

it up by picking up a medieval mace that was hanging from the wall. She hoped it was only there for decorative purposes.

"This is my secret," the mayor began. "I actively engage in BDSM as a submissive. It's the only way I can relieve the tension that comes with being in power. I'm aware that it's rather taboo, but it's the only thing in my life that provides satisfaction. It's very difficult to find willing participants, and because of the need for anonymity and privacy, I can't be seen visiting professional dungeons, so I hire dominatrixes to come here. That night I had hired a woman to come—it was a good night for it since everyone would be distracted by Halloween. I told the Thomsons I had a leak in my house so that I could leave their party early."

Olivia leaned over and whispered to Coco, "What's BDSM?"

Coco whispered back, "Look around you and figure it out."

"Where did she come in from?" Detective Casey asked.

"She was from Queens. Astoria. I found her on Craigslist. She was amazing: covered in tattoos, had nose rings and piercings all over, all the stuff I love. She was everything I thought she would be, and more. I brought her in through that private entrance," he said as he pointed to an almost unseen door. Her rate was a thousand dollars an hour, but I was having her stay the night, so I offered to pay her five times that amount."

Olivia leaned in to Coco and whispered, "That better not have been taxpayer money he used." Coco shushed her quietly.

The mayor went on to describe this woman and the finer details of her "outfit," which matched what Olivia and Coco had seen through the window.

"Anyway," the mayor continued, "I paid her up front, as we had arranged beforehand, and then she put me in this," he said as he pointed to a leather straitjacket. "And then she pulled a gun on me. At first I thought it was part of the scene, but then I realized she was going to rob me, or worse. She said she would take everything and that if I reported her or tried to have her arrested, she would expose me—she said she knew who I was, and I believed that she did.

"I couldn't have that. I struggled in the straitjacket, which she hadn't completely finished cinching. I was trying to free my arms, and I managed to get them in front of me. When I turned to stop her, I put my arms, which were still bound, over her head. She went crazy and started screaming at me—*'I'll kill you, motherfucker! You're a dead man. I'm gonna cut your fucking balls off.'* It scared the hell out of me. I was afraid for my life. We wrestled on the floor."

Detective Casey let out a low sigh. "And people wonder why we always tell them not to get involved in this sort of—"

Coco made a zip-it sign to Casey, out of the mayor's sight.

"This was not at all the sort of thing I had in mind," the mayor continued, looking askance at the detective. "I pay to be made afraid, but this was totally different. I was much bigger than she, and as we rolled around on the floor, she pushed her elbows into my ribs and kicked me in the groin while my arms were still around her neck. Eventually she started slowing down, and I thought I was tiring her out, winning the fight."

He paused, seeming to gather himself, and took in a sharp breath. "Finally she just stopped, and it felt like she'd given up. I was screaming at her, how dare she! I said I'd have her arrested. But she didn't respond. That's when she went limp, and I realized that I'd strangled her. I panicked." He searched the room for understanding but received looks suggesting he was pitiful.

"The whole thing happened in the living room. We hadn't even gotten over here to the guesthouse yet. I was thinking I was going to put her body in an old chest. I couldn't let it be discovered in my house! I was just going to leave her somewhere she could be found.

"So, that's when you saw me. Rolling her body up in the rug; I couldn't think of anything else. When I heard a noise outside"—at this, Olivia instinctively put her hand over her mouth—"I looked over and saw the strangest sight. Four Sarah Palins staring at me. I was certain it was the worst dream I'd ever had.

"The only thing I could think to do was to call somebody who knows how to fix things like this. I can't say who it was; let's just call him Blackbeard. He told me how to get rid of her body, so I did.

"The next day I found out she was a grifter. She'd been robbing a string of johns, so in a way she deserved it. But I'm not a killer, I swear. I'm not a killer."

"Well, in the eyes of the law you are," Detective Casey said, "and I hate that you'll like this, but turn around. I have to cuff you."

"Can *she* do it?" the mayor asked as he gestured toward Olivia.

"No," Detective Casey said, disgusted. He then led the mayor to his car.

After they were out of earshot, Coco turned to Olivia. "Okay, missy. Who are you, and what have you done with Olivia?"

"Umm . . . well . . . I don't know." Olivia trailed off, then turned and walked toward the door. Before she exited, she stopped, turned back to Coco, and said, "I guess I don't like bullies either."

At the police station Bailey, CJ, and Malcolm grew impatient waiting for the rest of the gang to arrive. When CJ got the call from Detective Casey, he realized they might be waiting awhile, so they went inside. Chief Bruno saw them come in and became effusive. This was a very different Chief Bruno than the one they had met the first time around.

"Hello, CJ, Bailey, Malcolm. What are you doing here?" he asked with a big fake smile.

Malcolm took charge right away. "Well, Detective Casey asked these two to come in, and I'm an old friend of CJ's, so he asked me to come along, to make sure everything's okay."

"Oh, in that case, why don't you get settled in the conference room and make yourselves comfortable? I'm sure he'll be right here."

As they made small talk, Bailey started texting CJ under the table.

- This is bullshit. Why don't we try that number for Blackbrd.
- Definitely. I'll do it since I'm closest to the door. What's the number?

Bailey sent the number, and CJ stood up to make the call.

"Would you excuse me for one second?" he said, as politely as his finishing school instructor would have liked, as he stood and walked toward the door. "The men's room . . . this way?"

"Yes, just down the hall," Chief Bruno said as he continued his small talk with Bailey and Malcolm.

Just outside the door, CJ dialed the number. As it began to ring, he contemplated hanging up, panicking that he was out of his depth. Meanwhile, Bailey noticed that the phone in Chief Bruno's pocket began to ring. She looked over at CJ and scrunched her face, nodding toward Bruno. But before they could figure out what to do, they saw the chief look at the caller ID, furrow his brow, then answer anyway. This all happened in an instant.

"Excuse me," he said to the room. "Hello?" he said into the phone. "Hello?"

He clicked the phone off but seemed suddenly alarmed. He excused himself and went into his office, shutting the door behind him.

"What the hell was that?" Malcolm asked.

CJ walked back into the room and held up his cell phone. "We just found Blackbeard."

* * *

By the time Detective Casey showed up with the others, Chief Bruno was gone. He was paranoid that something was going down, and he was right. CJ told the detective about the phone call and endured Casey's wrath—and rightfully so—for meddling where he'd been told not to. Just then CJ looked up and was shocked to see Olivia, Coco, and the handcuffed mayor in tow. He looked at Coco. "Are you kidding me? What happened?"

"Oh, Mary, you are never going to believe this one." Coco beamed. "You think Bailey being a lesbian was news, just wait. Your wig is gonna do backflips!"

"I told you, I'm not a lesbian!" Bailey protested.

"Dessert at the diner, everyone? I think we've earned some cake, don't you?" CJ said. "I can't hear this story on an empty stomach."

"Yes!" Olivia was excited. "I love cake!"

"I'll meet you there shortly. Gotta tie up some loose ends," Detective Casey said and leaned down to kiss Olivia.

"See you in a bit," she said to him as she linked arms with Bailey and walked out the door.

Coco smiled a knowing smile, and as she walked away she watched Malcolm steal CJ's silly Elmer Fudd hat off his head and run to the car. It made her think how nice it was to be there for the beginning of their relationship. Who knew how it would turn out? What she did know was that she would be there for CJ no matter what happened, and that he would be there for her as she worked through her issues with Sam, sexual and otherwise. Then she watched Olivia and Bailey walk arm in arm toward the car and thought how strange Bailey's newfound love was, but she felt comfort in the fact that she would be there for her too, and that Bailey was comfortable talking about it with her and the others. Coco also felt happy for Olivia and Rob, who seemed to be starting something wonderful. But what she was most happy about was that, no matter what happened with any of these relationships, the four of them now had the kind of friendship she had always hoped for.

Coco began to think about all the different kinds of relationships you have in life. There are relationships with everyone from the person who watches your dogs and the nameless guy who parks your car every morning at the office to work relationships that aren't that close but are necessary; and family, who are supposed to love you unconditionally. But nothing in the world, she thought, compares with the friendships you've created by choice. The ones with people who choose to love you, and whom you choose to love.

And sometimes those relationships come from the strangest places—if you aren't open to those moments, you limit the possibilities of building amazing friendships with people you would never have imagined choosing. Especially three people who wore the same costume as you, at a party you never wanted to attend, in a town where you didn't feel you belonged.

EPILOGUE

September, the following year

The Belle Haven Club was part of a long-standing tradition, but not the one you would imagine. This tradition had nothing to do with legacy, family, money, or even Greenwich. This tradition was about the vital economy of the wedding market.

That's what Coco always abhorred about weddings: the events themselves. In her circle, one wedding day could run you from thirty thousand dollars to hundreds of thousands. If you were going to spend money on a dream you'd had as a kid, why not buy that pony you always wanted, or rent out a candy store for a weekend? Of all the childhood fantasies to indulge, Coco could think of a lot better ones than the big wedding. The biggest insult was the year of planning, the arguing, and the hurt feelings. All over just one day.

Coco despised the whole concept of the American Wedding, yet there she was contemptuously wearing a white wedding dress and fabulous shoes because that's the other thing about weddings: you get to marry the person you love.

She realized that if a wedding was what Sam wanted, that was all she needed to know.

"Oh, Mary (sob) . . . you look . . . so . . . (sob)." CJ couldn't get the words out he was crying so hard. "I'm sorry . . . You just look beautiful. I'm so happy for . . . (sob) you both. That ceremony was . . . (sob)."

"Here," Malcolm said. "This is the last tissue. After this one I'll have to get you toilet paper from the men's room."

"Never!" CJ bellowed through his tears. "I need aloe tissues, you know that."

"Fine, I'll go out to the car."

"Thank you, dear. Isn't he lovely?" CJ said to Coco.

"Yes, he is," she acknowledged. "Is it next weekend that you guys go up to Martha's Vineyard?"

"It is. We're meeting my parents up there. Fingers crossed," he said.

Coco showed CJ her own crossed fingers before she was pulled away by a cousin wanting to know if Sam's friend from college was single.

CJ's life was relatively back to normal. After Nanny moved in with her ancient cardiologist, CJ had no choice but to go back to his own apartment in Chelsea, not far from Malcolm. He had also decided to try to mend fences with his parents. He took the sex columnist Dan Savage's advice and gave his parents one year to freak out, ask him stupid and inappropriate questions, sulk and be angry. But, he told them, after that year was up they had to be cool with his homosexuality and his relationship with Malcolm. After a year they had to respect him as an adult if they wanted him in their life. They had six months to go. He expected Martha's Vineyard to be awkward, but it was a step in the right direction.

After Coco introduced her cousin to Sam's college friend, she walked over to Bailey and Gertie, who were still sitting at their table.

"No, no. I was the love interest. Adrien was the one who sang the songs in *The Crooner,* not me, but thanks for asking," Gertie said to a guest who asked if she would go up and sing some of the funny songs she sang in that movie.

"*Sigh.* They've been bugging her all night," Bailey said to Coco as she took Gertie's hand.

"No, it's okay, everyone's been really nice. I don't mind," Gertie said as she turned back toward the other guests at the table.

"You sure you guys are okay? I don't need to call security on my uncle Bernie, do I?" Coco asked Bailey privately.

"No, no, she gets this all the time," Bailey assured her.

"I was," Gertie said.

"No, you weren't," Uncle Bernie said.

"I was," Gertie said.

"No, you weren't," Cousin Doug chimed in.

"I promise you I was on *King of the Hill.* I played one of Bobby's girlfriends, I swear!" Gertie maintained.

"You guys wanna come and sit with us?" Coco asked Bailey.

"Nah, your family is funny, we're having a good time," Bailey said.

"Okay."

"The ceremony was beautiful, by the way," Bailey said.

"It really was! I especially liked your friend the right reverend asking us all to 'testify.' Very funny," Gertie added. "Haven't you guys had enough testifying in the past few months after all your court appearances?"

"Thanks. Don't sit here all night, you two. Make sure you come dance later," Coco suggested.

"We won't," they said almost in unison, then said "Jinx!" together and laughed at themselves.

Just then Olivia came running through a crowd of guests, plowing into Coco, almost knocking her off her five-inch heels.

"Careful. I already have a bit of vertigo in these things. I don't know how long I can stay all the way up here," Coco said. "What's going on?"

"There is a major typo, *major,* on the cake plates. I don't know what to do!" Olivia was in full panic mode.

"What's the issue?" Coco asked.

"They wrote 'Just Marred' instead of 'Just Married'!"

Coco thought for a second. "Hmmm, seems more appropriate, don't you think? I say leave it, and let them eat cake . . . on them!"

Olivia had appointed herself maid of honor. Coco hadn't wanted a wedding party, or the obligation of inviting friends and making them suffer through the whole thing. Heck, she barely even wanted a wedding. But Olivia had insisted on it. "You can't get married by yourself!" she'd said. Coco had acquiesced and put Olivia in charge. She realized later what a good idea that was, since Olivia was willing to do everything Coco didn't want to, which was basically everything.

Coco secretly suspected that Olivia was only trying to make some good wedding planning connections, since she and Rob had just gotten engaged. He'd waited until he was promoted to chief of police, and then at his induction ceremony, when he got up to give an acceptance speech, he popped the question in front of his whole squad. They hadn't stopped giving him shit about it yet.

But it was because of Olivia and the Scooby-Doo bunch that he made chief. Arresting the mayor and taking down Chief Bruno was more than a regular detective would do, let alone a Greenwich detective. On the advice of counsel, the mayor pled to manslaughter and got four years plus an additional six months for blackmail and hiring a prostitute. Police Chief Bruno, who was known as Blackbeard to the FBI, was not an informant so much as he was a rat opportunist who would sell anyone out to save himself. But this time he had nobody to put on the chopping block since the mayor had already been arrested. When Rob Casey caught up with Chief Bruno, the FBI had several counts of corruption against him, so he wasn't getting away easily this time. Detective Casey turned him over to his buddies at the Bureau, and that was the end of him.

"When are you going to start dressing him better?" CJ said to Olivia. "This is Greenwich you know, not Arkansas. He's still in those cheap detective suits. Now that he's the chief of police, he needs better clothes. More Dolce and Gabbana, less Sears, Roebuck."

Olivia played with Rob's hair and said, "I love him for who he is, bad suits and all."

"My suits are *bad*?" Rob said, a bit hurt.

"No, sweetie, they're great, I'm just saying . . . See what you started!" she said to CJ.

"Girl, *you're* the one who has to look at him! I'm not expecting costume changes like at a Cher concert. I'm just saying, a little more panache."

Just then Coco and Sam stood to get everyone's attention and grabbed two microphones. Sam put his arm around the waist of his new bride and said, "We both have a song we wanted to dedicate to all of you. This was playing on the radio the day we met and it's been our song ever since, and appropriate even to this day." Then Coco turned to the DJ and said, "Hit it," and together they started karaokeing their song, LL Cool J's "Mama Said Knock You Out."

Don't call it a comeback
I been here for years . . .

Rory leaned in to CJ and said, "You know our Halloween party is a month away. You guys are coming, aren't you?"

CJ looked at him, rolled his eyes, and said, "Honey, you have a better chance of getting the Virgin Mary to give you a lap dance."

NAMASTE